D1525396

A SWEETHEART
IN
Paris

JENNIE GOUTET

In memory of Barb Kase Velasquez –
I'm so glad I got to hug you in Paris

Chapter One

I *need to end things with Christelle.* Victor Deschamps came to that decision in the short time it took to travel from the restaurant where they'd had lunch with his dad to the apartment he owned on Avenue Hoche. Sure, Christelle was pretty enough, but his father's subtle barbs had hit home. Her language was coarse, and her family flaunted their newly acquired wealth. Ironic coming from his father, these reproaches, since his dad's money was new as well.

Nevertheless, there was some truth to his father's criticisms. Money could buy life's elegances, but it couldn't buy elegance itself. It couldn't buy that confidence that came from old money, old families, sprawling apartments on Boulevard Haussmann, country manors in Normandy. Margaux had all those things. She had them in spades, so he supposed it was no surprise she'd broken up with him. Christelle was fun, but it was never meant to last.

The conclusion brought Victor relief, but not for long. He would be the one to end things, and Christelle always liked having the upper hand. It wouldn't be pretty. If only he could hire someone to tell her. Victor arrived at the building and hit the door button to enter, stepping over the metal door frame and walking through the cobblestone entrance that led to the court-yard. The trees in the open space were already beginning to bloom.

He didn't expect to see anyone because it was after the lunch hour and, by now, the professionals had returned to their offices on the first floor. So the sight of a brown-haired, disheveled woman crouched in the courtyard made him clench his jaw. They couldn't have beggars here, and apparently no one thought to ask her to leave. He'd have to deal with this one.

His impatient strides slowed once he got closer and saw an easel in front of her and a palette in one hand. She didn't hear him, so he had time to assess her ripped jeans and grubby sweat-shirt, the stool she perched on, and the movement through her thin torso as she applied her brush. Her long brown hair that glinted in the sun was tied on top of her head with chopsticks poking through the knot. Of course there would be chopsticks.

Her appearance didn't matter, though. The fact that she was here without permission did, and Victor opened his mouth to send her away.

The painting on the easel in front of her, however, gave him pause. This was not one of those touristy sketches of a Parisian building façade. It was the portrait of a girl, sitting with her hands looped around her bent knees, her face radiating innocence and hope. Separating the girl from the building façade was a jagged green shoot with spring flowers intertwined around the thin branch, up into the girl's hair, and across the canvas like a wisteria vine. The artist had painted the façade with precision and was clearly trained in realism. There were the four stone steps leading to the mirrored glass entrance, the large beige stones, the white shutters on the tall windows, flanked by black iron grates. It was perfect. Until your eyes were drawn back to the girl's hopeful expression, and your own hopes skittered off the canvas and up into the sky.

Okay, that was too fanciful for a man of twenty-eight years—a businessman, and a confirmed bachelor to boot. He needed to say something. Victor stared at the volume of curls, miraculously pinned up by those two chopsticks. The hair was the same texture and color as the girl in the portrait. Was this her?

"*Excusez-moi, mademoiselle.* This is private property. Who gave you permission to paint here?"

The girl turned, and Victor caught his breath when he beheld the same innocence, the same hope, with only a few years to add wisdom to the expression. She didn't have the worn features he'd expected from someone who looked like they lived on the street. The bones of her face were delicate, her brows perfectly arched, and her nose a cross between imposing and pert. She turned away from him without responding and threaded a thin line of white on one side of her building where the afternoon sun made the stones gleam. Belatedly, he realized she must have had permission from someone to have nearly completed her painting. Unless she snuck in regularly on the off-hours, like now.

"I live here." She turned her head again, back straight, and met his gaze over her shoulder. "*Monsieur.*" Her lush mouth settled in a straight line.

So the girl was American. Her accent was heavy and not cute like American accents could be. So thick, it was barely understandable. Quite atrocious, in fact. And it explained the outfit, though she was probably more authentic than the teens who wore down the streets of Châtelet-les-Halles with their imitation bohemian-chic. Americans most likely didn't know any better.

"Where do you live?" He knew his question sounded accusing, and that he was overstepping his bounds. Except this was his home, and he'd never seen her before.

"*Une chambre de service,*" she said. "Attached to apartment number four." She faced her painting again.

The *chambre de service* was a simple room on the top floor that once was used as maid's quarters. Each apartment in their

3

building had one, except his had been sold separately from the apartment before he purchased it. The number four apartment was owned by a lifelong resident and her no-good grandson. He was a couple years younger than Victor, and as much as Victor was a playboy, and not fit for much except work and partying, according to his father, Lucas was worse. Lucas's natural expression was an ugly sneer, and the girls on his arm—never the same one—he treated with a condescension bordering on hostility. Victor had no idea what these women saw in Lucas.

Victor wasn't really sure what women saw in *him* either. Unless it was his money.

This one was ignoring him, still intent on her work, and her hand moved automatically to capture the sunbeams angling off the stones, silver on top of white.

"How long have you lived here?" Victor asked.

"A month," she replied, and looked at him again, this time with a smile. "And I don't speak much more French than that, so if you have any more questions for me it will have to be in English." At least that's what he thought she said. Her French was abominable.

"I speak English," he said. "All educated French people do. Not all Americans who come to our country have managed to learn French, though."

"Perhaps they are not unwilling," she replied, her eyes teasing. "Perhaps they need more time than just a month."

Victor was momentarily silenced, struck by the truth of her words and the ungraciousness of his own. Yet she had not taken offense.

"What's your painting called?" he asked, as she turned toward it again.

"*April à Paris*," she replied, again with that atrocious accent. He could hear the grin in her voice.

"I think you mean, '*Paris en Avril*'—it's a common mistake for English-speakers. April is *avril* in French."

"Yes, but my name is April. So April is April in French too." Her lips turned up to match her smiling eyes.

Struck, he blurted out, "A pretty painting to match a pretty girl."

Her smile disappeared. "If my painting is 'pretty' I have not succeeded." She frowned at the canvas as he came to stand at her side.

The crease in her brows made Victor want to reassure her. "It's more than pretty. I just lack the vocabulary to describe it. I know nothing about art." He furrowed his brows. "Which probably doesn't make my compliment worth very much."

Her smile flooded back, and the vague point of tension in his chest lifted. "*More than pretty* is high praise from an art critic. Didn't you know?" April teased.

It was her colors, he decided, that made her so physically attractive. Light-brown hair set against pink-hued cheeks, lips as ripe as a peach, blue eyes under long black lashes. She looked like the Snow White princess he'd imagined when his babysitter read the story to him as a child—if you focused on her face and not the grubby clothes.

"My name is Victor," he said, surprising himself because he never had to introduce himself to women. They usually asked for his name. And his number. "I live in apartment number three. You can knock if you need anything. It must not be easy to be new in a country where you don't speak the language."

April raised her brows slightly, but the surprise vanished quickly from her face. "Where I don't speak the language *yet*." She pointed her brush at him and he stepped aside, worried she might accidentally flick paint on his jacket. "Thank you, Victor." She stood and held out her hand, another unexpected move. He'd heard Americans did not have good manners, and he didn't expect courtesies from Bohemian painters. He looked at her fingers and decided the risk of getting his own smudged in paint wouldn't be that high.

"I'd better go," he said, with some reluctance. "I have work to do." That last part was not precisely true, but he didn't mind if she believed it.

April turned back to her painting. "See you around."

She was clearly more interested in her painting than him, and he stared at her profile another moment, feeling strangely dismissed. Then again, he reminded himself, she had every right to paint here, and he would only make a fool of himself if he hung about, protesting her presence. Victor crossed the courtyard toward the entrance, catching a whiff of spring flowers. The scented breeze brushed his cheeks, and he noticed how pretty the sun was, reflecting off the building. It did have a hint of silver in it.

His eyes adjusted to the dim interior when he entered the carpeted foyer. He was about to take the stairs when he saw Lucas exit the elevator—the good-for-nothing grandson and landlord to the pretty American out there. Victor nodded and gave a curt *"bonjour."* Lucas responded in kind before heading out. They never bothered with more than bare civility, not since Lucas had followed one of Victor's girlfriends all the way to the train station and terrified her so much she broke up with Victor the next day. When the door closed behind Lucas, Victor peered out the glass panes to see how April greeted him. *Let's see whether she's telling the truth and really does rent their room*, he thought.

They did appear to know each other, but April flinched the minute she saw Lucas. Though she gave him a fleeting smile, her reserve could be felt through the glass. As Lucas leaned in to inspect her painting, April's eyes focused ahead and met Victor's through the glass door. He'd been caught. Embarrassed, he was about to turn away when Lucas reached out to finger a brown tendril of April's hair that had come loose from her chignon. She darted away from his hand, lifting her canvas off the easel in one motion before he could touch her, and Lucas backed off.

Victor relaxed. She was in no danger. And he was acting like an idiot. What business did he have watching her talk to other men?

April packed up her art supplies with that tight smile, her shoulders squared. With a smirk, Lucas dug his hands into his pockets and sauntered to the large wooden door that led to the street. Victor watched it close behind Lucas and turned to leave before April saw him again.

Mon Dieu. What was I thinking, about to act the hero for a girl I barely know? And an American, no less. He climbed the carpeted steps to his empty apartment. *I'm glad she brushed off Lucas, though.*

Chapter Two

"Your eyes are a really pretty light brown." April leaned forward and painted short lashes, thin strokes that cut into the whites of eyes that jumped off the page. She studied her subject again, who was facing her with his own canvas perched in front of him.

"You mean a really masculine light brown. That's because I'm from the part of China where men are extra handsome." Ben peered around his canvas, face deadpan.

April laughed. "I'll take your word for it."

They were silent, studying each other, then reproducing what they saw on the canvas. It was Ben's turn. "What's that scar from? The one along your hairline."

"Not many people notice that." April paused before explaining, but it was not so much to paint as to formulate the words. "It's from a car accident that took my mother's life." She saw Ben's face and was quick to do what she always did. "No, it's okay. I was only six, and I barely remember anything from before then. My dad raised me, and he was an awesome dad."

"The scar is tricky," Ben said. "I'm not sure I have it right. I'll have to ask Françoise. It's so subtle you almost miss it, but if you don't add it, something isn't right." He was studying the painting, then her face, with a critical eye.

"There's Françoise. You can ask her now." April was relieved only one other paired portrait class remained before they had to hand in their work. She didn't like the teacher's instructions to voice the observations as they painted. It felt too intimate.

However, she did feel calmer now than when she'd arrived. Painting always did that. Lucas's advances had felt more threatening than usual this afternoon, and she'd wondered if he was going to let her go when she said she had class. He always managed to approach her in a way that gave the appearance of friendliness, while actually invading her space, and he hadn't stopped asking her to go out since she signed the rental agreement to his grandmother's apartment.

Most *chambres de services* were bedrooms only, but hers had a skylight and a built-in bathroom with a tiny shower, toilet, and even a kitchenette. April knew she was lucky in her find, but Lucas was nuisance enough to make her rethink her decision about living there. If it had only been that one thing, she would leave. But it had proved much more difficult to get an apartment than she imagined without a steady salary or someone to guarantee she would pay the rent. April didn't know why Madame Laguerre had been willing to take a chance with her, but it wasn't something she could easily turn away. She had been homeless for two months before landing this apartment.

Lucas was someone to watch out for, though. Her instinct told her it was best she not be caught alone with him. April began cleaning her brushes, and her thoughts turned to Victor. The other resident she'd met today for the first time. Whoa. He was dangerous too, but in a different way, with those high cheekbones and Mediterranean skin tone, unfairly paired with hazel-olive eyes. She had rarely seen such perfect features on a man. *And I'd better stick to the clinical observation of a painter if I want to remove myself from temptation.* The man was good-looking and he knew it.

Actually, she reasoned, *I'm not tempted. I don't even know what his teeth look like (behind those full lips) because he didn't smile, not once. The man is so full of himself he'll have no room in his heart to care about anyone else, and my father loved me too well for me to fall into such a stupid trap.* "You find someone who recognizes your value and don't settle for anything else," her dad had often said. April scrubbed her brushes harder before realizing she was ruining the horsehair bristles. "Shoot!"

"Françoise said I'm close. A little more lapis mixed with white will do the trick," Ben said. "But you'll have to wait to see it. Coffee?"

April smiled back at him. Ben had no problem showing his teeth. He smiled all the time. "How about a cheap place to eat?" she said. "I skipped lunch, and coffee is not going to do it for me."

Ben's idea of cheap was not the same as hers. She usually ate at Flunch for her one hot meal a day, but with him it had to be a traditional brasserie. "I didn't come to France to eat at Flunch," he said, as they headed down the broad street. "Or McDonalds, so don't even think about it."

"I don't eat at McDonalds," she protested. "Well, not often. Just those times when only hot, salty fries will do." April grinned at his look of disgust. "You really should get more distinguished friends than me."

"I like you," Ben said. "Come on. This place looks good." He reached for the brass handle of the door, and she just had time to glance at the menu posted outside the restaurant. Okay, she could have a *croque monsieur* and salad for eight euros. She could afford that.

Ben ordered the full menu with appetizer, main dish, and dessert. When he saw what she was having, he chided her. "You said you were hungry."

"I am." April looked at him with wide eyes. "This will fill me right up."

"Huh." His brow crinkled. "Why don't you let it be my treat?"

"No, no." April shook her head. "Thank you, though." To turn the talk from her financial situation, she said, "Tell me about where you're from. What's it like at your house? Did you know I'm planning on going to China next?"

"You are? You definitely need to go then. There's no other place like it in the world." Ben sat back as the waiter brought the first course over. "How could you have forgotten to mention it before?"

"Oh, in the two weeks we've been paired up for the project?" April retorted. "How secretive of me."

Ben gave a snort and poured olive oil over his carpaccio. "All right. I'll tell you about Shanghai, but you tell me when you plan to go to China."

"In September," she replied promptly.

Ben looked up at that. "So soon?" he asked. "Why?"

April watched him wade through his appetizer as she nursed the glass of water she held. After taking a sip, she answered him. "I promised my dad. He told me not to commit myself to one style of art until I had studied everywhere, taking elements from each place I studied. My plan is to spend five years living in various continents and taking art classes in one or two different countries per year. I'll start with China in September for half a year, then move to India for the other half."

Ben had finished the appetizer and was mopping up the olive oil and lemon with a piece of bread. He glanced at her. "You can stay with my family for those six months."

"I don't think so, Ben," she said. "I couldn't impose on your family like that. But thank you." The waiter came with her *croque monsieur*, and April was grateful he hadn't waited until Ben had his main course, and that the sandwich was huge. "Now tell me about your family."

"I'm the only son—"

"Ah, so that explains it," April teased and took a large bite of her sandwich.

"You're funny," he retorted. "And I have a younger sister."

"Where is she?" April asked, pulling at the cheese and shoving it into her mouth. She wasn't even trying to be graceful.

"Jenny's at home. My parents would never let her go off on her own."

April frowned and set down her sandwich. "Don't tell me your parents are still so traditional."

"My parents *are* traditional, but they're open-minded, too." Ben had his hands folded in front of him, and there was something in his expression that made her feel like he was making fun of her.

"They're not all that open-minded," April protested. "I can't believe they won't let her travel just because she's a girl."

"They won't let her travel because she's eight." Ben smirked and picked up his cutlery as the waiter set a *tartiflette* in front of him.

"Oh." April felt herself blush.

"Admit it. You're prejudiced against Chinese people," he said without rancor. "You think we oppress women."

"I'll admit I held *that* prejudice," April answered, honestly. "I'm surprised your sister is so much younger than you."

"I didn't ask my parents why, and they're not likely to tell me," Ben said, grinning through mouthfuls.

"Of course not." April laughed. Ben was a touch arrogant, but she liked him. He was fun to be around. "What's your house like?"

"Well..." Ben paused. "Have you ever seen pictures of houses in China? My house looks pretty much like those, except it's bigger than most. My dad is one of the top businessmen in Shanghai, and he wouldn't settle for anything less than the nicest house in the city. The roof tiles are made of traditional red clay, and there's a veranda that stretches around the entire house. We're on the edge of the city, and we have a large property with a bamboo wooded area, a pond with golden carp, magnolia trees, and a mixed orchard with different fruit trees."

April stopped eating to listen. Ben was painting a picture with his words, and it made her even more excited to see it for herself. "The road that leads to my house has those plane trees that you see on the Paris avenues—you know, with the white mottled bark? We have those on either side of the road that leads to my house. So I don't feel homesick when I'm in Paris." He swallowed a sip of wine and added, "It sometimes snows in the winter."

"That sounds beautiful," April said, and picked up the remainder of her sandwich. "It doesn't seem foreign the way you describe it."

"It's definitely not foreign to me," Ben replied. "It's my home. You should come to Shanghai. Why not? It's a modern city, but there's still all the Buddhist temples with smoking incense, the Chinese songs, and the thousand-year eggs you'd want for a full cultural experience. And I'll introduce you to my calligraphy teacher, which is a must if you're going to study Chinese art."

"I might just do that." April put her napkin on her empty plate and looked up. "Plus, it would be nice to go someplace I have a friend. Unless—when do you plan to return home?"

"In August. So yes, I'll be there." He gave her a smoldering look. "Maybe we could go as more than friends."

April was obliged to laugh. "I don't think so, Ben. I have enough on my plate without the complexities of romance."

Ben shrugged. "It was worth a shot. Since this plate is clean, shall we go? I don't want the dessert after all."

April put her eight euros on the metal tray and said she'd meet him outside while Ben went to the counter to pay with a credit card. On the street in front of the restaurant was a woman, clad in a coat too warm for the season, with a scarf over her hair, sitting with a child and a cardboard sign in front of her that said *"j'ai faim, s.v.p."* April thought about her own situation and how lucky she was. Sure, money was tight, but that was only because it was tied up at the moment. She still had six of her father's paintings to sell, which would earn her enough to accomplish all her travel plans and maybe even put a down payment on a studio when she was done. She had more than enough to spare.

"Bonjour, madame." April handed the woman a two-euro coin. "What's your daughter's name?" The woman pointed to her lips and shook her head. April smiled, preparing to walk back toward the door, but the woman detained her. She held out a small bundle of fragrant white flowers, tied together with piece of twine.

"For me?" April asked, touched, though the flowers were already starting to wilt. The woman nodded, and April tucked the bouquet into the buttonhole of her leather jacket. "Thank you."

Ben came out the door and looked at the homeless woman, then at April. When she rejoined him, he said, "You really shouldn't encourage them, you know. They can get help if they want it. They're just taking advantage of you."

April started forward, piqued. "I don't give because there's a need. Or—I don't *only* give because of a need. I give because it's the right thing to do. It brings goodness and justice in the world when those who are fortunate share with those who are less fortunate, whether or not they are...worthy." She curled her fingers in air quotes. "God will sort it all out in the end."

"Your money," Ben said, with a shrug. When he saw April's displeasure, he put his arm around her shoulders and gave an affectionate squeeze. "Come on. Let's not fight. Are you coming to the student meeting before class tomorrow?" He stopped to turn down the street to his apartment.

"It's my plan," April said, offense forgotten and with a smile hovering on her lips. "Who can turn down free coffee and croissants?"

"See you then," he said, and tipped his hand in salute. April watched him walk away and turned toward her apartment. From an objective point of view, Ben was handsome and fun to be around, and he also had these moments of sweetness. But she wasn't sure he was a kindred spirit, and she would never settle for less. April's steps slowed. *I hope I don't find my kindred spirit until I'm done traveling the world*, she thought, *or he's going to be eating my dust.*

She punched the code to the wooden door leading to the courtyard, but when she opened the door, the movement was so unexpectedly easy she fell forward. Two strong hands caught her before she pitched to the ground.

"Easy there," he said.

Victor.

It took a moment for April to catch her breath. "You startled me," she said, with a nervous laugh. *I've never met the guy before, and now twice in one day?*

"I'm sorry," he said. "I was in a hurry, and I pulled the door quickly." Victor's face slanted into a frown as he studied her, then his eyes drifted down to her chest. Before she could find a coherent thought to express outrage, he said, "You have a *muguet*." It sounded like mew-gay.

"A what?" April asked, her brows wrinkled.

"Those white flowers. They're usually given out on the first of May. Where did you get them?"

"Oh, these." She looked down and pulled the flowers from her buttonhole, then met his gaze. "I gave some money to a homeless mother and her child, and she handed this to me."

"I'm surprised," he said.

"That I would give money? I know, I know." She didn't want to hear it again. "They could get assistance if they wanted it."

"No, not that," Victor said. "I'm surprised she gave you something back."

"They often give something back," April said, her expression serious. "I mean, not every time. But often. They give their gratitude, a smile, sometimes a piece of food, like a sandwich they think you might want."

"Which you don't," he said, his face in the form of mock horror. April looked at him in surprise, and he clarified, "You don't want the sandwich, I mean."

She laughed at that, and then she saw it. He smiled. And it was wholly unfair because his gleaming white teeth set in that perfect smile completed the look of perfection. She put her hands on her hips and shook her head.

"What?" Victor asked, a look of confusion coming over his features.

"Nothing," she replied. Nothing she could share anyway. "But you were running late, so I won't keep you."

He reached for the door handle. "Bye, April," he said.

She was already walking toward the courtyard and lifted her hand. "Bye, Victor."

Chapter Three

✦✦✦

"Mishou." Victor let himself into his grandmother's apartment and looked around. "Mishou?" He called again and knew a minute of panic before he heard her rumbling around in the kitchen.

"Victor, I'm in here." She came out carrying an old porcelain water pitcher that she brought to the table. "Oh, you brought me flowers *encore*. And yellow tulips, my favorite. You're always so thoughtful."

"It's not that hard to bring you tulips, Mishou. What I wish is that you would let me move you into an apartment closer to mine. One that has more space." He looked around. "And more light."

"What do I need with more space?" she asked with a shrug, the age-old argument. "My friends are here, and I would be lonely if I moved to another apartment. I promise to let you know if I need help. I'm not so foolish an old woman as to forget I'm no longer young."

"No, you are wise." Victor kissed her cheeks. "You are also important to me, which is why I keep bringing it up."

Mishou patted his cheek and proceeded to the hutch that held the collection of vases. "My dear boy, please get me that smooth glass vase on the top shelf. It's perfect for tulips." Victor obliged and went to fill it with water. "You've made *paupiettes de veau*," he called out from the kitchen when he spotted the tiny wrapped bundles of veal. "My favorite."

When they were seated at the table, the *entrée* of grated carrots and Dijon mustard dressing nearly finished, his grandmother touched his arm. "So, Victor. What have you been keeping busy at lately? Did you buy the company you were looking at? That international consulting firm?"

"Yes, although I didn't need to do much to close the deal. I'd already chosen who the members of the board would be, and Richard is handling the paperwork as usual. There's not really much left for me to do."

Mishou studied him, her gaze thoughtful. She never missed anything. "You said you were interested in trying out management for once. And this consulting firm—it was something you thought you could do. Have you changed your mind?" She reached for Victor's empty plate and served him a helping of rice and veal, giving him time to answer.

He *had* thought about it. He even had a window of time before he needed to choose a director for the firm, so he had time to consider himself for the role. But Victor knew that would be a mistake. He was good at acquisitions. Management? He wasn't so sure, and he wasn't about to claim a position at the helm of a multi-billion-dollar public company where his every move would be scrutinized by competitors around the world. He could just picture them plotting a hostile takeover while he blundered about. Maybe his own father would be the one to spearhead it. Victor cringed.

Plus, he had to admit, after leading the company up to this exciting stage where they'd acquired smaller firms in major cities around the world, all under the umbrella of Brunex Consulting, he couldn't step back from his visionary role only to get bogged down with the minute details of management. Not when the acquisitions he'd lined up would make this company his greatest achievement yet.

"I'm not sure I'm fit for management," he said, at last. "I would have to give it two years, and I'm not sure I want to commit to stopping all other business just to focus on this one branch. I might lose my edge."

"Or you might find you're not as good at it as you thought." Victor shot his grandmother a look, and she laughed softly. "No, that is not my own opinion on the matter. I think you will do splendidly as a manager."

Mishou sighed and, picking up her fork, continued. "You're still so afraid of failing after all these years, my boy. It's okay to fail. It's not okay to go through life having only the most superficial shot at it. Life is meant to be lived, *mon chou*. You're meant to embrace it and give all to life and love, even if that means getting hurt from time to time. Your mother understood that better than anyone. Even though her marriage to your father was not what she'd hoped, she never regretted it for an instant because it gave her you." She patted Victor's hand. "It will hurt a lot more in the end if you keep putting up walls to protect yourself."

Victor was used to his grandmother's idea of pleasant dinner conversation. It always went more or less along the same lines. Always hurting a little, but he didn't mind because it was a cleansing sort of hurt. It was the one time in the week where there was no superficiality. No hiding behind façades. He even looked forward to it. This depth wasn't something he could produce on his own. His grandmother was the magic ingredient in their relationship.

"How is your friend Christelle?"

Victor didn't answer right away. He unwound the string from the veal and put it to the side of his plate. "I'm going to end things."

"Of course that relationship couldn't last," Mishou said, kindly. "I saw that right away."

"You've never even met her!"

"I didn't need to." His grandmother raised her brows. "Any young lady who throws herself at a gentleman before she's had a chance to see beyond his wealth..."

"It wasn't like that, Mishou," he said, although it was a little like that. Her words confirmed his decision, though, and it brought him comfort. Just because another relationship didn't work out didn't necessarily mean it was all his fault.

As if she could read his mind, his grandmother said, "Listen. I have two pieces of advice for you." Victor shook his head with a grin, and she pointed a softly gnarled finger in his face. "Don't go looking for love. Let it drop into your hands like the heavy blossom of a fragrant peony." Mishou had always been a poet. "Love is not an acquisition like one of those companies of yours. It must come to you naturally. Unexpectedly. That's how you know it will last."

"Like how you met Grandpa at the bakery?" he asked, his eyes alight. Victor knew once he got her started on that subject, all attention would be off him.

Mishou sighed. "*Oh, mon Frédéric*. He was so handsome. Dapper, even. He never went to that *boulangerie*, except on that day because he was supposed to meet his date. A nice little woman—"

"Who never showed," Victor finished with a smile. "And once he got a look at you, he forgot all about anyone else."

Mishou's eyes went dreamy. "He never stood a chance. I had quite the figure in my day, you know." Suddenly, she laughed. "You've changed the subject, you naughty boy. But yes, let love find you."

An image flashed before Victor's eyes. *April.* Falling into his arms when he opened the door, a flower in her buttonhole. *Just like the heavy blossom of a peony.* He thought of her sparkling blue eyes and taffy-colored hair, her gleaming curls pulled back, and wondered what her hair would look like down on her shoulders. A chance meeting, he convinced himself before pushing the vision aside. That sort of thing was ridiculous.

Victor put his focus firmly on his meal. "What's the second piece of advice?"

With a sly smile, his grandmother asked, "What do you think the second thing is?"

"Taking risks," he answered, without missing a beat. "I should take risks in my professional life, as well as my personal life."

"Oh, you know how to take risks," Mishou said, surprising him a little. "Every acquisition is a bit of a risk. What you haven't yet dared to do is risk everything you have because you're so sure the prize is worth it. Sometimes it's only when you're stripped of everything you have—your possessions, your position, your heart —that you can see what you value in life. Being willing to risk it all, especially your heart. *That's* the risk you need to take."

Victor had a sudden and overwhelming urge to cry, which, of course, he would not do. Instead, he continued to shovel food in his mouth and chew, looking straight ahead. He had come close to finding himself when he was with Margaux. Being with her and her family, whose heritage was anchored and secure. *That* prize had filled every empty crevice of his being. Or at least that was how he'd felt.

But then she left him.

Mishou patted his hand again after he'd finished his plate in silence. "I bought some éclairs."

BEN WASN'T at the art studio today. April didn't know why, but fortunately the class was taking a break from the portrait painting to work on charcoal sketches of movement and she would not need him. There was an empty seat next to a girl named Penelope, one of the few French students in this school geared toward foreigners because the classes were mainly taught in English. Her first impression of Penelope hadn't been one of an overly warm person. Whether this was the typical French personality or simply Penelope's own style, April didn't know.

"Is this seat taken?" April asked her.

Penelope shook her head, her eyes on the sketchpad before her.

April sat down and took out her own blank pad to begin sketching the model, who posed in the front of the room, only to change positions each minute. After examining the model's overall physique, April quickly captured the movement with expert strokes, and at the end of the second sketch, Penelope stopped her work and leaned over.

"You're quick," Penelope said. "I've not been able to study it fast enough to get that much detail."

"I've been studying this my whole life. My father was an artist, and he taught me from an early age." April continued drawing, her eyes darting from the figure to her page.

Penelope went back to sketching, but April could see her looking over at her work from time to time. April was accustomed to the attention. She'd worked hard at honing her skill, and though she did have natural talent, it helped that her father had her drawing from the moment she could hold a crayon. If she had a gift, it was her job to grow it and use it well.

"Excuse me, class." Françoise called everyone to attention, and April noticed for the first time her teacher was not alone. An older gentleman had made his way into the studio and was examining the students' paintings, one by one, that were hanging on the shelves nailed into the walls. He turned to face the class and put his hands behind his back, looking like a benevolent father.

"I'm happy to introduce to you *my* art teacher, Mr. Chambourd, a respected maître at the *École des Beaux-Arts* in Paris and a member of the *Académie*," Françoise said. "He runs a studio there and has decided to honor us with his presence and, I suppose, to see how his former pupil is doing in carrying on his instructions."

Mr. Chambourd didn't look like he could be very much older than April's art teacher. "Now, I shall give you the fruitless advice to carry on as if he were not here." Everyone laughed.

The advice was indeed in vain, because as much as April attempted to continue her sketch uninterrupted, she couldn't help but risk surreptitious glances to where the maître was to see whether he was looking at her own completed painting, *April à Paris*. Finally, he did stand in front of it, even picked it up to look at it more closely, then put it down without a word and moved to the next one. April felt her heart sink.

"I wonder what he's doing here," Penelope whispered, deciding, it seemed, to let down her reserve and take April into her confidence. "He's very well-known in France. He's part of the *Académie*, and it's a huge deal that he's here."

April opened her eyes at that. "I've not heard of him. I can't imagine why he's here, but I do hope he sees something he likes." She smiled at Penelope. "Look. I think he's examining your painting, isn't he?"

Penelope craned her head, then sank down. "He is. I feel sick."

"No, don't," April said. "It's very good. Your attention to lines and contrasts is amazing."

"Ah, *merci*." Then, as if the words were pulled from her, Penelope added, "I've noticed your work too and admit to being a little jealous."

April laughed and shook her head. "No need." A movement at the door caught her eye. "Who is that, do you think?" A young man, whose hair had not been recently trimmed but whose clothes were tailor-made, leaned against the doorframe looking completely at ease, though he was standing in front of a room full of strangers.

"Oh." Penelope's voice shot up a pitch, causing April to turn to her. Penelope's face lit up as she soaked in the sight of the newcomer. That she knew him, or at least recognized him, was evident. "That's Arthur. He's my...he's my friend. Part of our circle of friends, though he's the latest addition and has only been a member of our group for the last year." Penelope leaned in. "He's a brilliant artist. Unbelievable. He must have accompanied Mr. Chambourd, although if he knew of it in advance, he didn't tell me."

Biting her lip, Penelope stood and seemed to gather her confidence around her like a cloak. It was an unusual look for Penelope, this need to garner her courage because, as much as April had found her a bit cold in the weeks she had known her—until today, that is—Penelope had always appeared supremely confident.

Penelope walked toward Arthur at the door, and April watched as he stood upright and smiled. *A seductive smile*, she thought. *As if he knows what it's capable of.* The feelings Penelope had for him, that were so patent when she and April had been talking, now disappeared, and the face she held up for him to kiss was nonchalant. Penelope spoke to him for a few minutes, nodding her head toward Mr. Chambourd.

April was impressed. She would need to learn how to be that relaxed with men. As it was, she was completely transparent. Though she'd been told she was pretty, and didn't appear to be all that bad when she looked in the mirror, there were never any men falling over themselves to ask her out—at least not anyone appealing. French women had a reputation for exuding self-confidence around men, and now April could see it was true.

Mr. Chambourd came to the doorway, all the while talking to the art teacher. After they'd kissed each other's cheeks in farewell —what April had learned was called *"les bises,"* and which they pronounced, *lay beez*—Arthur then introduced Mr. Chambourd to Penelope. They spoke for another minute before the guests took their leave.

Penelope returned to April's side. "You have no idea what a

huge thing it is for him to come visit our school. Arthur is in his atelier at the *École des Beaux-Arts*. I am so starstruck right now."

April turned to her in wonder. "If you are, you haven't shown it very much. You were completely natural up there."

"Ha." Penelope said. "That's in the genes. We French women can hide what we feel as easily as we can breathe."

"Lucky for you," April said. "I wear my heart on my sleeve, and it doesn't always serve me well."

Penelope studied her face. "You blush easily, don't you?"

"Mmhmm." April gave a nod. "No matter how hard I try, I can't hide what I'm thinking."

Penelope picked up her sketchpad. "It's not very practical, I'll admit," she said. "Other women will despise you for it, considering it a weakness. But the women who are sincere? The true friends? They will like you the better for it." She looked at the empty doorway and appeared lost in thought. Her feelings for Arthur were perfectly clear to April, but she wondered if he had any idea.

French women could indeed hide what they were feeling if they wanted to, and that was a mixcd blessing.

Chapter Four

❦

"I have an exciting announcement to make." The class was settling in, and Françoise clapped her hands above the bustle. "Mr. Chambourd, who I introduced you to last Tuesday, is hosting an art gallery event for potential buyers. After examining your paintings—oh yes, he was here for a reason, but I couldn't tell you until he was sure—he's agreed to consider the best paintings from this class. He makes no promises that any will be included because the competition is stiff and his own students are vying for spots. The selling will be done by auction and they will start the bids high, which gives you a greater chance at earning something. The buyers are international, and the theme will be Paris."

Françoise looked around the room, her gaze settling on April. "April, I think you should submit your painting, which I believe is nearly finished. Of all the canvases he saw, he mentioned yours as being well suited to the theme." All eyes turned to April, and her heart beat wildly. "However, don't let it go to your head. I recommend you begin another one and submit the best of two for consideration."

Addressing the class, Françoise said, "Your portraits should be nearly completed now, so work hard and get them done. Our next assignment will be—you guessed it—Paris. Traditional Parisian architecture should be included in the painting, but they're looking for a unique take on the City of Light."

The teacher took a moment to survey her class, her white coat buttoned wrong and covered with paint, but with a set of keen eyes under the cropped gray hair. "You are a talented group. I hope to see a few of your *tableaux* included."

Françoise turned then, and the class buzzed with excitement as everyone grabbed their canvases and art supplies and chose their stations. April was pink with pleasure. She tried to bite down her smile, but it was hard to make it disappear completely.

Ben glanced at her when he took his place. "You can gloat. I'm jealous, but I'll get over it." His words were teasing, but his tone was off.

April, at a loss for how to respond, finally said, "It doesn't mean that mine will be chosen. You heard her say it. Stiff competition."

"So you say." Ben picked up his brush and regarded her before leaning over to paint. Though she was used to his studied gaze by now, his frown disconcerted her. They had given up observing aloud what they saw now that the portraits were close to being finished, and she watched him in silence as he painted, putting her own finishing touches on his portrait. After a short while, his expression lightened, and she felt the mood shift.

"Now the eyes are all wrong." His tone matched the teasing words. "I'll have to include the light of victory."

April laughed. "Stop it, Ben."

APRIL WALKED up the Champs-Élysées and cut across one of the intersecting roads. The streets snaking off the main boulevard were narrower, with Chinese restaurants, small boutiques and functional stores that sold things like earbuds for hearing loss. It was not as nice as the broad avenue, but April found beauty in the teeming mass of humanity that stepped around construction sites, bought wrapped bouquets of flowers, and strolled out of the bakeries with fragrant baguettes under their arms. She considered her lunchtime options and settled for another *croque monsieur*. She really needed to eat better, but it was hard when she was so hungry and a little had to go a long way.

At home, April headed to the only bench in the courtyard, a blissful spot that was partially concealed from prying eyes by a corner of hedges and potted plants. She sat down in silence to think. What could she paint next? The *April in Paris* painting represented everything that was important about this first trip overseas—this first trip that honored her father's dying wish. It held so much emotion for her, it spilled over onto the canvas, and she wasn't sure she could do better.

She chewed her sandwich over the lump that rose in her throat, forcing it back down. There was no need to allow her emotions to carry her away. It had been a year, and this was a moment for celebrating. Her art teacher had mentioned *her* canvas in front of the class as a potential for the prestigious art gallery. She would honor her father's memory best by painting.

Swinging her feet, April took another bite and enjoyed the stillness, the early spring warmth of the sun, the bird that was chirping in one of the two trees on the other side of the court-yard. The door opened to her left, and she glanced up to see Lucas exit the building. Any hope that he might not notice her was lost when his gaze fixed on her.

"There you are, April." He spoke English with a strong accent and said her name *Ah-preel*. "I haven't seen you in a few days. Have you been avoiding me?"

"Yes," she said.

"Well you shouldn't," he shot back. "My grandmother rents your apartment, and you won't find another place for that price in all of Paris. I'm not one you should try to avoid."

April thought it better to say nothing. She couldn't eat any more, so she wrapped the remains of her sandwich in her napkin, picked up her bag and stood. "Have a good day, Lucas." She walked past him, afraid he was going to grab her arm, but he didn't. As she marched toward the door, the back of her neck prickled with awareness. It was only when the door closed behind her that she breathed more easily. The elevator was on the top floor, so she took the stairs.

In less than a minute, the door opened again, and she turned. Lucas began climbing the steps behind her. "I thought you were going out," she said. It took an effort to keep her voice calm.

"No. I saw you out there from the window and came out to see you. Now that you're coming inside, I've decided to come inside too." He gestured up the stairs. "After you."

April reflected on what to do. The safety of her room was a couple floors up. She could lock the door. Even if he had a key, she also had a deadbolt. But a lot could happen on the stairs, especially as they got toward the last floor where there were only students like her, whose paths she rarely crossed. Maybe it was better to go back outside where there were people around.

Just as she was debating, Lucas took a step closer. "I think you should go out with me."

"Lucas. Going out with you is the last thing I will do. I won't get mixed up with my landlord." *Never mind the fact that you give me the creeps!*

"There are benefits to getting mixed up with your landlord," he replied, his voice still urbane and teasing, but with an underlying threat that was hard to ignore. His persistence in pursuing her had crossed the line to stalking almost immediately after she moved in, and her own reaction to it quickly went from annoyance to something akin to fear. Most of the time, however, she thought she could handle it. He would not take things further— not when she knew who he was and where he lived.

Lucas lifted his hand to brush her hair off her neck, and a door opened upstairs. April moved out of his reach and looked up the stairwell, trying to keep her face impassive. She could not let Lucas see any fear. Someone was coming, and that someone would be her salvation. She hoped the savior would be willing.

It seemed an eternity as she heard the key in the lock and the muffled sounds of footsteps on the carpeted stairwell. Using the distraction, April stepped away from Lucas, who was listening, too, and didn't make an effort to move toward her again. In another minute, Victor rounded the stairwell, his hand resting on the smooth brass railing.

"Lucas," he said, studying him with hard eyes. "*Rien à faire?*" April knew what that meant. *Nothing to do?* She appreciated his ironic tone and wished she could have his insouciance. She wasn't sure, as a woman, she could ever be that carefree. Maybe there was some form of martial arts in China she could learn that would give her more protection.

"What's it to you?" Lucas retorted.

Victor ignored him and turned his regard to April. "Bonjour, April," he said, then switched to English. "I've been meaning to talk to you about your painting. Do you have time now?"

April managed a nod. "I do." She couldn't manage a smile, though. She was still standing stiffly, irritated, and with threads of fear that had begun to dissipate when she caught sight of Victor.

"Well then." Victor nodded to Lucas. "We won't keep you."

That was smooth, thought April. But apparently not obvious enough for someone like Lucas, since he made no move to let her pass. Victor didn't bat an eyelid and turned to her instead. "Shall we go to my place?"

"How about a café?" she replied.

He nodded, taking her elbow with his back to Lucas, and staying at her side until they reached the bottom step. A few more strides across the hallway, and they were at the door to the courtyard. He opened it and allowed her to pass through. "Well," he said. "I'm surprised my coat is not burned off my back from the force of his glare."

April couldn't muster a smile. "He scares me."

"He's not someone to get involved with," Victor said.

"An understatement," April said. "Thank you for rescuing me."

"It's my pleasure," he replied. "And I want you to know that you can come knock on my door any time you feel threatened, day or night. I don't keep normal business hours and often work from home, so you have a good chance of catching me."

"Thank you," she said again. "This is the most relief I've felt since I moved in."

VICTOR DIDN'T KNOW what had prompted him to offer his help, except for the fact that he couldn't bear to let any girl be hounded by the likes of Lucas. He had been pleased to see April again after not running into her in over a week, but he hadn't missed how tense she was or the threatening posture Lucas displayed when hanging over her. Why didn't she just tell him to get lost?

"Why do you encourage him?" he asked when they'd arrived at his favorite café, three doors down. It was one of the dwindling typical Parisian cafés, with small round tables and two chairs over-looking the street—a favorite with locals. They managed to get the last table outdoors.

"Do you think I encourage him?" April's eyes went wide, her voice leaded with irritation. "Do you think I have much choice in the matter? It took me two months to find a place to live because I don't have a guarantor. Lucas keeps threatening to evict me if I'm not nice to him. On top of that, there's the phys-ical threat of his presence. I can walk away from him, but he follows. I can push him away if it comes to that, but he's stronger. You have no idea what that's like." She sat back, blinking her eyes hard.

"I don't," Victor admitted. April's difficulty stirred some feeling in him, something like anger over injustice that he usually found easy enough to dismiss. He wasn't sure what to say, so he rubbed the bristle on his chin and finally settled for, "Like I said, I'm here for you if you need it."

"Thank you, Victor." She offered him a smile that made his heart beat a little faster, but he talked himself down from imagining a second date. *Not this one. I will befriend this little Bohemian, but nothing more.*

When they had ordered two *cafés*, Victor said, "I didn't really have anything to ask you about art. It was just an excuse to get you away from Lucas. But...are you painting anything new?"

April smiled at the waiter as he put an espresso in front of each of them, and she opened her little square of chocolate before answering. "Our art teacher announced this morning that a maître of the most important art school in Paris is hosting a gallery with some colleagues of his, and they've invited our class to submit our best work. The theme is 'Paris.'"

"Is it *l'École des Beaux-Arts?*"

When she nodded, Victor's lips crept upward. "My grandfather went there for architecture. He told me about some of the pranks the students have pulled—they're known for that. Once, during the Second World War, the director of the school was forced to give a tour to the Nazis. Everyone knew about the visit, and when the director brought the Nazis to the nude painting class, he walked in and saw that the model was fully clothed." Victor paused for effect, then added, "And the students were all naked."

April couldn't help but laugh. "Oh my. You wouldn't think it with such a prestigious school. Did they get in trouble?"

He shook his head. "The director just shut the door quickly and took his guests to the next classroom. You should submit that painting you were working on the last time I saw you."

"My teacher said the same thing. But she encouraged me to work on a new one and decide which of the two is better. So I need to come up with a new place to paint."

"Huh." Victor toyed with the handle of his cup. "I'll see if I can think of something. I know the city pretty well." It would be good for him to be doing something other than working anyway. It was not often he set his mind to searching out a place in Paris just because it was pretty. It could be an interesting challenge, and fun. "How long are you here for?" he asked.

"Just through August." April picked up the tiny espresso cup and took a sip. "After that, I plan to spend six months in China studying art—maybe Shanghai, although I'm not sure. And then I want to go to India, and South America, and...I'm not sure where else. I want to study art in all these places."

Victor's mouth dropped. "That's ambitious." When he didn't say anything more, she smiled and gave a shrug. The truth was, he felt a little jealous of her freedom. Or maybe he was jealous of her courage. Who did that?

After a silence, April asked, "What do you do? You mentioned you work from home."

"I'm in mergers and acquisitions," he said. "I invest, and I acquire businesses. If the one I purchase is not doing well, I put new management in place to turn the business around. Then I sell it at a profit."

"How many businesses have you bought and turned around?" she asked.

"Oh, maybe twenty? I've only been doing it for six years, and I'm learning from my father."

"It sounds interesting. What type of businesses?"

"It varies," Victor said. "Small stores, consulting firms, payroll companies. Each one is different."

"Do you like it?"

"I like the money," Victor said with a laugh.

April shook her head. "It's not enough, though, is it? Or—it must get old just doing something for a love of money. There has to be a love of the process, right? For instance, with painting, I can't just want to have a beautiful painting as an end result. I need to love the process of producing what I see in front of me, and the inspiration to paint a greater significance into it. Like the hope represented by the girl in my painting. Or, at least, that's what I hope is coming through."

He gave a weak laugh. Hope was *exactly* what came through. "Not everyone can find such satisfaction in their jobs. Investment is not like painting."

"I'm not sure I agree." April seemed to remember her coffee and took a sip. "If you're really good at something, you can love it, even if to someone else it seems like it doesn't make a big difference in the scheme of things."

"Well," he conceded. "I like doing one thing differently from my dad. He's pretty ruthless and doesn't take into account the feelings of the companies he buys out. I try to keep the owner in an advisory position if it's something that's important to him or her, with the understanding that the company has to continue to turn a profit."

"See? You do enjoy it. I was sure there was more there than simply making money, or you wouldn't be doing it."

They had finished their coffees, and Victor debated whether he should prolong their time together or propose they go back. He didn't want her to get the wrong idea. Not that she seemed to be under any illusion that he was interested in her. Finally, he said, "I'll get the check. Shall we head back?"

"I can pay my share," April said, reaching for her wallet.

He stopped her with his hand on her arm. "No. I'm the one with all the money, remember?" He gave her what he hoped was a disarming smile. "It's just a coffee."

As they were walking back, Victor raised his voice as the light changed and the traffic surged. "Where does your family live?" He almost missed her response.

"I have none."

"Why? You've disowned them or something?" He drew his brows together. "Everyone has family."

"Not quite everyone," April replied, a bit louder now. A

motorcycle sped up as it swerved around the cars in the street. "My parents were both only children, and their parents are all dead, some before I was born, and one as late as when I was in my teens. My mom died when I was very young in a car accident, and my dad just died last year. So I really have no family."

He looked at her and was not surprised to see a sheen over her eyes. He had heard the slight tremble in her voice, though she was far from asking for sympathy.

"I see." He had no idea what else to say, so he was glad to reach their building.

When they had gone through the wooden doors, they both looked around the courtyard, searching for Lucas, he assumed. The guy was nowhere in sight. "Come on. I'll walk you to your room," he said.

At her door, April turned, the heavy key in her hand. "Thanks for the coffee, Victor."

He shrugged and pursed his lips. "It was a pleasure."

Her answering smile lit her eyes. "I'm happy to have a friend in Paris."

The comment pleased him. "Then let's meet again for coffee next week," he found himself saying, and it surprised him how much he meant the invitation. They would go out as friends.

Chapter Five

A week went by where April managed to live her life without bumping into Lucas even once. She began to feel more secure as she went to and from the building, but she no longer had her lunch in the courtyard. It was beginning to be warm enough that she could eat in the small park outside her school, though she was still searching for that perfect spot to paint. Perhaps Victor would come through and show her something a little out of the way.

Ben appeared and took a seat next to her on the park bench. "Thought you might be here."

"You mean because I told you this is where I've been having my lunch lately?" April bumped his arm with her own. "Have you begun your Paris painting?"

"I think I've found the spot. I'm going to paint the street artists next to the Georges Pompidou center. That should give me all the bold colors and unusual characters I need. We have enough paintings that show the historic stateliness of this majestic city. It's getting boring."

April's mouth fell open. "Ben, how is it that your English is so good? No one talks like that."

"My family spent a few years in Hong Kong for my father's work, but I think I would have spoken English fluently even without it. My parents made sure my sister and I were bilingual. Well—trilingual if you count the French, but I'm not as fluent in French."

"Better than me," she said.

April leaned back on the bench beside Ben, and they watched a man throw a stick for his dog, who caught it and returned it. Two high school boys played Frisbee, looking from time to time to see if the group of girls sitting on a blanket were watching them. They were, but discreetly, only risking glances when it seemed the boys were occupied. April sighed. Her own teenage years had not been all that carefree.

"Have you thought more about your plans for China?" Ben asked when the silence stretched. He had been watching her, she noticed with a jump, and with an intensity that was new.

"No. It's enough for me that I plan to go. I don't want to rush my time here thinking about my next move. I want to be fully present in each place I live, even if it's just for a few short months."

"Don't you feel a little...unrooted? You know, since you don't have any home to go back to?"

The reminder felt like a physical punch, and April fought the tears that sprang up instantly. Unable to answer right away, she stood, wordlessly crumpling her napkin into a ball and walking to the garbage can. She dropped it in and stayed there a minute, face averted, pretending to watch the man with his dog.

When April returned to the bench, she pasted on a smile. "Why should I feel like that? My situation is not much different from other kids my age who are off having adventures without their parents nearby." She opened her cloth bag and stuffed in the notebook she'd been carrying for her impromptu sketches.

"It is different," Ben insisted, in a way that seemed as if he were determined to pour salt on her wound. "They have the security blanket of family to go back to, and you don't." Why was he forcing her to face what was painful when it was nothing she could change?

"Ben—" April stood again, now mad. She started walking, hoping he wouldn't follow, but she had no such luck.

"April, wait. I'm sorry. I didn't mean to make you upset. I just wanted to get you to think more about China. I can offer you a place to stay, so you won't feel so homeless. That's all."

April wiped the tears away from her face in an angry gesture. "Fine. You want to invite me over? That's nice," she said in a tight voice. "But stop making comments about my life. Let me live it the best I can with the situation I've been dealt. You're not in a place to make any observations about how I should feel."

"Okay," he said. He put his arm around her. "Let me walk you home."

It was all she could do not to push him away. Instead she smiled and took a step aside. It wasn't like she had a zillion friends in Paris. "That's nice of you, but I had plans to go exploring the city to try to find my new spot to paint. That's something I need to do on my own."

"All right, fine. No hard feelings?" Ben was looking at her in concern.

"No hard feelings." This time she softened toward him. It wasn't his fault she was so prickly. But as she hoisted her bag on her shoulders and walked away, she couldn't help the tears that leaked down her cheeks. And she couldn't help the fact that it was quite some time before she was able to view the future stretching before her in any but the bleakest of terms.

❧

VICTOR ENTERED his apartment with a spring in his step. He had decided to go knock on April's door and see if she wanted to have another coffee together. Hadn't they said they would meet more often? It was nice to have a friend. That's what she had called him, and it wasn't something he was used to. There were not many people he'd stayed in touch with from school, and most of the girls he met tended to regard him with a predatory look. April seemed to study him, rather, her blue eyes shining with irony and laughter. It had been a week, and the more time went by, the more determined he was to meet her again.

His keys went on the antique console under a gilded mirror, making a soft clink when they hit the marble. Everything in the apartment had its place, and Victor liked it that way. His study was the only room in the apartment that was the least bit modern. He had chosen a plain white desk, and furniture with red and black accents. He didn't care that he set the modern paintings in between wall panels that were decorated with nineteenth-century molding. He had respected the requirements for decorating a traditional Parisian apartment in every room, but the office was his.

As he crossed the living room, his phone buzzed and he pulled it out of his pocket, then froze. Margaux. It took a few seconds to steady his beating heart, and then, before he could lose his nerve, he cleared his throat and answered.

"*Allô?*"

"Victor, is that you? You sound different. It's Margaux."

He swallowed before answering. His throat was so dry, just from hearing her voice after a year, he wasn't sure any sound was going to come out. "Bonjour, Margaux. Yes, this is still my number. What a surprise to hear from you." His voice cracked a little, and he hoped she hadn't heard it.

"Yes, well. I've been away. You knew that, right? I went to Monaco."

"You told me before you left, but I didn't think you'd be gone so long." Victor tried to keep the peevishness from his tone but wasn't sure how successful he was. "You just broke it off and left, and I haven't had a single word from you other than a postcard with no return address. You didn't even return my calls."

"I just..." There was silence on the line. "I just needed a clean break. I was feeling pressure from my parents. They liked you, you know."

They had. It'd been the one thing that gave Victor confidence their relationship was going to work. Her parents accepted him, even if they were so formal as to be stiff. They liked his work ethic, and the money he brought in, of course. They even approved of his decorating taste, something which made him feel proud. While they didn't seem overly impressed with his father, they hadn't held that against Victor. Surely with all that going for him, Margaux wouldn't just dump him. But she had in the end.

"Why are you calling me now after all this time?" The question begged to be asked even if he was afraid it would turn her away.

"I need to see you."

Victor heard the urgency in her voice, and his heart leapt. She missed him. That was it. She missed him, or she wouldn't be calling him after a year. Maybe they could work things out after all. "Okay. When?"

VICTOR SAT on the steps of the Grande Arche de La Défense. Not too far up since she'd specified the base of the steps, but far enough that he could see her coming. He rubbed his face and exhaled. She was late again. People scurried across the esplanade, but no familiar face stood out of the crowd, except for...the woman looked like Margaux if it weren't for the baby carriage she was pushing.

Bile rose in Victor's throat as he stood, and he felt his fingers go numb. He took a couple steps down, then there was no mistaking her. She waved at him as he approached, a tentative smile on her face.

Wordlessly, they stood in front of each other before she offered her cheek for him to kiss, a movement that brought them close, their cheeks warm as they each grazed the other. Shock kept him nearly speechless, but he turned to look inside the carriage at the sleeping infant. "Yours?" he asked.

Margaux nodded.

"Who's the dad?" he asked her.

She looked at him for a minute, then took the handles of the stroller and said, "Come. Let's walk down the esplanade. It's nice today." Without waiting for him, Margaux turned and headed toward the fountain in the middle, and after a second's hesitation, Victor followed.

"Why'd you get back in touch, Margaux? What do you want from me?" The pain Victor had felt over their breakup rushed over him, and it was just as intense as if it were yesterday. He could hear the pain in his own voice when he asked, "You're with someone else, is that it?"

Margaux stopped and turned to him. Her sleek brown hair was pulled back in her usual style, and she wore the gold pendant earrings he'd given her for her birthday. Victor couldn't help but admire the beauty that came from her simplicity. A white crisp collar turned out over a navy blue sweater. A beige trench coat that fell to below her knees, revealing her jeans and brown moccasins. She always managed to look perfect.

"The baby is yours," she said.

He had been staring at her, soaking in the sight of her, though it would cost him when he had to rip her out of his heart for the second time... "Wait. What?" He couldn't have heard her correctly.

Victor looked at the baby again, this time searching for proof. Searching for something that would show he carried the same genes as this newborn. Could it be the nose? Or the shape of the face? But no. It just looked like a baby.

Margaux was still looking at him, and he could only ask, stupidly, "Is it a boy or a girl?"

She laughed. "It's a boy, Victor. His name is Matthias."

The blood rushed to his head, and he began to heave. "Victor, are you okay?"

Stumbling over to the modern statue in the center of the esplanade, Victor tried to hide behind it as he threw up everything he had eaten that day. It was not private enough. Businessmen and women, and more than a few tourists, gave him strange looks as they passed by, many turning away in disgust. He stood upright, shaking. *I have to get a bottle of water or something*, he thought. He looked at Margaux, and it wasn't a nightmare. There she was still. There the stroller was. Still.

He returned to her side. "How many months is he?"

"A mint?" she offered, and he took it. "Matthias is three months. So you see, I went to Monaco pregnant, but not knowing it. I can't explain why I didn't come back, but I...couldn't."

She was being secretive again. Victor couldn't stand when she kept these most private parts to herself, especially when they involved *him*. That was how she could leave, with almost no word, at a time when he thought they were at their best. He'd thought they were on their way to getting married.

"So why did you come back now?" he asked.

Margaux hesitated, her gaze drifting to the Arc de Triomphe in the distance. "I had to let you know," she said. "It wasn't fair to keep it a secret from you."

And the trouble with that—he could see it in her expression— was that she didn't even see the irony.

Chapter Six

Victor couldn't stop thinking about the baby after he left Margaux, and that was rather speedily as he needed time to process the shock. The baby—Matthias—hadn't opened his eyes, so he didn't know what color they were. Matthias had just slept right through his first meeting with his father. No big deal. Victor would have slept through it too if he were in Matthias's place. It wasn't as if the dad were very impressive.

He'd promised Margaux he would be in touch soon, and he meant to. He should probably tell his family, though he was reluctant to do so. His father, frankly, would probably not even care. Or, he'd make some snide comment—or worse, make use of his uncanny ability to read into his son's soul and mock him for finally having figured out a way to burrow back into Margaux's life, against her will and better judgment. His father really was something.

He could tell Mishou, but even with her he was strangely reluctant. He felt like the news would let her down. Sure, she wanted him to settle—wasn't she always telling him that?—but she didn't want him to settle down with Margaux. "You're not yourself around her," she had said. "You're trying to be someone else, and that can never last. Or, it might endure, but you'll live only as a shell of yourself, and that will destroy you in the long run." How could he now tell her he had a reason to make it work?

Victor walked into the courtyard, and his half expectation of seeing April there made him realize he'd gotten sidetracked in his intention to meet her again for coffee. Perhaps he could see if she were home now. He wouldn't talk about the baby, of course, but it might help get his mind off things.

He climbed to the last floor and knocked on her door. There was no immediate answer, but he thought he heard shuffling inside, so he called out, "April, it's me, Victor. I don't have your telephone number. But I thought you might like to have a coffee with me or something."

The door opened and April stood there, smiling, her hand on the knob. There were lines on her face from what was probably a nap, but he wisely said nothing about it.

"That sounds nice," she said. "Can I meet you downstairs? It'll just take me a minute to get ready."

She was wearing jeans and a plain navy blue T-shirt that brought out her eyes, and he thought she looked nice as she was, but he just nodded. Five minutes later, she jogged down the stairs, and he was relieved to see she hadn't changed. The lines on her face were gone, though, and it looked like she had put on some makeup, though it was hard to tell. He smelled mint as she walked up to him. It was an automatic impulse to lean forward and kiss her on both cheeks, and she seemed to have caught on to the French tradition because she kissed him back naturally enough.

"Thanks for the invitation." April stuck her hands in her pockets and swiveled forward. "Where shall we go?"

"How about Le Marais?" he proposed. "It's a little further. It's in the third arrondissement, but I was thinking about a place I could take you for your painting—"

"Oh good," she exclaimed. "I've been walking everywhere this past week, but I haven't found any place I loved. Do you have something in mind?"

"Yes. It occurred to me when I had a business meeting near there this week. It's Passage de l'Ancre," he said. "You'll have to decide for yourself if it inspires you. It's not like a grand monument or anything—more like a secret passage that few people know about. And it's got a lot of color."

"It sounds interesting, at least. Different. Not something I could find on my own." April looked up at him and blinked against the sunlight as he held the door for her.

"Are you up for walking a bit?" They turned down the broad street, and Victor began to feel lighter and more free with each step. "We can take the métro."

"I love walking," she said. "It's the best way to see Paris."

Victor and April cut across some of the side streets, then across Boulevard Haussmann to the métro station. April filled the silence by talking about her beginning French lessons, even practicing French with him until he begged her, laughingly, to switch back to English so he could understand her again. He was relieved to see she took his teasing in good fun. She talked about the portrait she'd finished of some guy, Ben, and how her art teacher was different from the one in Seattle. Françoise focused on the gradations of shadows, and April was learning to look for reflected light there that she had not noticed before.

They climbed on the métro, and the door hissed shut. Victor liked listening to her speak English because her voice was low and melodious—something she lost when she was trying to speak French. Suddenly, April stopped short, and a self-conscious blush covered her features. "I've been doing all the talking this entire time. I'm so sorry. I'm not usually such a chatterbox."

"I don't mind," Victor said. "What's a chatterbox?"

They were at the next stop, and the métro chimed to signal

that the doors would close. "It's someone who talks way more than she should." April laughed. "How've you been this past week?"

Victor pinched his brows together, suddenly at a loss for words. He no longer felt like keeping his news a secret from her, and he didn't know why. It wasn't like he knew her all that well, but without the physical attraction—not that she wasn't attractive, but that just wasn't the way their relationship was turning out—he was comfortable around her. Like one of those friends everyone seemed to have, except him. Maybe it was the fact that she was a foreigner that explained why she didn't seem to run from him, or want something from him.

She was waiting expectantly, so as the train lurched forward, Victor said, "I'll tell you. But how about when we're at the café and not here in the métro."

April accepted his request without teasing or pressuring him, and he was grateful. They stayed mostly silent during the ride, their hands grazing on the cold metal pole whenever the train swerved.

When they got out at République, she asked, "Are we going straight there? To the Passage de l'Ancre?"

"No. Coffee first," Victor answered. Then, as an afterthought, "If you don't mind." April shook her head, and he couldn't resist adding, "We're going to a café that's perfect for you."

"How so?" But Victor just shook his head, the corner of his mouth lifting.

However, when they stood in front of the Lily of the Valley café, all April said was that it was pretty. She liked the marble counter. Victor looked at her searchingly. "*Muguet?*" he said. "Doesn't ring a bell?"

When she shook her head, he pointed to the name of the café. "I looked it up. Those flowers you were wearing were lily of the valley. *Muguet.*"

"Oh! I had no idea what they were. I just knew they smelled good." April glanced at the café again and turned to him with a look of mild surprise. "That was actually really thoughtful of you to bring me here."

He felt a flush of warmth in his chest. "What would you like to eat?"

"Eat? Cheesecake," she exclaimed, having looked at what the other diners were having. "I miss cheesecake. And I'd like some coffee too, but a *café au lait*, not a tiny espresso." April gestured to a spot in the corner that seemed private, and Victor went to the counter to order.

THAT WAS SURPRISINGLY ROMANTIC, April thought, *for someone I'm determined not to get involved with*. It was nice to have a friend in Paris, and she didn't want to lose that. Plus, he seemed preoccupied and not out to seduce her or anything, which was for the best. She watched as he squeezed by someone and came to where she was sitting.

"Cheesecake," he said, and set it down with a flourish.

"I forgot to give you money," April replied, embarrassed.

"Don't. Please." Victor shook his head. "When we go out for coffee, let it always be my treat. I have enough money. If we ever go out to eat, I'll make sure you don't send me into bankruptcy."

"Was that a joke?" she asked in mock surprise.

That only elicited a smile, so she leaned forward. "Okay, Victor. I can tell something big happened this week. Do you want to tell me about it now?"

He looked young, she thought, while he stirred a sugar cube into his coffee. Then it dawned on her. No, he looked vulnerable. That's what was different.

Victor met her gaze. "I went out with someone for a year and a half, and she was important to me. I wanted to marry her. Her name was Margaux." He stopped, and April waited quietly, unsure where he was going with this but knowing he needed to get it out.

"A year ago, she left me. Told me she was going to Monaco for a short while, that she had a friend there. She didn't want to tie me down while she was away because she wasn't sure how long she was going to stay."

April bit her lip. "That sounds...painful."

Victor blew out a breath in frustration. "Yes. Because she didn't give me a chance to say what *I* wanted. She just said that even though she still loved me, she needed a break. So I let her go."

April waited, fiddling with her fork and letting her coffee grow cold. When Victor didn't say anything more, she asked, "When's the last time you saw her?"

"A year ago. Until today. I did try to contact her a couple of times while she was away, but she had turned off her phone. It was no longer her voice on the message. I didn't even think she still had the number, but then she used her old number to call me. And I saw her today for the first time."

Victor paused before adding, "She didn't come alone."

April couldn't help it. He looked so forlorn, she placed her hand on his arm. "She's with someone else, is she? And she came to meet you with *him*?"

He looked at her strangely, then let out a half laugh. "No. She came with a *baby*."

April was so surprised she jumped in her seat. "A baby?" Then she looked around and lowered her voice. "Whose baby?"

He narrowed his eyes and mumbled, "Mine, apparently."

April's mouth dropped. Okay, so what was she supposed to say to that? She swallowed. "And how did you feel about that? I mean, what did you say?"

"I threw up," he responded, then shot her a look. Was it embarrassment? He was hard to read.

There was humor in all this somewhere, but she didn't feel the

48

least desire to laugh. "Well, I should say so," she said. "What a shock."

Taking a bite of her cheesecake, followed by a sip of lukewarm coffee, April tried to put some normalcy in the situation. This was heavy news for a budding friendship. *Good thing I have no expectations*, she thought. Glancing at Victor again, it seemed he had some of his color back. "What's the baby's name?"

"He's called Matthias."

"Well, hey," she said. "I think you're going to be a great dad."

"You do?" His eyes widened in surprise. "What makes you think that?"

"It's just a hunch. Not everything in life is a certainty. We can't map out how everything is going to go. We can just do our best. If you're willing to be invested in the baby's life, then he will love you. You don't need to be a perfect dad or anything. Kids are forgiving."

"I'm not," he said under his breath.

"Well, maybe that's another thing to work on," April said with a smile. "Look. It's a life-changer, sure. But it can be a really good thing. Do you and Margaux have a future together?"

He shrugged. "We didn't talk about that."

"She'd be crazy not to at least be considering it."

"You think so?" Victor looked more hopeful, and she suffered a tiny pang that it was what he wanted. It would probably be the best thing for him and the baby, though, so she would support him.

"I do," she said. "Hey, if you're almost finished, why don't we walk a little."

He put the last bite of macaron in his mouth and stood. "Okay, let's go. I'll show you the secret passage."

THEY ENTERED the doorway on Saint-Martin, which looked like it led to someone's private property. As soon as the brightly colored, verdant street unfolded before them, April's eyes went wide. Walking slowly, she fingered the bushes that lined the walls and peered in the shop windows that bordered the street. She stopped short. "I could paint this place in the rain and paint someone walking with an umbrella by that umbrella store."

"Pep's. It's also an umbrella repair shop," he said. "Last one in Paris."

"This street has got so much character. It's like I'm in a village in France rather than in Paris. It's perfect, Victor. Thank you." She squeezed his arm, and the solid feel of it under his sweater brought her comfort.

"Are you going to feel comfortable painting here?" Victor asked.

April looked around. "It's got a couple benches and private corners. I think if I can find a spot and bring my portable stool, I'll feel comfortable. I hope people won't mind seeing me."

"I think once they see what you're painting, they'll be happy to have you here," he said, causing April to smile.

"Oh, Victor," she breathed, taking in the whole street in one broad sweeping gesture. "This is truly magnificent. I imagine there aren't many spots like this left in Paris"

"There are some," he said, "but no, not many."

"Well, I've found my spot," April said. "And, an added plus is that it's going to feel like a friendly, cozy sort of refuge, which is just what I need right now."

Victor looked at her keenly. "Is Lucas leaving you alone?"

"I haven't seen him. Thank goodness. But it's true, I'm always afraid I'm going to bump into him."

"And you can't leave?" he asked. "I mean, not that I want you to. I like having coffee with you."

She smiled. "I really can't. Unless there's some way to get housing that I haven't learned of that doesn't require sharing the room."

"Ah. That's just what I was going to propose. You don't want a roommate?"

"I feel too old for that. I'm twenty-three. I also need time alone and want to be free to paint at three in the morning, if the mood strikes."

They had sat on one of the benches in front of a shop with bushes planted on either side. There was no one walking by, and April felt as if they were in their own fairy-like world with nothing to disturb them.

"Does it strike often at three a.m.? The mood to paint," Victor asked curiously.

"No, not really. I have more traditional sleep habits." April chuckled. Stretching her legs forward, she asked, "I don't mean to bring up the subject again if it's painful for you, but do you plan to have an active role in Matthias's life? The whole sleep thing made me think of it because apparently that's something new parents don't get much of."

"Margaux didn't say whether she wanted me in his life—or hers—and it didn't occur to me to ask. We're going to have to get together again when I've had time to sort out what I'm feeling."

"I see."

It seemed like too monumental a subject to drop, but she was unsure if he wanted to discuss it any further. A comfortable silence had fallen when he suddenly said, "I should probably buy him a gift, right? What should I get him?"

Considering the matter, April replied, "Yes, that would be a good thing to do, I think. You can never go wrong with a gift."

Victor gave a short laugh. "You haven't met my ex-girlfriends. They never seemed happy with my gifts. They were never big or expensive enough."

April looked at him in surprise. "Victor, what kind of women are you dating? I mean, where are you dredging up these people? They sound horrible." She clapped her hand over her mouth. "I didn't mean—"

He laughed. "No, it's okay. My grandmother has been telling me I need better taste in women. It's no secret." He thought for a minute. "Margaux never complained about the gifts I gave her. She seemed happy to get them. She just tended to complain about me."

April gave a small snort. "Well it sounds like she was happy enough with your contribution to the baby."

Chapter Seven

The sun disappeared and the air began to feel cold, and Victor stood. "Shall we go?"

April nodded and gathered her things. They exited the passage on the opposite end they'd come in and headed toward the métro. As they were walking, they passed a baby boutique, and Victor stopped, hesitant. "Should I get the baby some clothes or something? What do you get a baby?"

"I don't know." April shrugged. "I know less than nothing about babies. I've never even babysat."

"Ah." Victor started forward again. "I know nothing about babies either, except for the fact that I'd like a big family." These words were accompanied with a flush of embarrassment. He had told April way more than he'd ever shared with other women. Or anyone else for that matter.

"I want a big family too." April looked at her feet, hiding a smile. 'I mean, not right away. I want to explore first and maybe start having babies when I'm thirty? Provided I find the right husband, of course."

"You don't need to get married. Not many people get married

in France. Not around our age anyway. Although...I asked Margaux to marry me before she left, and she said no."

"I think I'm too traditional," April said. "It's like saying...yes, I would like to have all the benefits of building a family with you, but I want to keep my get-out-of-jail-free card in case it gets too tough. That's just not my style. If we're in it, it's for the long haul."

"Yeah." Victor nodded. "Even though it's less common here in France, I feel the same way. I would want my kids to have more stability than I had growing up."

"Mmm hmm." April turned down the stairs of the métro. "I guess I had stability growing up, but man it was hard being an only child, and it's been hard having no family left. I don't want any of my kids going through that. I want to build them a brood."

Victor laughed. "A football team. You only need eleven."

"Just ten more for you," April said, gaily, as they pushed through the turnstile and jumped on the train that was pulling up.

When they had changed trains and finally exited at their stop, Victor guided their steps toward the Champs-Élysées, and April said, "I think you should get him a little stuffed animal. I'm sure his mom already has his clothes for the next year or so. Most moms would be at least that prepared. But I'm sure he'd like a stuffed animal."

Victor considered it. "All right," he said. "Do you still have some time? We could go to Petit Bateau up there. I think it's a pretty traditional store for babies."

"I have time." April smiled and gave a little skip. "I have fun hanging out with you."

Victor felt his heart lift just watching her, and he hooked his fingers around her arm. "I never understood that expression, 'hanging out.' I always imagine people hanging on a bar, like monkeys or something, while they talk."

April just laughed. "Well, I have no French comparison, but I'm sure you say equally silly things."

"I'm sure we don't," Victor said, lengthening his lip. "We're too civilized." April grinned.

Upon entering Petit Bateau, Victor asked the saleswoman to show him where the stuffed animals were. "Do you want a *doudou*?" the woman suggested. Victor had to explain to April that it was a stuffed animal for babies and smaller children, usually a stuffed rabbit or bear head with a bit of cloth attached that babies could hang on to. Not a soul knew this, but Victor still had his own *doudou* that his mother had given him as a baby, stashed in a box in the cupboard—the one Mishou said he wouldn't let go of at age three when his mother passed away after a swift bout of cancer.

After sharing a glance with April, he answered the saleswoman. "Yes, I think that could be nice. He's three months old."

"You might want to think about getting two," the woman said. "Babies can get attached to their *doudou*, and if you ever lose it, it can be quite traumatic. You can alternate the two and use one while the other is being washed so that they get worn to the same degree."

When the woman moved away, April said under her breath, "She's a good salesperson."

But the lady heard and called back in perfect English, "Parental guilt is lucrative." April burst out laughing.

They settled on a blue bear with a square flat cloth body and paws on each of the corners. Victor picked up a second one.

"You see? You're a good dad." April nudged his arm. The salesperson asked if it was a gift, and wrapped it, and they took the white and navy shopping bag and left.

"Okay, so I have a gift. Now I just need to ask Margaux what she wants from me."

April sympathized. "That's the hardest part."

VICTOR SAID goodbye to April and headed to his apartment.

Armed with the baby gift, he finally felt like he was ready to call Margaux and talk about next steps. It helped to have something to offer Matthias. As the phone rang, he mused that he would've liked to have had a say in picking out a name. Margaux picked up on the second ring.

"Hi, Victor." She sounded like she'd run to answer the phone.

"Margaux." Suddenly, Victor was at a loss for what to say next and knew that whatever it was, he couldn't say it over the phone. "Are you free to meet me tomorrow?"

"It depends on what time," she said. "My parents expect me to be here for lunch, but I can be free after that."

"Do you want me to swing by your parents' place to get you after lunch? How about three o'clock."

"Yes, that's fine," she said. "I'll see you then."

When he came to her parent's apartment the next day, Victor wasn't sure if he were supposed to call her to come down or ring the bell. Would her parents be glad to see him? What did they think of the baby, and what did they think of *him*, considering his role in it? Victor comforted himself with the fact that at least he had asked her to marry him. He'd done the right thing by her.

In the end, Victor rang the bell. He'd told her he would come to her parents' place to get her, so that's what he would do. Her father answered the buzzer, and Victor pushed open the heavy gold and mirrored door. He climbed the stairs, too nervous to wait for the elevator, though she was on the fifth floor. The white, molded door to their apartment opened and Margaux's father stood there. With a gruff nod, he held out his hand. "Victor."

Gesturing inside, her father walked into the living room, expecting Victor to follow. "Margaux is feeding the baby and will be out in a minute. Why don't you have a seat." Victor wondered about the fact that her father hadn't used the baby's name.

He sat. And waited until her father said something, not feeling it was his place to break the silence. Finally, Mr. de Bonneville—

they had never been on first-name basis—spoke. "So, Matthias is yours."

"I guess so," Victor said. "I didn't know anything about it until a few days ago." When the words were out, he felt so stupid. What guy answers the question *Is this your kid?* with, *I guess so?* What dad doesn't even know about his own kid? Never mind that Margaux had not chosen to fill him in on the fact that he was a father, he still felt vaguely guilty about his role in it. He'd always imagined his first child would be an occasion for an ecstatic joy that nothing else could give. The child would come into the bosom of a family that wanted it, where the mom and dad were happily married. He didn't expect guilt.

"I know I don't have to worry about you doing the right thing," Mr. de Bonneville said. "Although this was not what I would have wanted for her. Not at all." He glared at Victor through bushy brows as if it were his fault. "When do you plan to set a wedding date?"

Victor gulped. Wasn't this what he'd wanted all along? He wanted to belong to this family that would justify his existence, in a way, by including him as a full member of the centuries-old, aristocratic line. He would call Mr. de Bonneville by his first name. Baudouin. He would be there for Christmas morning. Their kids would open gifts and the de Bonnevilles would all be smiling. His mind took off at the vision, but he felt empty.

"Sir," he said at last. "I've asked her, and she said no. I'm not sure anything has changed since then. She hasn't brought up the idea of marrying me."

"But you're still willing." Mr. de Bonneville eyed him keenly. "Margaux may not have said anything, but she will change her mind now that Matthias is here. She knows what she owes to the baby, and she knows what she owes to this family."

Victor nodded but was saved from having to reply by Margaux entering with the baby against her shoulder, the blue blanket draped across the sleeping infant's back. "Hello, Victor." She walked over to receive his kisses on the cheek. "I'll just put Matthias down in the stroller."

Victor followed her into the vestibule. "I bought something for him. It's a *doudou*. Actually I bought two in case he loses one, which is what the salesperson said to do." He darted a glance at Margaux's father, but Mr. de Bonneville just stared at Margaux as she buckled Matthias into the stroller and stood straight.

"Thank you, Victor." She reached out for the white bag and peeked inside, adding, "He has a *doudou* that he seems to like, but you know how it is with babies. It's always nice to have other things to offer in case they grow tired of the one they have."

Of course the baby would already have one he liked. Victor was late to the game. "Well, anyway..." He watched Margaux put on her coat and reached out to shake her father's hand.

"Shall we go? *Au revoir*, Papa." Margaux gave her father a kiss on the cheek. She was calm and poised as usual, and gave her father the same dose of affection she'd always shown, but something in her had changed. Was she truly ready to settle down now? Victor wondered what she wanted from him, but he couldn't see any great contentment in her features, and he doubted his ability to meet whatever that need was.

They walked down the broad street, heading toward Trocadero by habit. It was where they always used to go when it was nice out and they had time for a picnic or wanted to soak in some sun. It was nice out today, but as soon as they turned to walk along the Place du Trocadero, the rays of sun shone in Matthias's eyes. Victor still hadn't seen those eyes open. He supposed Matthias was a cute baby, but he didn't feel any particular attachment. *I must not be a very natural father.*

"I'm not sure where to begin," Victor said. "I was a little shocked last week when you showed up with a baby." He turned as a group of male college students, wearing pink feathers and making chicken noises, were about to intercept their path. It was their school's equivalent of *bizutage*. Hazing. Having safely skirted the motley crowd, Victor continued. "However, I do plan to be involved in Matthias's life. And yours," he added, "as much as you want it."

Margaux tucked the blanket around the baby as the sun hid behind a cloud. "Thank you. I knew you would. I don't want you to do anything out of a sense of obligation. I know I didn't give you fair warning, and I'm sorry about that."

She didn't look sorry, but then he knew she showed only the barest glimmer of what she felt. Assuming she felt things. Victor wasn't always sure. He couldn't figure out when he'd stopped being so gracious about Margaux's quirks. Perhaps he was done making excuses for her. But then maybe their relationship needed to get to that new level. Maybe this was part of getting on the path to maturity. Margaux becoming more vulnerable and Victor idolizing her less.

"Your dad talked to me about marriage. Did you know that?"

"To me?" Margaux nearly jumped.

"Who else?" he asked, smiling weakly. "It makes sense for us to marry, right? After all, the baby is mine."

She didn't return the smile, or say anything at all, so after an uncomfortable moment he said, "The baby *is* mine, isn't it?"

"Victor, we went over this," Margaux replied, weary. "If I told you he is, then he is. But if you want to take a paternity test..."

He shook his head. That would be a bad way to begin. "No, I trust you."

She sighed, and turned the stroller down the ramp that led to the stretch of lawn below. "I'm sure my dad is ready for everything to be tied up in a neat little bow, but I need some time. I'm ready to talk about you being in Matthias's life, but not necessarily you being in mine." She looked at him, her expression guilty. "Is that okay?"

"Of course," Victor answered. What else could he say? They walked to the only free bench set in the shade, and she parked the stroller in front of it. "Do you want to talk about Monaco?" he asked, after a pause, looking up as a group of women jogged by them on the path.

"No. Let's talk about you. How has business been going?" Margaux adjusted the baby's blanket, probably just to do something with her hands.

So Margaux wanted to talk about his business and keep her own life secret? Fine. He could do that. He could fill the entire afternoon with talk of business. He could fill an entire married life with talk of business. Throwing an arm over the back of the bench, he crossed his leg, his movements urbane and controlled to hide his anger. "Remember the stationery supply store you advised me not to buy because it was too bourgeois? Well, I sold it for a huge profit, and I've bought and turned two more like it since you left."

Chapter Eight

April sat on the floor of her room and leaned against the bed. She had all six of her father's remaining paintings in front of her, perched against what little wall space the apartment had, as well as along the tall wooden armoire that came with the furnished room. Most of her father's paintings had been sold to private collectors, but two had been donated to museums. The painting the Seattle art gallery deemed most valuable had been her least favorite. Her father told her it was the one he painted when her mother died, and the feeling it evoked when she looked at it was of a bleak void so deep, it could never be filled. The canvas had been too large to carry with her and, before coming to France, she'd made an impulsive decision to sell the painting and donate the money to charity. The sum had been considerable.

She hadn't looked back. The ones in front of her were most precious to her, and they were well worth the red tape required to get them through customs just so she could have them with her. There were three of his earliest work—realist paintings that showed his natural genius and reflected the good instruction he'd had from the beginning. These were various sizes. A small painting of a dog looking up at a boy, a larger painting of a dock he had told her was from Chile, and the largest painting of her as a toddler, running through a field of wildflowers. The emotion she felt looking at the painting was partly evoked by her connection to it, and partly by her father's skill in capturing it. She wanted to reach out and caress the strokes, but she knew the oil on her fingertips could ruin the varnish, and she didn't dare.

The other three paintings were from the end of his life, and there were few of those out in the world. He had taken to painting abstracts. Although the forms were only vaguely delineated, it was possible to tell what the subjects of the paintings were by the colors he used. The ones April had before her were of their garden in three different seasons: summer, fall and winter. He died before he could begin spring.

April kept the shutters open wide, allowing the sun to stream in. It warmed her face, but didn't touch the paintings. She always kept them lined up next to the armoire, away from the heat of the window and the radiator, and cloaked in a protective darkness.

When she'd had enough of looking and connecting with her father in the only way that was left to her, April got up and wrapped the first painting, carefully, and went to slide it along the armoire. The phone rang before she could finish, and she glanced at the caller. Ben.

"Hey there. What are you doing?" he asked, as soon as she picked up.

"Not much. I was about to head out to paint."

"Have you found your spot yet?"

"As a matter of fact, I did." April held the phone with one hand while picking up another protective cloth with the other. "And wild dogs won't drag the location out of me, so don't even think to ask."

"Oh come on," he urged. "I told you where I was painting, and I even showed you the beginning of it."

"I know, and it's very good. But I'm keeping mine hidden until it's done. Anyway, you've already seen my other one so we're even."

"Meet me for dinner," Ben said, suddenly.

April paused, tempted. She hadn't spent time with anyone in a couple days, outside of meeting people in class. She was starting to feel lonely, and Victor must have been busy with his new baby, because she hadn't heard from him since their coffee date. "All right then. I'll meet you later. Around seven?" April looked at the paintings she still needed to wrap. "I want to make sure I have enough time to paint."

"Sounds good," he said. "And wear something nice. This time it's my treat, and I insist."

"Ben..." April stalled. She didn't want to go out on a date.

As if he could read her mind, he said, "It won't be an official date. But let me take you out anyway."

"Fine. Where?"

"It's near Métro Alésia, and I'll text you the address," he said. "Seven o'clock. I'll make reservations."

As soon as she hung up the phone, there was a knock on her door. *Victor!* April glanced at the mirror over her sink—although *why* she would do so was anyone's guess. Victor was her friend, nothing more. She pulled open the door, and her upturned mouth fell when she saw who was standing there.

"Bonjour, April."

"Hello, Lucas." She glanced beyond him down the hallway. There was no one. "What is it you need?"

Lucas was looking past her at the paintings she had not yet had time to put away. "What are these?" he asked, pushing his way in. April felt helpless to stop him, and she opened the door wider in case she would need to call for help. Not that anyone would answer. This building was like a tomb. He walked over to the canvas of her running in the wildflowers and picked it up, his thumbs directly on the paint.

"Please put that down," April said. "These are my father's

paintings and they're important to me." She tried to reach for it, but Lucas turned a quarter of a degree. Ripping the painting out of his hands was not an option. April had to do whatever it took to make sure the paintings stayed intact.

"They're really good," Lucas said, his voice soft with interest. He examined the paintings on the floor, then looked again at the one in his hands. "You could get a lot of money for these if you sold them. I know someone who works for an art gallery. I can ask her what they're worth and help you sell them. They're not going to bring you any money just sitting here on your floor."

April kept her voice steady. "That's nice of you, but I already have a plan for selling these. I don't want to do it right away. They're the last thing I have of my dad, and I want to keep them until I absolutely have to sell them. Here—" She gently pried the painting from him. "Let me wrap these back up to avoid any more exposure to the sun."

Once the painting was out of his hand, Lucas leaned against the doorjamb with a sneer, becoming more of the man she knew. "Come on, April. Let's go out for a drink. You went out with Victor, so I know you won't mind going out with me."

April kept her back to him as she carefully wrapped each painting, trying to think of the wisest course of action. She could not show fear, though it was what she felt. She could not be rude. That would be like poking a bear for a reaction. No matter what, however, she had to be firm, and when she was finished wrapping, she faced him squarely. "Lucas, I appreciate your asking me, but I'm not going to go out with you, so please stop asking. When I go out with Victor, it's as a friend. Nothing more. But I don't think that's what you're asking me for. I don't want to get into a romantic relationship right now." When April had gotten all the words out, she braced herself for his reaction.

It was just as she feared. Lucas turned beet red and glared at her before pivoting on his feet and walking toward the staircase. She heard a curse in English and something in French she didn't

A SWEETHEART IN PARIS

catch, but his tone made it sound like a warning. April closed the door softly and locked it, then sat on the bed. A feeling of unease washed over her, the mood oppressive and ominous in her room that had been cheerful only minutes before. Somehow, she didn't think she'd seen the last of Lucas. Maybe she should try again to find another place to live, but just thinking of it made her feel exhausted. Where else could she go?

AFTER FOUR HOURS of painting in her new spot, April returned, cautiously, afraid to cross paths again with Lucas. She didn't, but as she dressed in a red, fitted cocktail dress, she knew she would also need to leave the apartment to meet Ben, then return unscathed, before she could be sure of escaping him for the rest of what felt like a very long day. With trepidation, she walked down the stairs, and when she saw Victor instead of Lucas, her relief was all out of proportion.

"Victor," she called out in a squeaky voice. He'd been about to enter his apartment, and he turned in surprise, his eyes softening as soon as he saw her. That little detail, and the camel-colored sweater he wore that looked soft to the touch, made her want to leap into his arms. *Oh boy.* Sometimes she forgot about her resolution just to be friends. However, this was the only option open to her, and she wasn't going to miss out.

"Hi, April. Were you out painting again today?" She nodded, then chewed her lip as he examined her more closely, from her fitted dress up to her face. His eyes narrowed. "Are you doing all right?"

"I'm fine. I must be out of breath from the stairs." April leaned against the railing. "Yes, I was in the magical spot you showed me. And you? Have you been able to give your gift to… Matthias?" She almost said "your baby" but worried someone would overhear, and she imagined Victor was not ready to let the world know.

His shoulders slumped. "I did. Apparently he has a *doudou* he likes already."

"Yes, but he doesn't have one from his father. Or," she corrected herself, "he didn't before you gave him two. He's a really lucky baby, you know." April smiled at him.

Victor shook his head, but she caught a begrudging grin. "Are you doing something now? Do you want to..."

April felt a pang of regret but jumped in when he hesitated. "No, I need to go back out again. I'm meeting my friend, Ben, for dinner."

He looked at her more closely then, a slow perusal that made her feel breathless. "The one from the portraits."

"Yes, I, uh..." April knew she was blushing, and between the red dress and the red runner on the stairs, there was no hope of his not noticing it either. "He's the one I spend the most time with outside class."

Victor glanced at his keys then back at her, his expression inscrutable. "I won't keep you then. Have a good evening."

"I will." April turned to go, a weight of despondency settling on her already dark mood. Unwilling to end the conversation, she said, "I'll have to show you my progress on the painting."

The gaze he flicked her way showed interest. "I'd like that. I feel like I have a small part in its success." When she raised her eyebrows, he added, "Just a small part."

April laughed. "I'm teasing you. You do. I could not have found the place without you. I've already drawn in the contours and blocked the shadows, so I think I'll have something to show you by the end of the week."

"Let's have lunch then. You can show it to me, and we'll go and eat afterwards."

She paused before answering, but when she saw him seem to pull inward, as if to steel himself from rejection, she quickly explained. "I would love that. It's just, Victor—I really need to watch my budget, and I'm uncomfortable letting people pay my way. Tonight, with Ben, is an exception. He insisted, and I couldn't say no *again*. But I don't plan to make a habit of it, and you already treated me to coffee. Could we just get sandwiches instead?"

He surprised her. "Let me bring you to my grandmother's apartment. She makes me lunch once a week, and there's always too much food for the two of us. I think she will like you."

April broke out into a grin. "You've never mentioned family before, except for a not very favorable comment about your dad. I was thinking you didn't have any family you were close to. I think it's absolutely perfect that you have lunch with your grandma every week, and I would love to join you. That is, if you're sure she won't mind."

"I'm sure," Victor said. He stepped toward her. "Let me at least say good night properly since we're in France, and it's what we do." Leaning forward, he brushed each cheek with a kiss. His skin was soft, with only the slightest stubble, and he smelled like some unidentifiable masculine cologne. Understated and expensive.

"Good night." April turned and went down the stairs at a clipped pace, trying to slow her beating heart. It was for the best anyway. She was glad he had a baby in his life. It seemed like he needed the focus. And *she* needed to be focusing on her art. That was her baby, and it would be for a long time.

Chapter Nine

Victor had been mulling over the idea ever since he left his meeting with prospective clients, and as soon as he entered his apartment the decision was made. It was time to tell his father about the baby. He also needed to tell his grandmother, but he didn't seem to be able to bring himself to do it. Maybe it was because she would care the most.

It wasn't often Victor felt the urge to open up to his dad, but maybe being a father did that to you. He also needed to warn Mishou he'd be bringing a friend over for lunch. That was easier since April was *just* a friend, like she said. It was nice having a female friend, though if he were honest with himself, it was hard ignoring how beautiful she was when she wore a dress like that red one. Seriously. That Ben character was lucky. Victor was sure Ben didn't look at April just as a friend. How could he?

Best get this over with quickly. Victor picked up his phone and searched for his dad's name. "Papa," he said, his voice curt. "I need to see you about some business. When do you have time?"

His father mumbled something to whoever was in the room with him, telling him—or her—to put the papers in front of him. He got back on the phone. "What's it about?"

"It's about the Marseille subsidiary. I have some documents to show you that you'll want to see." He knew his dad well enough to predict he wouldn't agree to see him if it were for any reason other than business. This would make the meeting worth his while.

"All right. Be here tomorrow at three," his father said. "Bring the papers with you. You can't afford to lose this deal."

"I know what I'm doing, Papa. I wouldn't bring this to your attention if it weren't for the fact that we're sharing the deal." He also knew his dad respected him more when he stood up for himself.

"Hmm." His father grunted in reply, then hung up.

Victor looked at the phone. "So nice to talk to you, too, Papa." He hung up, then headed over to favorites to dial his grandmother. It was like the spoonful of syrup after the bitter medicine.

❧

APRIL WAITED at the entrance of the restaurant until her eyes adjusted to the dim interior. Ben was already at the table, and he stood when she entered. His eyes went wide. "I didn't even know you owned a dress like that."

"Why, thank you, Ben," she said, sitting when he held the seat out for her. "It's nice to know you have confidence in my ability to rise to the occasion."

"That's just it," he said, sitting. "I wasn't sure you would."

"Ben, you're obtuse." April scanned the menu. "What are you getting?" She had agreed to dine out with him on this one occasion and now she was going to eat well, even if she would try to choose the least expensive things on the menu.

"We're getting an entrée, main dish, and dessert, okay? So choose whatever you want from each."

"No arguments here," she said, deciding on the salmon terrine

69

for the first course. It was a cozy seafood restaurant, and though she wasn't crazy about fish, she did like salmon and knew it could be her fallback if nothing else worked. They did have a small selection of meat, however, so she chose from there.

"Lamb?" Ben exclaimed, when the waiter walked away. "But this is a seafood restaurant."

"I'm not a fan of seafood," she retorted with a smile. "But thank you for inviting me. I do like salmon."

"No seafood? That's too bad. It's my mom's specialty. You may change your mind when you try it."

"Anything's possible," April said, lightly. "But not everything is probable. How far along are you in your painting?"

"I have the full sketch done. Now I just need to play with the colors."

"You're further along than I am, then. Isn't Penelope painting George Pompidou as well?"

"Yes. I see her there sometimes. But she's focusing on the Parisian buildings around the center and is contrasting the two."

"We should invite Penelope out with us sometime," April said. "She seems pretty cool."

"She's Parisian. I'm sure she already has enough friends," Ben retorted.

April pursed her lips. "You can never have too many friends, and she doesn't seem to have any in the class at least. I'll invite her."

"Fine. But let's focus on *us* since we're enjoying this good dinner."

"Ben, might I remind you there is no 'us.'"

He flashed her a grin. "Just thought I'd try."

April rolled her eyes and accepted his attempt at humor, but she detected a serious undertone, which worried her. This was why she didn't like accepting meals. There were expectations underneath, and she wanted no expectations where her own were disregarded. A change of subject was in order.

"Have you talked to your family lately? Do they know about the art competition?"

Ben poured her a glass of sparkling water and grimaced. "Yes. I shouldn't have told my mom. She told my dad, and he's already told everyone my painting was accepted."

"Yikes. That's a lot of pressure. What if you don't get accepted?" April put her napkin on her lap and stared at the candle on the white tablecloth, soothed by its flickering light. She shouldn't have been surprised by his cocky answer.

"I will."

"No, seriously, Ben. How can you know? Now that your dad has told everyone, that puts a lot of pressure on you."

He shrugged and his look was uncertain. "I'll do whatever it takes, just as I'm sure you will." He smiled then, as if he were trying to put on a brave face, and her heart went out to him. She sincerely hoped for his sake his painting would be accepted.

"So tell me how to say fish in Chinese," April said, as the waiter came and deposited a plate of salmon in front of her.

"*Eu,*" he replied, breaking off a piece of bread.

April raised a brow. "Ew? Like gross?"

Ben laughed, his handsome features lit with amusement, and whatever tension was there flew away. "No. You have to make your voice swing upwards. *Euuu.*"

Grinning, she attempted to imitate him. "Euu."

"You just said 'rain,'" he said.

"Oh dear," April replied, mildly. "I'd better practice some before I get there."

❦

VICTOR OPENED the glass door to his father's office, a modern suite in a mid-nineteenth-century stone building that overlooked the Seine. "Victor, good to see you, my son. Have a seat." This warm accolade was for the benefit of a harried-looking man

Victor had never seen before. A middle manager by the look of it. "We're just finishing up here, and then you and I can get to our business. Did you ask Marie for a coffee?"

"No. I'm fine." Marie was his father's latest fling, but considering the predatory looks she threw Victor's way, he wasn't sure how long she would last.

When his father had seen his associate to the door, he returned and sat at his desk, all appearances of cordiality gone. "So what have you got for me?"

"It's these documents they want us to sign. They say they won't sign the contract until we agree to these conditions. I can't move forward without your approval on them, but I don't think you're going to like number three."

His father scanned the page. "Keep his no-good son-in-law on as CEO, with all power attached to the title? I don't think so. Tell him we'll think about it, and then let's organize a hostile takeover with his remaining board. They've had enough of the son-in-law too." His dad tossed the papers back toward Victor, then grabbed the stack of documents at his right and slid them in front of him. When Victor didn't get up right away, his father looked up from under the severe brows that had terrified Victor when he was young. "Anything else?"

Yeah. You're going to be a grandpa. Victor put the papers his father had tossed at him inside his leather bag. "I ran into Margaux," he said. He leaned back, gearing up for battle.

"So, she's come back, has she? I didn't think she would." His father started skimming the document and writing notes in a legal pad to the side. Finally he looked up, irritated. "And...?"

"And she had a baby. Who is mine, apparently." The last word came out small.

His father went back to writing. "Is that all? Well, I suppose she'll marry you now. Then you'll have everything you've always wanted. A happy little family." His father's sneer showed what he thought of that plan. "I suppose her dad will be glad to have your money."

He'll take me in spite of my relationship with you, Victor thought. "His dad would like us to get married, yes. But I'm not sure Margaux wants it."

"Can't say I blame her. Listen, tell Marie to get in here when you go, will you? I've got a letter I need to have her type out as soon as she can."

There would be nothing more. Victor slung his bag on his shoulder and pushed the glass door to exit.

VICTOR SAW Margaux again the next day. This time, she suggested that she and Matthias come over to his apartment so they could talk, and the baby could sleep more peacefully. He'd only thought about cleaning the apartment in preparation, and not about providing refreshments, so he ran out to the local market an hour before she was supposed to arrive. As he entered the building, his arms full of groceries, Lucas was coming out, and Lucas stopped him with a gesture.

"Hey, can I ask you something? Are you and April together?"

Victor, accustomed to Lucas's lack of civility and impatient to get home, answered brusquely. "April and I are friends. Nothing more." When Lucas didn't take the door that Victor held out to him, he let it fall shut behind him and started to walk across the marble foyer.

"So that means she's free to date other people?"

At this, Victor turned slowly. "April can date whomever she pleases. But I wouldn't expect anything from her right now. Her focus is on her artwork."

Lucas's laugh was nasal. "Oh, girls always have time for an extracurricular activity. It's all they can think about."

The words left a bad taste, not only because they lacked respect, but because they expressed what he, himself, had thought in the past. April was unlike any woman he'd ever met, and in seeing her passion, he knew Lucas's idea of how women thought was completely untrue. It made him ashamed of how he'd treated women in the past. "That might be true for some women," Victor said. "But not April."

He couldn't help himself. He had to add, "Listen. Just stay away from her, okay? She's not interested in you."

"How do you know that? It might just be jealousy since she's clearly not interested in you. In any case, don't tell me what to do. *Occupe-toi de tes oignons.*" Watch your own affairs.

Victor laughed in disgust. "I might say the same for you. Leave April alone," he repeated.

When he got to his apartment, Victor wasn't sure he had done the right thing by sticking up for April. It might make things worse for her if Lucas knew he cared. But he couldn't help himself when faced with the leering, skinny, overgrown adolescent in front of him. Oh, how he wanted to punch him.

Several of Victor's classmates had already gone on to find partners and have children, and he had wondered if he was too immature. As if he needed that extra time to grow up. Now Victor saw that he'd at least come partway. Lucas was a shining example of a person he *didn't* want to become. Mishou would be proud of him for his revelation. She was forever telling him it was time to grow up, but in the nicest terms possible. Only she could talk to him that way.

Margaux rang, and he let her in. She seemed tired as she unwound her scarf and leaned forward to receive his kisses on the cheek. It was different than when Victor kissed April. With April, there was a little spark and a smile in her eyes, probably because she wasn't used to greeting people that way. With Margaux, it was colder. A routine and nothing more. Perhaps it was better she hadn't wanted marriage.

Victor looked in the carriage and saw that Matthias had his eyes open for once. The baby studied him curiously, and Victor felt some deep stirring of the heart. Perhaps he should introduce himself to the baby. Say, "I am your dad," or something like that. He waved his fingers at Matthias, who watched him with a serious expression, and Victor felt stupid.

"He's awake," he said.

"Yes, I just fed him before coming here. He'll probably fall asleep in a bit."

"Do you want some orange juice?" Victor asked. "Or a *pastis* or something?" Her family liked the anise-flavored drink.

"No alcohol while I'm breast-feeding. A glass of water will be fine."

They sat on his spindle-legged embroidered couches, which were not all that comfortable, he realized. He'd gotten them to match the apartment, but never used them. In fact, he rarely had company.

Victor felt like he had to say something. "How is he sleeping?"

"He still wakes up every three hours," Margaux said. "But at least in France, my mom can watch him during the day while I take a nap. It was hard in Monaco."

"Did you stay with your cousin the whole year you were there?"

"Not all of it." She got up suddenly to get the baby out of the stroller. "Here, do you want to hold him?"

"Ah, okay. Sure. I don't really know how to..."

"Just make sure you support his neck. Like this." Margaux showed him where his hand needed to be placed, and as soon as he had the baby properly secured, she moved back to her seat, her signature scent of Hermès perfume trailing in her wake.

Victor looked more closely at Matthias. "I don't really see the resemblance. Not to you or to me."

"Well, babies change all the time, you know." When Victor continued to study Matthias, Margaux took a deep breath. "I've been thinking about your proposal."

"My proposal?" His heartbeat went up a notch. Surely she

couldn't be thinking of his wedding proposal that she'd turned down, not once, but twice.

"Yes. I know I told you I needed to think about it, and it's true that my dad is putting a lot of pressure on me to marry you, with you being the father and all. He also said the devil he knows is better than the devil he doesn't. The thing is..." Margaux toyed with her skirt as her last words hung in the air. "I think it would be a good idea after all. I think it's better for Matthias to have two parents and, you know, I can't exactly live with my parents again like this. You can't go back to your parents' house once you've left it. It's suffocating."

Margaux looked up at him now, meeting his gaze. He hoped his panic didn't show. "So yes, Victor, I'll accept your proposal. We can start planning a wedding."

Victor didn't think a sense of dread was a very promising start to a marriage, but he had offered, which was like giving his word. He swallowed down his panic and managed a smile. "Well that's great, Margaux. I think it will be for the best." He wasn't able to say anything more, however, so he studied Matthias while she swung the leg crossed over her other knee and stared at the paintings. It was unlike her to make random movements—to be anything but poised.

The silence was loud as each was lost in his own thoughts. Finally, Margaux turned to Victor with an artificially bright smile. "Well, that's settled then. I'll tell my parents so they can make the announcement."

Chapter Ten

I t was a beautiful day. The lilacs in the courtyard gave off a rich
perfume, and as soon as April stepped onto the sidewalk, a
soft breeze carried the smell of budding leaves that swept away
the motorcycle fumes that so often filled the street. The sun
glinted on the beige stones and lit up the gleaming black grates in
front of each window. April walked with a spring in her step,
contemplating her luck to live in such a beautiful place, even if it
were just for a few months.

Her painting was rudimentary and contained only a sketch of
the storefronts and trees, and she'd left it at home. Today, she just
wanted to soak in the atmosphere of this colorful, quaint little
street. She watched people come and go, deciding which
personage would appear in her scene. There would be the little
woman in a red beret and beige trench coat, walking a fluffy white
dog. There would also be the young couple: the man in the navy
and white striped Breton shirt and his girlfriend with long, sleek
black hair. Goodness, this place was a gold mine with its myriad
characters that could represent Paris. She would also include the
gypsy girl begging at the entrance to the passage, putting her at
the base of the first storefront. This, too, was Paris.

Once she'd sketched some of the possibilities, April decided to head to the art school, though there was no class. Perhaps there were students there, and she could see what they were working on, or invite them to go for coffee. She could call Ben but was reluctant to do so. Despite all his protests to the contrary, she had the feeling he was looking for something more from her than she was ready to give. She was even unsure about the wisdom of accepting his offer to show her around Shanghai when she came. Then again, who says no to introductions and a personal tour given by a local?

There was no one in the school. At least that's what April thought until she heard sniffling coming from behind one of the canvases in the corner. With a small frown, April went and peered over the canvas. "Penelope, is that you? What's going on? Do you need help?"

Penelope looked up quickly. She appeared startled, as if she hadn't heard anyone come in, and swiped at her face with her hand. Her smile looked more like a scowl. "I'm fine. Really. I didn't think anyone was here."

"So you let yourself have a cry. I understand that." April pulled out a tissue from her purse and handed it to her. "Don't worry. I won't be a bother. But can I help you with something?"

Penelope stood abruptly and started putting her unused art supplies into her bag. "No, really. I'm okay." She forced a more natural smile this time. "What are you doing here?"

April shrugged. "Actually, I didn't have anything to do, so I thought I'd come here and see if anyone was working. I don't suppose you want to go have a coffee with me?"

Penelope hesitated. "No, I'd better get going." She took her canvas and brought it to the racks where people left their paintings to dry and, calling over her shoulder, said, "You're from America, right?"

"Yes." April drummed her fingers on the table at the edge of the room, wondering if she should work on something or go somewhere else. She didn't like having all these hours to kill, and for once, she wasn't in the mood to be alone and paint. She considered again calling Ben.

"Are you from New York, by any chance?"

"No, from Seattle," April answered. "I've never even been to New York."

"Huh." Penelope picked up her bag as April sat on one of the stools by the door. "I'd love to go. It's always been my dream."

"You should then. What's stopping you?"

"Well, that's easy for you to say," Penelope said. "I'm sure you had family support to come here. My family does not want me to study art or travel, so I'm not going to get any help from them."

April paused before responding. "I suppose you could say I have family support—or I did anyway. But everything I'm doing is on my own. I'll have to depend on what my father left me for future trips. For this first one, I'm using the money I earned while studying. So you see, you can do anything you set your mind to."

"If you have a firm enough mind." Penelope stared straight ahead, then sighed. "And generally I do, but..."

"I know," April said. "Sometimes circumstances make it tricky."

"You do understand." Penelope looked at her curiously. "Do you know a lot of people in Paris?"

April shook her head.

"You know what?" Penelope said, suddenly. "Why not. Let's go have coffee. I have a few hours to kill before I go to a party later, and maybe I'm in the mood for company after all. Plus, I like you, and I don't like everybody."

Coffee led to an invitation to the party Penelope was attending that evening. She explained that she had some good friends from high school who lived in the area, and they were hosting a dinner party, but that they wouldn't mind one more. "And Arthur will be there too. The one who came to the studio with Mr. Chambourd."

"But I don't speak French very well," April put out nervously.

"Don't worry about that. People are always eager to practice their English."

The sky was starting to darken when they arrived at a simple building that was only four stories high, with large bay windows in each apartment. "Nice place," April said. "Your friends from school seem to be doing well."

"Oh, Guillaume's parents bought this place for him," Penelope replied. When they entered the apartment, Penelope was met by a chorus of greetings with a few curious faces turned April's way.

"This is April from the art school. You're going to have to practice your English with her because she only just arrived in France."

The mood in the apartment surprised April. Instead of smoke and beer glasses and the loud noise of a party, she found a group of sober, neatly dressed young people cooking together and sipping glasses of wine or sparkling water. The kitchen was larger, she suspected, than most French kitchens, and they were able to work around a center island with a wood top. One was tearing salad into pieces, another was seasoning steaks to be cooked, and yet another was mixing dressing in a brown ceramic bowl.

"Would you like to help, April?" one asked, in English.

"I don't know much about cooking," she replied, "but I'll do my best."

They gave her tomatoes to slice and she tried to match her slices to the ones already on the wood platter.

"I'm Guillaume." A thin man with tousled brown curls, and sideburns that suited him, came and gave April a kiss on each cheek. "I'm Penelope's boyfriend, but she doesn't know it yet."

Penelope rolled her eyes, but April laughed. "You have a really nice apartment, Guillaume."

He bowed. "You're an artist like Penelope?" When April nodded, he added in a stage whisper, "She's very talented, but she'll be the last one to tell you that."

"Well, having seen her paintings, I can confirm she's very talented." April ignored Penelope's noise of protest. "And, so, what do you do?"

"I'm a physical therapist," Guillaume replied. "I put people back together when they're broken. That's why Penelope is so perfect for me."

"Stop teasing, Guillaume," Penelope said, without rancor, but April didn't think his words were empty. Guillaume's eyes followed her when she left the room.

"I'm done with the tomatoes," April said. "What are you making?"

"Tomatoes, mozzarella and basil for the entrée, steak au poivre with green beans for the main dish, and chocolate fondant for dessert. After the cheese and salad, of course."

April looked around at the group of eight people, who were chopping, drinking and making jokes. "Have you always done this? You cook together? Do all of you know how to cook?"

"I'm the one who likes it best, and I'm the one who organizes it, but everyone here knows how to cook or is learning fast."

April sighed in appreciation. "Thanks so much for having a novice like me. This is really great. We never did anything like this back at home."

Guillaume lifted his eyebrow. "No hamburger assembly parties?"

"Now you're just teasing," April retorted, with a bump on his shoulder.

When they sat down to the meal, it was with cloth napkins and chunks of warm baguette that someone must have just gotten from the bakery. The tomatoes were a festive red against the green basil leaves, and someone had cut the mozzarella in thin slices and drizzled olive oil over the top. When they got to the main course, April was surprised there was no starch to accompany the meat and green beans, but she figured nobody needed it with the baguettes, and then the cheese course that would follow.

She had been right. By the time she finished sampling from the cheese selection, choosing the pungent chèvre, camembert, and Roquefort, as well as the hard Comté, she was certain she couldn't hold another bite.

Penelope sat on the other end of the table, looking much more cheerful than when she had arrived. The epitome of French, April thought. Her brown hair was cropped close to her face and it framed large brown eyes. She had delicate features that matched a slender frame, and when her smile appeared, it made her glow with beauty. No wonder Guillaume was smitten. Next to her sat Guillaume's sister, Aimée, who looked a little like him, except for the shape of the mouth and the absence of sideburns. Then there were Théo and Martin, who were practically glued to the sides of Auriane and Morgane. She'd have to ask if they were dating.

Only Arthur sat apart, and Penelope shot him covert glances that he didn't seem to notice. He leaned back at the table to April's left, aloof, but not unfriendly. In fact, she was never made to feel that she was a third—or rather ninth—wheel. She'd have to get to know Penelope better. Anyone who had friends like these must be a good person to know.

Guillaume brought the chocolate fondant right from the oven, and April couldn't believe her mouth could still water when she was so stuffed. But she salivated with the first bite. "This is amazing," she exclaimed, then clapped her hand over her mouth in embarrassment. That was louder than she'd meant it to be. Everyone gave a small cheer then went back to their dessert.

"*C'est incroyable*," Théo said. "You'd best start practicing your French if you're going to spend time here."

April nodded her head. "*C'est incroyable*,' she repeated, badly, and put another spoonful in her mouth.

"So you're studying art. Are you here for the year?" Arthur had finally come out of his shell, and she was conscious that his question was not mere idleness since she knew he was an artist himself.

"Just for the spring semester and the summer. Although I'd like to go to Arles for the month of August when school is closed and tour there."

"A fan of Van Gogh, are you?" Arthur made a hard *g* sound at the end of the name, rhyming it with cog.

April stared at him. "How did you pronounce that? Isn't it pronounced like van *go?*"

"Not in France. It's pronounced van *gog.*"

"Oh. Well I won't make that mistake again," April said. "One ought to know how a name is pronounced."

"Especially an artist's name if you're an artist." Arthur lifted an eyebrow as he held the espresso that Auriane had just set in front of him.

So even the reserved Arthur had decided to open up at last, and they talked about Mr. Chambourd's style of art over the constant volley of teasing and light-hearted sallies that flew back and forth across the table. When one or two comments were directed her way, April grasped enough of the French to hold her own, though she answered in English.

"We're not going to let you off that easy. You need to speak French," Théo said with a wink, enunciating the words slowly so she would understand.

As she was preparing to leave, April realized she'd not had such a good time with a group of people her age...ever. No drama, no trying to impress, no love triangles (although it seemed like there was some unrequited love). No hard feelings, anyway. What a treasure to have friends like this. *I wonder what had happened to Penelope to make her sad...*

Penelope came to see her out. "I'm going to stay behind and help Guillaume clean up."

"I should help too," April urged.

"No, we have stuff to talk about." Penelope smiled and shook her head. "And no, there's nothing between us. He was just joking."

Hmm, thought April. "If you insist. But I feel bad leaving a mess."

"It's fine. Thanks for cheering me up." Penelope had put on bright red lipstick after dinner, which completed her pixie look, and she gave a dimpled smile.

"It was nothing. You have the best group of friends," April said. "Seriously."

"You'll have to join us again then." Penelope leaned in to give her the *bises*.

"I would love that." April hoped her invitation was sincere.

It was only ten o'clock when April got on the direct train line to come home. Perfect. When Penelope had first proposed that April join her, April feared the evening would just be starting about now, and she was not the type to stay up all night for social activities. In fact, an hour was generally about all she could handle. What a pleasant surprise that the evening had been so rich in friendship and laughter, and that it ended early enough for her to get home at a reasonable hour. She'd be tucked away in her bed before eleven and ready to start tomorrow's adventures fresh. It was time to incorporate her sketches of the figures into the painting.

Chapter Eleven

✦❀✦

Having entered the door code, April's footsteps echoed on the cobblestones as she crossed the quiet courtyard. She pressed her key fob against the second door, hesitating by the elevator. No, she would take the stairs. The exertion would clear her mind, and the exercise certainly wouldn't hurt her body. The lights in the stairwell didn't work. It was the second time it had happened this month, and she'd heard there was a glitch in the electricity from time to time. Good thing she wasn't stuck in the elevator. She heard the sound of her own breathing as she climbed the stairs.

A window in the sloped roof let in light from the moonlit sky that showed the contours of the steps and railing in dim relief. April could see well enough as she rounded the stairs and approached the top floor. Normally, she hated fumbling through the dark. It made her nervous. But the meal and convivial atmosphere she'd just shared with new friends made her feel invincible, like only good things could happen. At the top of the stairs, she pulled on the railing and headed left to her apartment, but a movement on the right brought her head around. A man got up from the window ledge.

It was Lucas.

April's skin prickled. Her pounding heart and breathlessness were not just from climbing six flights of stairs. Some primitive instinct told her Lucas was not here to chat. Danger crackled in the air.

"Why are you sitting there in the dark?" April strove to keep her voice neutral and turned to face him, another instinct warning her she'd best not have her back to him.

"The apartment is dark too." He stood, only an inch taller than she did, but with a raw energy that felt menacing, especially when he moved her way. "At least here is some light," he said. "Why don't you stay out here with me where there's light, April?"

April shuddered. She couldn't help it, though she was going to continue to pretend everything was normal. She had a sense that showing fear would be the thing to flip him over the edge.

"If there's no electricity, I'm going to a café. There's no sense in staying here." April could hear the breathlessness in her own voice and hoped he didn't see how afraid she was. She turned—her back to him now—and went for the stairs.

"I'm coming with you then," Lucas said.

"No." April took the steps at a fast pace. "I'll go by myself." When he started trailing her, close enough to touch, a hysterical sob rose in her throat. She shoved it down.

"It's a free world, and you can't really do much to stop me from coming." His reminder of how little power she had frightened her, as it was meant to do.

It was too dark to run. April quickened her steps past the fifth flour, then the fourth, the silence between them ominous. Clutching the rail, she circled down, with Lucas stalking only a step or two behind her. He touched her arm, and she leapt at the contact.

"Careful, April. In this dark you could break your neck."

She shrugged off his hand, and for only a moment, anger won out over fear. "Get your hand off me."

Lucas allowed more space between them, and she breathed a sigh of relief, but she wasn't sure if he was just biding his time. When he touched her again, her panic came back full throttle. She was being tracked like an animal.

The third floor landing was her chance. April darted away, flying to Victor's door, and pounded on it. "Victor! Victor! It's April. I need you." She thought she heard an answering noise in the apartment, but Lucas grabbed her arm and hauled her back toward the stairs.

"You can forget about me being nice now," he growled.

"Victor!" she called out again. One door opened in the hallway, but a face that didn't belong to Victor peeked out and quickly shut the door. She wasn't sure she would have any help from that quarter.

"Shut up," Lucas said. He pulled her again, and she almost lost her balance on the step.

"Let go of me. I can walk on my own." April strove for anger, but was engulfed in fear. There was no one in sight. She had to find a way to break his punishing grip.

They were in the foyer now, and as if he read her hopes about coming across another resident—anyone who might help—Lucas yanked her toward the door that led to the alley where the garbage cans were. It was a dead end, except for the other door that led to the courtyard, which was locked on that side. There weren't even any windows overlooking the alley. No one would see them here. With one hand on her arm, Lucas buzzed the door open with his key chip and pushed her outside.

I can't let him drag me out there. An incoherent dread suddenly crystalized. *It may not be enough for him to assault me. He's completely out of his senses right now. He may kill me.* "Let go of me," April yelled, again. She ran to the door that led to the courtyard and yanked it open, running through it, but as soon as she was out, Lucas hauled her to a stop and pulled her back toward the alley. She clenched her teeth together and kicked him.

Immediately, there were pinpricks of light in front of her eyes as he brought his arm up and slammed his hand against her face. There was a dizzy shock that left her weightless before her cheekbone throbbed in full force. April doubled over with the pain of it, but in an instant Lucas had his hand around her neck, and he pinned her to the wall.

A door slammed. April heard the sound of running and felt someone pull Lucas away from her. She could breathe again.

"*T'es fou?*" A voice called out. *Are you crazy?*

Victor.

April staggered forward, reaching out a weak arm to steady herself, but she found nothing and fell to her hands and knees. Through the haze, she saw Victor take a swing at Lucas. "You—" His fist made contact, but Lucas had punched Victor back in the gut, cutting off the rest of his words.

In a swift movement, Victor stood upright and punched Lucas with a left hook. "You ever touch her again, you're dead," Victor shouted and gave another punch for good measure. Lucas slumped to the ground.

Someone above the courtyard opened the window. "Take your party somewhere else. Some of us are trying to sleep."

"Mr. Poulain," Victor called back, breathless, his eyes on Lucas who was slumped on the cobblestones against the door leading to the alley. "Instead of complaining..." He took a breath and seemed to be mastering his anger. "May I suggest you make yourself useful for once and call the police."

There was a pause. "*D'accord,*" Mr. Poulain replied, in a surprisingly meek voice. He pulled his head in to shut the window.

Victor's breathing slowed, his eyes not leaving Lucas's form, which was still on the ground. He darted a glance April's way. "Are you all right?"

She nodded, then realized his eyes were trained on Lucas again, who was coming to consciousness. Victor hadn't seen her nod. "I'm all right."

"I can't come to you yet. I don't know what this *crétin* might do. Stay there. We'll get him put away, and then I'll give you a hand. You'll have to give a statement to the police. Are you up for it?"

April nodded again and got to her feet. After a minute, she added a weak, "Yes."

Victor watched warily as Lucas sat up and leaned against the wall. In an instant, he attempted to pull himself to his feet, but Victor shook his head. "Don't even think about it. You're staying right there."

Lucas spat in his direction. "You can't make me do anything. This is my apartment building, and I'm going home."

Victor sighed, wearily, and put up his fists. "If you haven't had enough, we can go another round. But you're staying here until the police arrive—" He was not able to finish his thought before Lucas leapt up and barreled into Victor's stomach, before starting for the door that led to the street. With a grunt that turned into a surge, Victor hurled himself after Lucas and grabbed him around the waist, but Lucas pulled forward until they were at the stone archway that led to the street exit. April noticed Victor was not wearing any shoes.

"*Lâche moi!*" Lucas grunted, straining against Victor's grip.

"*Je t'ai dis que non.*" *I said no!* Victor stopped pulling and let Lucas go forward suddenly, which sent his head crashing into the wall. Instead of being dazed, Lucas slammed his heel on Victor's bare foot and darted the few steps forward, punching the button and yanking open the door. He took off at a sprint.

Victor swore and limped after him, leaving April alone in the alley. She forced herself to take steps toward the stairs that led back into the building. The forlorn sound of the wooden street door clicking shut greeted her ears.

VICTOR HALF SPRINTED until he reached the end of the block

before realizing how futile the exercise was. How could he hope to catch him barefoot when he had no idea which direction Lucas went? Heart heavy, he turned his steps back toward his building. Giving the door a shove, he crossed the courtyard in silence until he reached April's side.

"I'm sorry, April. I lost him. I checked the side streets and alleys nearby, but I have no idea which direction he went, and now he has too much of a head start."

When she remained mute, his eyes sought her out. She had picked herself up and was leaning against the wall, but she looked shell-shocked. Victor heard the faint sound of sirens that grew louder as they approached the building. Mr. Poulain had come through. The car screeched to a halt followed by four car doors slamming shut.

And then they were in—four officers with walkie-talkies that went off with clipped messages and garbled static. They moved as one toward the stairwell, taking in the scene. The leader signaled to Victor. "Are you the one who called?"

"No, someone in the building did, but I can take responsibility for making a statement. Lucas Laguerre was attempting to molest April..." He turned to her. "I don't know your last name."

"It's Caleigh."

He turned back to the officers. "Mr. Laguerre—he's a resident in the building—was dragging Mademoiselle Caleigh over there to the alley where the garbage cans were when I caught him. We fought, but he fled the scene." He looked at April again. "Come," he said, with a gentle wave. She stood straight, not quite steady, and walked toward him.

"Tell them what happened and I'll translate for you."

In a whisper that was difficult to make out, especially in English, she described finding Lucas outside her room and her flight down the stairs with him trailing her. Victor clenched his fists when she described how he seized her in the dark, and he turned to the officer to translate her words.

April faltered when she got to the part about Lucas dragging her into the alley. "I told him to let me go," she said, "but he hit me across the face."

Victor translated. "*Elle lui a dit de lui laisser tranquille mais il l'a frappé. Là.*" Victor pointed to her face, where he noticed the swelling for the first time on her perfect, translucent skin. Fury surged in him, and he felt only the overwhelming desire to beat Lucas to a pulp. If only he were still here.

The police officer finished writing.

"April," Victor said. "Let me bring you back inside." He could settle her on his sofa, maybe get her some *tisane*. Did he *have* any calming teas in the kitchen?

The officer put an end to that thought. "She needs to come to the station, so I can make an official statement and have her sign that. Does she agree?"

Victor translated the request.

"Absolutely," April replied, her eyes on the officer. Her voice sounded firmer now, and that brought Victor some measure of relief.

"We'll follow you there. Where is the *préfecture* located?"

The officer gave the address and signaled for the other policemen to follow him "We'll be right behind you," Victor said. "We'll take my car."

The officer waited for April to confirm this with a nod, then tucked his black notepad under his arm.

"You'd better bring ID," Victor said. "Do you have it on you?" April nodded, and he addressed the officer. "We'll be right there."

When the officers left, silence reigned and Victor took a step forward. "Come with me upstairs so I can get my papers." He looked down. "And my shoes."

April nodded, but didn't move. Her eyes were glued to the ground, and Victor's heart sank. She was traumatized. Nothing like her usual self. "Come," he said. "I don't want to leave you alone for even a moment."

Inside, he hit the light switch without thinking, and only when they came on did he remember there had been a power failure earlier. April followed him up the first two of the carpeted steps, but stopped short. "Victor." Her voice was soft. "I don't think I can walk up the steps."

He rushed to her side and lifted his hand to touch her arm, but paused. *Would his touch be welcome?* He pushed the doubts aside and put his arm around her waist, giving her support.

"The power's back on. We can take the elevator." Victor pushed the button on the ancient contraption, and when the elevator arrived, he opened the cage and pushed the door open. As the door closed, he followed his instinct and gently put his arms around her and pulled her into an embrace. It lasted only a couple seconds, but she didn't pull away. In his apartment, he retrieved his papers, and they re-entered the elevator before anyone else called it.

April gave a look of confusion when he led them back outside and toward a door on the side of the courtyard. He explained. "This leads to the garage where I keep my car." It was satisfying to hear the alarm beep twice and to deposit April safely into the front seat. Nothing could happen to her when she was with him. If only she would talk, maybe then he could ease her pain. It had been nice when she was in his arms.

THE VISIT with the police did not take long. April sat on the folding chair in the office of the lieutenant, while an officer went to get a second chair. The lieutenant typed the statement and printed it out. "Read through this and if everything looks correct, put your signature here," he said.

Victor read everything out loud, translating as he went. April bit her lip then nodded in agreement. It was not pleasant to relive the event by telling the story and hearing it read back to her. She slid the paper to the spot in front of her and signed. Then the lieutenant made a photocopy of both their IDs and handed them the originals.

"Once we find Mr. Laguerre, he will be put in a holding cell until he goes before a judge at the tribunal to decide whether he is found guilty."

"Should he not automatically be guilty if we know who did it?" Victor asked before she could voice the same question.

"The word of one witness carries weight, but we will be looking into all the details of the case. If it takes more time, he will be allowed to return home and check into the station each week, but he will not be allowed to leave the country."

"He will be allowed home?" April's voice rose a pitch, her brows drawn together. "But that's also where I live. How will I then be protected from him? How can the attacker be allowed to return to the place where he attacked someone?"

Victor translated the question, then he and the lieutenant spoke back and forth in rapid French. It was hard to read Victor's expression, though at one point he raised his brow in surprise. He turned to April. "Yes, he is allowed to return, but only if they don't have sufficient evidence to hold him. They should, based on your testimony and whatever I've contributed. I can also comment on his character."

The lieutenant said something else and Victor turned back to her, but she knew what he was going to say. She'd caught the word, *médecin,* and knew she would have to see a doctor. Victor explained, adding, "And we'll have to bring the report and photos back to the station to join with the statement."

"Of course." April sighed. It could not be over so easily, but it must be done. Whatever she could do to make sure that Lucas didn't get out any time soon, she would do.

When the doctor's visit was finished, and the report dropped back off at the police station, April climbed wearily into Victor's car. They drove down the broad streets, still teeming with life, but the interior of the car was an oasis, with only muted sounds from the street reaching them above the classical music. "I just hope they can find him," she said.

"They will," Victor assured her. "As far as I know he only has one home, and it's here. Where else would he go?"

April had been incapable of saying a single word more than was necessary in the two hours since he had first rescued her. Now she did.

"You saved me. Thank you."

Victor glanced at her and put his eyes back on the road. "I'm sorry it took me so long," he said. "I was in the shower."

She smiled weakly. "I thought I heard someone in there. And you didn't even take the time to put your shoes on. Victor—" April rested her hand on his arm as he shifted gears. "I was scared. Really scared. I will never forget what you did for me."

Victor took his hand off the gear and held hers. "I'm glad I was on time." He squeezed it, then pulled his hand back and pounded on the steering wheel. "I want to kill him."

This time it was April who reached for his hand. "No murder necessary," she said, attempting to smile and failing. "You were there for me, and that was enough." They held hands until he was forced to change gears.

Chapter Twelve

At home, they walked in silence from the garage through the courtyard, the trees making gloomy shapes near the stone façade. A light went on in the stairwell before they walked through the front door of the building.

"Are you going to be okay?" Victor headed for the elevator and punched the button. There was the sound of the elevator cage, then door, snapping shut upstairs, then the old elevator box arrived at a leisurely pace. April shoved down her fear of parting ways with Victor, of going back to her empty room alone.

"I'll be fine. I mean, I'll not be at ease until he's caught, but I can deadbolt my door." Their gazes met, and she attempted a smile, shifting hers to the stubble on his chin. His eyes remained fixed on her—she could feel it in the silence of the marble hallway—and it warmed her.

The moment was interrupted by the "*bonsoir*" of a man exiting the elevator, and Victor held the door as she entered. "You know what?" he said, as the door shut behind him. "Why don't you stay with me tonight?"

April's heart leapt while at the same time a feeling of alarm stole over her. She felt no fear from Victor's presence. On the contrary. The problem was that she was not a woman who...who was easy, and she wasn't sure what his proposition entailed. Plus, didn't he still have feelings for his ex-girlfriend? *I mean, they had a baby together.*

Victor must have seen her hesitation because he was quick to reassure her. "I have a guest room. The bed is comfortable, I'm told. You will have complete privacy. Even your own bathroom."

"Um..." The offer was tempting. What was the alternative? Going back to her tiny room on the quiet sixth floor and hoping she didn't hear a key turn in the lock in the middle of the night? Who would hear her if she screamed—or come to help if they did?

"Come on, April. I promise you'll be safe with me. And I won't try anything." He held his hands up. Then he froze. "Also...I didn't get a chance to tell you this, but Margaux decided she wants to get married after all, so..."

"Oh!" She lowered her voice a pitch. "You're engaged."

"Yeah. I'm engaged." Victor looked at his feet, then back at her, and she could not be certain, but was that regret she saw in his eyes?

"So is that a 'yes'?" he asked. Only when she nodded did he press the button for the third floor.

"Oh wait," April said. "I need things from my room. Can we take the elevator further?"

"Of course. I'll go with you." They took the elevator to the fifth floor and walked the last flight up the stairs. Victor said, "I'm not leaving you alone for a minute. At least not for tonight."

What will happen to me the rest of the time? April thought, but did not voice. At least she had a friend for today and she was safe for this night. She would worry about tomorrow when the time came.

Entering her room, she saw her father's paintings shrouded in white linen and felt reassured. Here was something continual. With the physical reminder of her father's presence, she felt less alone. April grabbed the most modest pajamas she had—the ones with navy leggings and a white flowered top with long sleeves. She took her towel and toiletries and a change of clothes for the next day, and shoved it all in a cloth bag before stepping into the hallway.

"Ready?" Victor asked with a smile.

"Ready." This time they took the stairs down, and she followed him into his apartment. As soon as he turned on the lights in the living room, smaller spotlights illuminated the blue and gold-specked contemporary paintings he had placed on the white walls. April took two steps in and saw another smaller room beyond, painted yellow. At her side, Victor suddenly looked unsure of himself, his gaze darting around his own apartment, as if he were looking at it for the first time.

"These paintings." April spun around once. "Where did you get them?"

Victor shrugged. "I buy them when I see one I like. The streets between here and the Champs-Élysées have a lot of art galleries, as you may have noticed. When I have time, I go in and see what's there. I buy whatever catches my eye. Plus, I like to support artists."

Wide-eyed, she turned to him. "You're like a dream come true."

Victor laughed and rubbed his neck. "I don't have any real taste. I just buy what I like."

"Well, taste..." she said. "It's subjective. But it seems you knew where to hang them, and you knew to put that painting of the sunflowers that has the country feeling on the yellow wall in this...what is it? A library?"

"Yes," he said. "It's the only room in the apartment that I decided needed a different color on the walls."

"And then you put these three modern fluid art paintings here on your white wall, above an embroidered sofa with threads in the same color scheme. You have great taste. I think hidden under that businessman exterior is the soul of an artist."

"Now that," Victor replied, with exaggerated shock, "is not something anyone has accused me of before. Here, let me show you to your room." He stopped and opened a linen closet in the wall that was distinguishable only by the tiny white knob and a thin crack around the cupboard. He pulled out crisp white sheets. "It's in here."

April followed him into a medium-sized room, whose focal point was a simple bed with a wrought-iron bed frame and a mattress that seemed new. There were no paintings here, just black and white photos of what looked like an ancestor and shots of a stone house in the mountains.

Victor walked over to the window and opened it so he could close the wooden shutters on the outside, then pulled the thin white drapes to hide the windowed alcove. The switch on the wall turned on the lights in the wall sconces, and the only thing overhead was the ceiling molding and a hook that once would have held a light fixture or a chandelier. There was a larger lamp on the antique wood desk in front of her bed, and to her right was a wooden cupboard, taller than her, that seemed to open with the key that was sticking out of the keyhole.

Victor had taken the duvet that was folded on the bed and started stuffing it into the cover. He was efficient, and in two shakes it was made. Wanting to be useful, April took the pillow and slipped it into the white pillowcase while he put the sheet on the bed. It felt intimate, this making the bed together, but it didn't feel weird. She sat on the bed and made a little bounce, looking up at him. "I think this is going to be the best night's sleep I've ever had."

Victor laughed. "I certainly hope so." His smile faltered, then, as he reached out his hand and grazed her cheek with it. "Let me get you some ice for that."

April felt tears sting instantly in her eyes, but he left for the kitchen, giving her time to master her emotions.

When he returned, he held a blue ice pack wrapped in a white cotton cloth and she pressed it, gingerly, to her face. "I forgot I had that," he said. "Good thing because there was no ice."

"Thanks," she whispered.

Victor watched her, unblinkingly, then cleared his throat. "Have you eaten?"

When she nodded, he went on. "Okay, then that door leads to the bathroom, which is yours alone so you won't be disturbed. Just call me or come knock if you need anything at all."

He came and stood in front of her, so she got up, too, and let her hand with the ice pack fall limply to her side. Facing her, he put his hands on her arms and rubbed them. "Good night, April. I'll have breakfast for you in the morning." He kissed her on each cheek, tenderly on the bruised side, and left.

April kicked off her shoes and lay on the bed, the cold sheets soothing her aching head, lulled by the room and the sense of peace that pervaded her. Here she was, in a friend's apartment in Paris, feeling secure for the first time since her dad was on this earth to root her to it. She sighed. How she'd missed that feeling of security. Shifting to her side, April left the cold pack to balance on her check so she could hug her arms to herself.

With Victor, there sometimes sparked this awareness of how attractive he was that pulled at her insides. Most of the time, he was like a warm blanket, comforting and secure—surprising for someone whose attractiveness was sort of the first thing you noticed. April was grateful he treated her like a friend and not like a potential conquest. She was feeling vulnerable enough as it was. However, as she drifted off to sleep, her heart was not so reasonable. The image of Victor putting his arm around her to comfort her, and leading her to his apartment so he could keep her safe... his face, close, as he gave her the *bises* before going to sleep. These images caused little tugs on a heart that did not want to listen to reason.

JENNIE GOUTET

Victor had slept deeply and was shocked into reality by the insistence of his alarm. He had left it on the desk, and he stumbled across the room trying to get to it before it woke April. He wanted to have time to get some *viennoiserie* and fresh fruit before she woke, so she would have breakfast to wake up to.

Having silenced the alarm, he grabbed a pair of jeans but was more careful in choosing a shirt to fit his mood. It was sunny out, and despite what April had been through last night and what had brought her to his apartment, Victor was feeling good. His olive green shirt was tight around the arms, showing his dedication at the gym, and girlfriends had told him it was the best color to bring out his eyes. The shower was quick, and he jotted down a note before he left the apartment.

There was a line in front of the *boulangerie* with the warm smells wafting out to tempt the buyers. He was not used to getting up this early, but he saw the old ladies with their rolling caddies and a few young people in jogging clothes walking out with fresh baguettes under their arms. Perhaps he would get a baguette too, but did he have any jam in the house? He wasn't sure. In the end, he purchased a baguette, a couple of croissants, *pains au chocolat*, and *pains aux raisins*. She would have a good selection to choose from.

Next he went to the marché a half block away and bought fresh strawberries, a liter of freshly squeezed orange juice and a pot of homemade jam. He was fairly certain he had butter at home, so he headed in that direction, thinking, for once, how practical those rolling caddies were.

Stepping through the heavy wooden doors of his building, he was aware of a feeling of excitement, or of well-being, that he knew came from seeing April. As he was about to cross the courtyard, Victor stopped short at the sight of Margaux raising her hand to press his buzzer.

"Margaux," he called out, his voice loud from shock. It reverberated throughout the courtyard.

She jerked her head up and dropped her arm. Coming down the steps, she put her hands on the stroller, which was still perched at the base of the stairwell. "Hi, Victor. I was about to buzz. I'm glad to see you haven't left for the day yet. Not that you have a nine-to-five job or anything." She waited till he arrived and offered her cheek.

"What are you doing here this early? I wasn't expecting you." Victor felt a strange sort of breathlessness, or a sense of foreboding. He wished she hadn't come when April was here. How would he explain her presence? And how would April feel to see him walk in with Margaux?

"Matthias wakes me up early every day, so I'm used to being up. It's just that today I felt like taking a walk with this beautiful weather. I didn't think you'd mind if I came here. I thought we could start planning the wedding."

"Of course," he murmured, averting his eyes, as he busied himself with getting out his keys. He reached down to grab the bottom of the stroller while she lifted it up the three steps. His mind was whirling with possible ways he might handle the situation.

They didn't both fit into the elevator without folding the stroller. "Here," Margaux said. "You can walk up with Matthias, and I'll handle the stroller."

Victor's heart gave a lurch as he was handed a sleeping baby, who shifted as he was transferred out of the warm cocoon of his stroller and into Victor's arms. Matthias immediately began to wail. "Um. I don't think this is a good idea..."

Margaux had already folded the stroller and pulled it into the elevator after her. Victor quickly handed her the heavier of the two bags with the orange juice, strawberries and jam while he adjusted the bag of patisseries plus Matthias in his arms and began the ascent. Matthias's cries resounded in the stairwell.

Victor had hoped to reach the door before Margaux so he could see if April was awake, but now that was impossible. As soon as he got to the third floor, Margaux was already out of the elevator with the stroller open and the bag of groceries underneath. She reached for Matthias, and he stopped crying immediately. Victor was a little bothered at how easily Margaux was able to comfort the baby, while he seemed only to be able to make him cry.

He opened the door, prepared to explain the presence of April and Margaux to each other, but was met with silence. She was not yet awake. Now what should he do? Should he explain to Margaux the reason April was here before she appeared? After all, he was innocent of any wrongdoing. It wasn't like he had set out to seduce April. She was his friend, and she needed help. But Margaux would not see it that way, and he had not exactly created a good reputation for himself by his past behavior.

His decision to explain did not exactly go as planned because Margaux began talking—loudly, he thought, when there was someone sleeping in the next room. And didn't her voice scare Matthias? She barely paused to breathe. How could he not have noticed this before?

"—so my father can get the Tiara Château Mont Royal. You know, the one in Chantilly that my family likes? It can host all our guests and yours too, although I don't think you will have many coming, right? I suppose you'll have your grandmother and your father, plus whoever his latest girlfriend is. And I don't think you keep in touch much with your friends. What about Bertrand? Oh no—I think you had a falling out over a girl, if I remember. So your crowd is not likely to be as big but we'll need a place large enough to host all the people our family has to invite, and we must be careful not to leave anyone out—"

Victor heard the bedroom door open, and Margaux must have heard it too because she stopped short. "What's that?" she asked.

April appeared a moment later and, except for a pink tinge to her cheeks that accentuated her bruised eye, met with calm Margaux's look of shock and subsequent fury she shot at Victor.

April, glancing at the baby carriage, smiled and advanced into the room. "Bonjour," she said, then switched to English. "You must be Margaux, and this must be Matthias." She met Margaux's gaze head-on, which must not have been easy since Margaux was rigid with anger.

Turning to him, Margaux said, "I should have known when you came home with all those groceries you were not alone. And now you're telling your *amoureuses* about me and my baby?" Her steely tone screeched upward. *Our* baby, Victor wanted to correct.

"Margaux, this is April." Victor strove for an even voice, though he was both angry and guilty. Though why should he be guilty? He had done nothing wrong.

April took a step back. "Well," she said. "I can see my presence is causing you problems, so I'm going to head home. Victor, I'm just going to get the rest of my things in the room."

She appeared at the entrance to the living room a moment later, and Victor left Margaux and went to April's side in the hallway. In a low voice, he said, "I'm sorry. I bought breakfast for us, but I won't offer it to you until I have a chance to talk to Margaux."

She gave a weak smile. "I wouldn't dream of staying another moment. I hope you get things sorted out with your fiancée."

They had arrived at the door, and Victor kissed her on both cheeks before seeing her out.

Margaux's posture was glacial when he came back in, and now the baby was crying too. With a brusque movement, she took the baby out of the stroller and sat down to feed him. "Honestly, Victor. I was a fool to think we could pick right back up where we left off. Were you cheating on me when we were together, too?"

He sat. "No. It wasn't like that then, and it's not like that now. April stayed here because she was attacked last night. Remember Lucas who lives on the fifth floor? His grandmother rents the service room to April, and he took advantage of her. He was waiting for her when she returned home last night. I just happened to hear the struggle and came to help her. There is nothing between us. She stayed in the guest room."

Margaux said nothing, and Matthias squirmed on her lap. "You're making him fussy," she said in a peevish tone. Settling the baby more comfortably, she looked at him. "I don't want to be made a fool of. Are you sure you want this wedding?"

"Yes," Victor said. His voice cracked on the one word, and he felt how weak his persuasion was. But it was the right thing to do for the baby. And hadn't he spent an entire year dreaming of just this? That Margaux would honor him by agreeing to marry him, and he would now be a full member of her family? He had to say more. "I definitely want to be there for you and Matthias. We can start planning the wedding now if you want. I'll set out the breakfast."

"Wait." Margaux put the baby up and burped him. He gave a feeble cry, and Victor wondered if he'd had enough to eat. How much did babies eat anyway? "I'm not in the mood to plan the wedding now. It was a stupid idea to come—"

"No," Victor protested.

"Let's just plan it with my parents. They'll probably nix any idea I come up with on my own." Margaux stood to leave and put the baby back in the stroller, securing him in place. "Shall you come by later this week?"

Victor kissed one frosty cheek, then the other. "Sure. Just call me and let me know when." He opened the door and watched her walk to the elevator. "Let me help you with that."

"No, it's fine. I'm used to folding the stroller with one hand. Goodbye, Victor."

Chapter Thirteen

Victor's door clicked shut, leaving April in the silent, dim stairwell. A bead of light streamed through the narrow glass pane on the wall and made a diagonal patch on the floor. The morning had been idyllic up until that point, with her waking up slowly to the yellow morning light that poured through the sheer curtains, and stretching her toes in the soft down duvet. The room was almost feminine in the way it cocooned its inhabitant. April had had time to shower and get dressed before she heard the door open. Had Victor gone out for breakfast? Her stomach rumbled in anticipation.

But then she heard him talking to a neighbor from the sound of it. And there was an answering voice, but this time it was the proprietary, nasal tone of a Parisian woman inside the apartment. April went still. Her mind whirled with whom it might be and came up with only one solution. His fiancée.

Noiselessly, she pulled on the clothes she had brought, taking care not to touch the ones she was wearing from the night before. Those she wanted to burn. Then she squared her shoulders and reached for the door handle. In the living room, Victor's expression was one of private agony, and any embarrassment over the situation fled. Her one thought was to reassure him. She wouldn't give his fiancée any cause to feel she was competition. So she had tried to put her at ease and admire the baby and show that she was nothing to Victor. The stiff French woman did not bend. Well? April would let him do the explaining as to why she was there after she'd left.

She climbed a flight of stairs. All the fear from last night was gone, but she knew the sense of security would be short-lived until the police found Lucas. Surely he couldn't hide forever, could he? As she rounded the stairwell, she calculated what she'd need to do now. There was no question of her staying in the same apartment. She'd need to find a new place to live. Even if there were no security issue, how could she continue to live in an apartment owned by the relative of a man who had attacked her?

At the top of the stairs, the sun beamed through the skylight, and she stopped, lifting her face to its warmth and letting it wash over her. When her eyes adjusted to the dim corridor beyond, they settled on the door to her apartment.

It was cracked open.

The shock of it stole her breath, and a buzzing filled her ears. With the sluggish fog overtaking her that she knew for fear, April walked forward and pushed the door open. Her gaze landed on a scene of pure chaos. Her clothes and belongings were strewn everywhere, and it seemed that all the drawers had been emptied. Worse. Her father's paintings lay bare against the furniture and the wall. All of them removed from their protective linen. All of them shredded with a knife.

April staggered toward the first painting. The one of her when she was little. This one had been cut most severely with slashes on the face and neck. It was as if *she* had been stabbed. With a strangled sob, she scanned the other paintings, turning each one until every torn canvas was in view. Not one was salvageable.

She slumped against the bed and wept. All her dreams had been wrapped up in these paintings. They were the last link to her father, and they were supposed to pay for her travels and art studies around the world. That was her father's dying wish, that she would sell his canvases for this purpose. A buyer had already expressed interest in the painting of the dock in Chile, and April had been holding on to it as long as she could before she needed to part with it. She turned the painting and fingered the torn canvas from behind. She could repair it—perhaps. But not enough to sell it. Her dad had been particularly pleased with this one.

Examining each painting in turn, she took them in her hands, and by habit held them aloft so her tears wouldn't touch the canvas. None of them could be sold. The damage was too extensive. She shook her head as the tears came afresh. Some she might be able to have repaired and keep just for her. Allowing that thought to console her, April imagined an apartment where these paintings hung on the wall, even had the spot of honor. Could she create an accompanying painting, a twin? What message would that portray? Beauty from ashes. Honoring our scars. Perfect imperfection.

It had almost calmed her, this thought. But it wasn't enough. What would she live on? And her even greater chagrin—*why* hadn't she taken the insurance, no matter how costly it had been? Now she had only about a month's worth to live on. There was no way she could afford even a move to a new apartment.

A sound in the stairwell made April leap to her feet, gasping for breath, her heart racing. Wasting no time, she rushed into the hallway and tried to pull the door shut, but the handle had been damaged and it wouldn't close. Who cared now? She had nothing in there left to lose.

That's not true, she thought. *Even in their damaged state, those paintings are the most precious thing I have.*

Circling her way down the stairwell, April paused on the third floor. Should she knock on Victor's door? No. It would only complicate things for him. Surely she could find her way back to the police station and explain what happened. Just as April turned to go, Victor's door opened and she saw him exit. He held the door for his fiancée, who pushed the stroller into the hallway, her face stony. They exchanged a few words.

Then, both Victor's and his fiancée's gazes landed on April, shoulders hunched and tears streaming down her face. She was caught.

"April, what is it?" Victor asked. He started toward her, and Margaux's gaze hardened.

April shook her head, not trusting herself to speak. Finally, she raised her hand, a mute gesture of supplication, of sorrow, the polite wave of *let me not burden you* and began the descent.

"April," Victor called again, but she didn't look back. She heard their exchange, him placating and the fiancée's sharp, angry retort. She was out the front door, running across the cobblestones. *Préfecture*. That's what the police station was called. She just needed an Uber.

There was already an English translator at the police station, who had been brought in for another case, which was lucky, she was told, because usually she'd need to wait. April explained what had happened, and they checked the police report from the day before. "It looks like we have a suspect. We'll need to go back to the apartment to document the evidence." After conferring with the officer handling the case, the translator said, "We'll meet you there in fifteen minutes."

April nodded, refusing to think about what another Uber car ride was going to do to her shrinking budget. She was in the building minutes before she heard them on the stairs and half hoped that Victor would hear them too and come out of his apartment. He must have left because the lobby and stairs were silent. Three policemen crowded into her small room before one of them shooed the others out to take pictures.

"Is this how you found the room?" the officer asked, analyzing the room through the camera viewfinder.

"No." April shook her head when it was translated. "I picked each of the paintings up to examine them, but I did put them back close to where they were when I found them."

He frowned at her. "You shouldn't have touched anything."

"I didn't think..."

At last, photographing the broken doorknob, he asked, "Do you have somewhere else to stay?" April understood the question before the translator asked it. She didn't have another place, but she wasn't sure the police officers were going to be able to do anything about it, and she didn't want to face complete humiliation.

She nodded.

"Don't stay here tonight. Until we catch the criminal, you're not safe here."

Nodding again, she watched them walk down the circular stairwell, stopping at Lucas's apartment. His grandmother opened the door only a crack, as if she were afraid the officers would try to shove their way in. "You again? I told you he wasn't here." The old woman looked up and caught April staring down at them, and her glare was malevolent. Never had April noticed how unfriendly this woman could be.

April returned to her room, sat on the bed, and wrapped her arms around her torso. "All right, April." Her voice was soft. She wasn't used to talking to herself. "You need to figure out what you're going to do about this mess." She stared, unseeing, at the paintings then at her clothes. She could ask Victor to put the paintings in his cave—one of the cement blocks in the basement that belonged to each apartment and that came with a key. But she wouldn't ask Benjamin or Victor if she could stay with them. She had already seen the strife she was causing between Victor and his fiancée. Ben would just get the wrong idea.

Penelope. Could she ask her? *Hmm.* April could at least inquire about youth hostels. Or wait—she could become an *au pair*. That came with housing and food and even a small monthly stipend. Surely there were families searching even now. Perhaps their first au pair had gotten homesick and left the post. Okay, so maybe that was not very likely since the school year was almost over.

April stood up, determined. There was nothing she could do about protecting the paintings since the door was broken. Lucas had the key, so he must have acted from pure spite. She would take a few of her most precious items and see if Penelope was at the art studio.

Victor was entering the courtyard as she headed out. "April," he called, his voice loud with relief. "Where did you go? What's going on?" He was alone.

She went to him, relieved in her turn to have found her friend. "Victor, I need a favor. Can I store my father's paintings in your cave?"

His brow wrinkled in confusion. "Yes, sure. Or we can put them in the guest room. I don't mind. What's going on? Why were you crying?"

She didn't answer right away. "I'm so sorry to have caused you problems with Margaux. I really did not want that to happen." Fairly certain of the answer, she asked anyway. "Were you able to sort things out with her?"

Victor shrugged. "We'll be fine. Don't worry." He insisted, "Why were you crying?"

"Oh, Victor." April stopped a moment, choked up at the thought of having to explain it. "Lucas—at least I think it was him—shredded all my father's paintings. They were my last memory of him, and they were also my source of income to travel. I was planning to sell them one by one, and the auctioneer recommended against bringing them with me, but I couldn't bear to part with them any sooner than I had to. *All* the paintings were slashed through with a knife, Victor. Some of them are completely destroyed."

Astonishment turned to rage, and Victor stepped away, walking a few paces with his back to her. "How dare he?" he ground out. When he strode back, he pulled her into an embrace, caressing her hair, wordlessly. April was shocked into immobility. His arms felt right.

Victor pulled back suddenly. "Let's go look."

April was still reeling from the physical contact and had to focus to consider his words. Either Penelope was there or she was not, and though she had to get the paintings to his apartment, she also needed a place to stay tonight. "Listen, Victor, can you get them without me? I need to find a new living situation. Lucas also broke my doorknob. And no," she added when she saw that Victor was about to speak, "you have been so, so kind to me, but I can't cause your fiancée any more problems, and it will not work to have me staying with you."

"I know." He shoved his hands in his pockets. "I mean, if you had no other solution, I wouldn't care what Margaux thought. But as it is, I do have a solution." Victor's eyes glimmered, as if with a secret.

"What?"

"Come," he said. He took her by the elbow and led her to the bench in the courtyard by the fountain. When they sat, he said, "I was just visiting my grandmother to see if she might let you stay for a few days. You know, at her place? That will give the police a chance to find Lucas. She said she'd be very glad to have you. To tell the truth, I think my grandmother can get lonely."

April didn't know what to say. Her eyes fixed on his, she finally broke the gaze and leaned forward to trail her fingers in the fountain. "It sounds like a dream come true. Honestly, I'm at my wit's end. But I don't know how I can impose like that."

"What does 'wit's end' mean?" Victor frowned. "And what do you mean by impose?"

"It means I don't know what else to do. Where else I can turn. The paintings were not just sentimental. They were my financial security. They were what was going to enable me to travel and study around the world."

"So staying with my grandmother is a good thing, right? You have a solution." His brows were still furrowed.

She knew it probably didn't make much sense the way she was explaining it. "A temporary one, but even that...I've never even met your grandmother."

"Remember I told you I was going to bring you to lunch? She's already heard all about you and was waiting for me to give her your availability so she could invite you. Trust me." Victor laid his hand on her arm. "She wouldn't offer if she didn't want to. She's not like that."

April shook her head. "I just can't, Victor. I hope you can understand." She saw from his expression that he didn't. "I need to find my own way in life. I can't wait for people to rescue me."

Victor was still frowning, but he gave her a perceptive look. "Because they might not come?"

She raised an eyebrow, shrugged, then finally nodded. "I need to prove, if only to myself, that I can come up right again when life knocks me down."

Victor sighed. "It seems ridiculous to be so adamant when a perfectly good solution has presented itself, but I understand. I'm the same way. And now that I'm not on the receiving end of this particular solution, I have to agree with Mishou. Stubbornness is not always a sign of strength. Come on."

"Who's Mishou?"

"My grandmother. I'm still going to take you to meet her for lunch." He guided her elbow, the pressure of his fingers light, and she had a strange sensation of well-being though everything was falling apart. She also had a strong desire to weep.

"When, now? I can't." Her voice squeaked.

"No. Next Tuesday if you can. Now I'm going with you wherever you were headed to help you get a place to stay."

"Victor." April's tears leaked again as they walked, and she wanted nothing more than to stop and sink into him for another hug. "I think that's the nicest thing anyone has ever done for me."

Chapter Fourteen

"I hope Penelope is here," April said, as they entered the stark room filled with canvases in various stages of completion. "She mentioned the other night she'd be spending extra hours here to get her painting ready for the gallery selection. Also—" April scanned the tops of the easels, looking for movement behind the ones in the back. "I would like to introduce you to her. She and her friends are so great. I think you would like them."

Victor hadn't dared ask whom she was planning to seek out for help but was conscious of a relief that it was not that guy, Ben, she was relying on to save her from her current situation. He was ready to accept that she would not rely on *him*, but he hated to think it was only because she liked Ben better.

Not that he had any vested interest in the situation. He didn't. He was engaged. *But I care about April as a friend, and I would hate for her to care for someone who was not good enough for her*, he told himself. As soon as that thought crossed his mind, it was replaced with the memory of holding her in his arms. She was soft, and when her chin was tucked into his neck that way, he could smell her shampoo. For a minute, the sensation was so strong he was unable to move from the doorway.

At the back of the room, April asked the only two students who were present, "Hey, have you guys seen Penelope?" Victor saw them shake their heads.

"That's a small setback," she said, when she returned to his side. "I'd hoped to find her here. But that's okay. My next step is to look at some of the housing opportunities on the FUSAC website. I'm sure there are hostels advertised there—"

There was a clatter of shoes in the hallway, and Penelope whizzed into the room as if summoned by April's wish. "April, you're here *again*. Don't you ever leave? You made a big hit with all my friends last night." She stopped short when she saw April's cheek, and she dropped her bag to her side. "What in the world happened to you?"

April didn't answer right away and glanced at Victor, her mouth in a straight line. "May I introduce you to my friend, Victor? He's my neighbor."

He found himself being assessed by a petite woman whose shrewd brown eyes seemed to miss nothing. "Nice to meet you," she said, and with an inquisitive lift to her brow, "*Français?*" He nodded, and she switched to French. "I assume you're not the author of the black eye."

"Far from it. I'm actually here to give April a hand because she's had a bad run of luck lately. April?"

April dipped her head and continued in English. "I'm wondering if you know of a housing situation on short notice. For instance, an au pair situation where the family needs to find one quickly? I was just about to check the FUSAC for short-term rentals, although what I really need is some sort of apartment in exchange for a job so I can make ends meet."

Penelope pursed her lips. "All right. But something has happened since we saw each other last night. You seemed perfectly fine, and you didn't have a big black eye."

April set her jaw, fighting back tears. "Everything has

happened. I was attacked last night, but fortunately Victor came to my rescue." She gave him a wobbly smile. "So Lucas didn't hurt me...much."

"You know your attacker's name?" Penelope looked to Victor for confirmation, and he nodded. "Go on."

"So I stayed in Victor's spare bedroom for the night just in case Lucas came back, and apparently he did because my room was broken into and all my father's paintings were ruined. The paintings were worth a fortune."

Penelope's eyes hadn't left April's face, but now she looked at Victor again. "The police are involved?"

He answered in English so April could follow. "Yes. It should be a clear case because they know who it is—at least for the attack, although it seems evident for the paintings too."

April continued, "But in the meantime, my door is broken and I can't stay in my room, even if I were courageous enough to stay there, which I'm *not*. And I have no source of income now that the paintings are ruined. I need to get on my feet. First order of business, a place to stay, even temporarily. Even for tonight."

"And you can't just stay with Victor again?" Penelope looked at him, and he shrugged.

"No. It's causing problems with his fiancée—"

"Oh." Penelope's mouth went round. "That would."

She appraised Victor again, and he felt like defending himself, but what would he say? That he didn't think he loved his fiancée but they had a baby together, so he was stuck? The thought came unbidden, slid into his consciousness, then whirled around and hit him square in the chest. He didn't love Margaux. He had been so focused on what he used to want—being tied into a good family with the security he once craved so strongly. Not only did he not love Margaux—at least, he was starting to doubt the fact—he didn't really like her family either. Her dad was calculating, and her mom was a shadow of a woman, faded into the background.

Was Margaux going to become like that too? Or, perhaps worse, would she become like her dad?

April had continued. "And, so, if you know of anyone, or of a cheap place that you think is reasonably safe, I know I'm asking a favor of you as if we've been long-term friends, and we've really just met, but..."

Penelope exhaled. "I can see I've been making a fuss over nothing in my own life when I look at the challenges you're facing." She put her hand on her hip, then turned her gaze on Victor. "Wait. Why are you here?"

"April's my friend. I wanted to help." He stepped back but toppled a painting from the easel behind him, which he caught before he wreaked havoc.

"And you don't have any solutions for her?"

"I do. I offered one, and she refused it." April was now giving him a look, and he gave a pointed one back.

What kind of *solution?*" Penelope's gaze narrowed.

"No, no, not like that. I offered to let her stay with my grandmother." Victor laughed when Penelope's look of mistrust turned into shock.

She rounded on April. "Are you crazy? Why'd you turn that down? I assume he meant it for free."

"I can't impose on her," April protested. "And the truth is, I need to earn some income. Even if I don't have to pay rent, I need to make ends meet. That's why I was thinking au pair."

"Hmm." Penelope chewed on her lip, thinking. No one rushed her, and after a minute, she did not disappoint. "Then here's what I propose. You said your door is broken? Let's go back to your place and get your stuff, and...how much is there?"

Victor answered. "It's a small *chambre de bonne* worth of things, and she can store everything she doesn't need immediately in my spare bedroom."

"Which shouldn't anger the fiancée too much," Penelope

mused, though Victor doubted it were true. "April, you can come and stay with me for tonight. I have to make a few phone calls, but I'm sure I can figure out someone who is desperate for an au pair. Do you like kids?"

"Uh...I don't really know much about them, but as long as there are no diapers involved, I should be able to keep them reasonably safe."

Victor laughed. "What other credentials could a parent ask for?"

April didn't protest when Penelope decided to forego her afternoon painting project and help move April's things into Victor's spare bedroom. As they walked toward the train station, Penelope was on her phone with a former employer, then one cousin after another. Finally, she covered the phone to whisper, "I think I may have something." She finished the call as they reached the subway station, and she paused at the top of the stairs.

"Our former nanny, Miriam, is about to start a new job. Her husband does quite well, so I think she doesn't need to work, but a spot opened up in a local private school for a guidance counselor, and she decided to take it. She only needs someone to do after-school pickup and homework in exchange for room and board, and she's willing to give a generous stipend."

"Your nanny?" April gulped. "She sounds like a tough act to follow."

"Aw, you'll love her. She's wonderful. The only thing is that her husband's boss had already recommended someone, and they need to see that through first. So this is not a sure thing. In the meantime, I can put you up for a couple days, but unfortunately not as long as I would like since I'm still living with my parents."

"I understand," April said, in a small voice.

Victor followed the instinct that had been dogging his every step and finally put his arm around April. She looked vulnerable and scared at the thought of being an au pair, and he just wanted to comfort her. She leaned into him slightly, which felt good. Penelope eyed him even more shrewdly, and he had to force himself to let go.

"We'd better get on the train, right?" Penelope said. "I promised Miriam I would bring you to see her today if we don't finish too late. She's anxious to meet you."

As they headed down the stairs to the métro, a tall Asian man with handsome features put his hands out to block their path. "April," he said. "I was just coming to see if you were here. *Bonjour, Penelope.*" He reached over to kiss her on both cheeks, and turned to do the same to April. Only then did he notice the bruise, which was shadowed in the stairwell.

"Whoa. What happened to you?"

"It's a long story, Ben, but I'm fine." He looked skeptical, so she continued. "Honestly, I'd rather not get into it in the public métro station, but I'm fine."

His questioning gaze settled on Victor, and his mouth turned downwards.

April turned to Victor. "Ben, this is my neighbor, Victor."

Victor stuck out his hand, and Ben shook it, reluctantly. "The one who showed you the spot for the painting competition that you haven't let anyone see?"

"The very one," she replied, attempting a smile. "He's here to help me find a new place to live."

"I could have done that," Benjamin said. "I have contacts in the city, you know."

"Well, in the end, it's Penelope who has saved the day. Although, I still have an interview to undergo. We're about to move my stuff into Victor's apartment—"

"What?" Ben exclaimed, whirling to look at Victor.

"My *stuff*, Ben. I'll be staying with Penelope until I can move into my new situation."

"I'm coming with you," Ben said. "And I'll expect to hear the whole story at some point."

April didn't answer, and Ben turned to follow the group to the train.

PENELOPE TOOK charge of the conversation the whole way there. She had a natural-born ability to lead, which made finding her crying in the studio now seem like a distant memory. It was odd that their budding friendship was forged when Penelope was acting so out of character. Perhaps, though, April would never have offered to have coffee with her if Penelope hadn't shown her vulnerable side.

Victor answered in deep, confident tones and revealed a different side to him than he usually showed April. She couldn't tell if it was simply because he was French, and he was communicating in his own language, or if Penelope brought out the best in him. Or maybe April was seeing the best in him more and more as their friendship deepened. Honestly, apart from his good looks, her first impression of him left much to be desired. Cynical. Mistrustful. Shallow. That's what she had thought.

Funny how wrong first impressions could be.

Ben walked at her side in silence, and she felt bad for being short with him earlier. They had spent enough time together in the recent weeks that he deserved more than that. "Thanks for coming with us to help," she said.

Victor and Penelope were deep in conversation, and Ben shot a look at Victor under his lashes. "Why are you putting your stuff in his apartment? What's going on, April?"

She sighed. "I was attacked last night. I can't even believe it was only last night. Victor happened to be there and he scared the guy away. I spent the night in his apartment—" She put her hand on Ben's arm when he scowled, suddenly bone weary from explanations. "I stayed in his guest room. I was afraid Lucas would come back."

"Lucas? So you know who attacked you then?"

She began to wish she could have told Penelope and Ben at the same time. It was not an easy story to hash out again and again. "He's my landlord's grandson. I stayed with Victor because I was afraid, and it turns out I was right to be. He did come back."

Ben raised his eyebrows and Victor called out, "Next stop is ours."

"And?" Ben prompted.

"He destroyed all my father's paintings."

"Your father was a painter? You never told me that."

April got to her feet as the métro slid into the station. "Yes. He was very good."

THE WORK of shifting her belongings to Victor's spare room was quick with four of them helping. Penelope directed the men to carry the paintings down first, wrapped, and with care, though they were no longer worth anything. Ben paused over each painting before moving them, and he and Victor seemed to have declared an uneasy truce. In the meantime, Penelope helped April to pack one duffel bag to take with her until she could get settled in her new apartment, leaving the winter clothes and some extra things in the larger suitcase.

"Now let's go get your deposit back," Penelope said, heading for the landlord's apartment.

"There's no way." April shook her head.

"Let her try," Victor said, with a small smile. "I'm beginning to think your friend is capable of anything. Here. Let's stay out of view."

Penelope knocked on the landlord's door with a crisp *tat tat*.

There was a shuffle from inside and the sound of the peephole moving. The door opened.

"Yes?"

"*Bonjour, madame.* I represent Mademoiselle Caleigh, and she will be leaving the apartment now that your grandson attacked her and came back and slashed her priceless paintings. She will need her security deposit returned."

The old woman slammed the door shut but was stopped by a designer shoe in the door. "I would advise you to comply quickly and go write her a check for the amount due. What is it? Two month's rent?" She turned a questioning gaze to April.

"Four," April said.

"Four!" Penelope whistled under her breath. "*Ecoutez, madame.* Like I said, you can write a check for the amount you owe Mademoiselle Caleigh, and steer clear of whatever crime your grandson is involved in, or you can face my father in court for improper rental proceedings. You decide."

"The doorknob is broken. I'll have to pay someone to repair it," the grisly old woman complained in a peevish voice.

"True. I suppose it'll be quite a bit cheaper than paying for the six paintings your grandson destroyed. How much is that, April?"

"Four hundred thousand dollars," April replied, her voice grim. "Give or take."

"*Four hundred thou...*" Penelope's jaw dropped. "Well, madame. It doesn't sound like you have much choice." The four of them waited while Madame Laguerre shuffled down the hall. She came back five minutes later and shoved a check at Penelope.

"She'd better get her things out of the room," the old lady called after them as they turned toward the stairs. No one replied and she slammed the door.

"Four hundred thousand euros..." Ben said.

"Dollars," April corrected.

"No wonder you're upset," he replied.

"She's upset because she lost the last remaining link to her father," Victor interjected.

"Well, yes," April admitted. "That and the loss of four hundred thousand dollars because I don't know how I'm going to carry out my plan to study in several countries, much less purchase a ticket home." When she noticed all three looking at her with somber faces, she added, "But I'll figure it out."

Chapter Fifteen

✿❦✿

At the entrance to their apartment building, Victor gestured for Ben to follow Penelope out, then turned and took April gently by the shoulders. "I'll take care of your stuff. So lunch at my grandmother's house on Tuesday? Let's meet here at noon."

April nodded and felt her eyes fill with tears. "I don't know how to thank you."

"April." Victor reached up and brushed his fingers on her cheek, too close to the bruise, and he winced in sympathy. "You're really incredible, you know. I mean, you should have taken my grandmother's offer, and she may scold you when she sees you." April smiled through her tears and shrugged, inarticulate.

Victor continued. "But I don't doubt that you'll always come right side up, no matter what life hands you. I hope, as your friend, I'll be there to see it." Hands still on her face, he leaned down and kissed her gently on each cheek, then reached over to open the door.

April didn't know what she was feeling when she followed Ben and Penelope, who had fallen into conversation. She missed Victor's presence already. Her cheeks still tingled with his kisses, and her heart was raw, as if it were as bruised as her face. She missed him in the way someone missed a person they loved. But she didn't love him. She couldn't.

There had been a crush once in college. Somehow, any kind of crush had escaped her all throughout high school. It was probably because her father had begun to be ill by the time she was sixteen, and care for him occupied all her free hours. In college, she spent guilty hours away from him, knowing she needed her degree, and that in some way this was her sanity too. The art classes let her escape from a difficult reality, and she plunged herself into her work. That was where she'd met Dave.

They spent a lot of time in the art studio, and she never let on that she had any feelings for him because she didn't want to mess up the friendship. He didn't seem to notice her in any way other than a classmate and a buddy who shared the same passion. So she stuffed the feelings until one night, when she was working in the studio until one in the morning, he came in from the bar, just tipsy enough to reveal how he felt about her. It turned out he'd been hiding his feelings too. But that was a week before graduation, and they didn't live anywhere near each other. She knew her father was going to take up all her time once she graduated. Her dad had hung on for years, but his strength was drawing to a close.

April sighed, trailing behind her friends. Her father had died right after she graduated, and she'd had to settle his affairs. It took a year of working through grief and working at the ice cream parlor before she could find enough strength to put his plan into motion. She was accepted into the art school in Paris and left a few months after that, her feelings for Dave a fading memory.

It all came rushing back now. The crush. It was not Dave she thought of, though the feelings were the same. Those tingly sensations that suggested the world had tilted on its axis. She was constantly aware of Victor's presence, and also comforted by it. April walked along, thankful Penelope and Ben were still lost in their conversation. Her own thoughts were too personal to be shared.

❧

PENELOPE'S FATHER gave April a reserved, but not unkind, greeting. Her mother was much warmer, kissing April on the cheeks and clucking over her bruised eye. She followed them up to Penelope's room, on the second floor of the duplex, and indicated a box in the corner. "I had time to bring the air mattress upstairs, but have not blown it up. It should be pretty easy to do, and I'll go get you some sheets. How long do you need a place to stay?"

April looked at Penelope, who answered for her. "We're asking Miriam if April can stay there. Miriam decided to take a job at the *lycée*, and she needs a nanny so we're going to try that first. If that doesn't work, we'll go look at the ads at the American church."

"I'm sure something will work out." Her mother stood for an instant, staring at April, then clapped her hands together. "Well, let me go get those sheets."

"I'm an imposition," April said, as soon as Penelope's mom left.

"You're not," Penelope insisted, coming over to take April's bag off her shoulder. "I think...I think my parents are not very happy right now. And I think that's what's causing the reserve. This is why I didn't offer to let you stay longer. But I believe both my parents think it's the right thing to do to let you stay here until you get on your feet, especially after what's happened to you. They can agree on that, at least." Penelope gave a strained smile and opened the box to the air mattress, just as her mother walked in with a set of sheets.

FIVE DAYS PASSED. The opportunity with Miriam fell through, and there were few index cards proposing work or housing at the American church. April had followed up on two of them and was waiting to hear back. She went to school and worked on her series of sketches on motion, and began sketching in the figures on her canvas. The portrait was done and ready to be graded as well. April may have been unsettled, but she was not unproductive, and the thought gave her grim satisfaction. In truth, it would be some time before she could find joy again after the loss of her father's work. She'd had to contact Sotheby's to let them know the paintings would no longer be for sale. The expert expressed polite sympathy that was painful to hear. By the time their phone call finished, he seemed more interested in sourcing the next lot than her ruined legacy. Yes, April was sad about the lost income, but what hurt was that the hole her father left in the world could so quickly be replaced to everyone but her.

It was time to meet Victor for lunch at his grandmother's apartment. April went back to her old building, and as she approached it, her heart rate picked up. She hadn't realized how nervous she would be coming back here. When she crossed a side street to get to their building, a black-headed figure swiveled suddenly to walk the opposite way when he saw her, and she could almost swear it was Lucas. April couldn't quite make him out as he mingled with the crowd, and he didn't look back so she could be sure of it. But...surely it wasn't him? He couldn't be anywhere near his old residence, where he was most likely to be caught. Her face was troubled when she walked up to their building and saw Victor standing in front of it.

"April." A broad smile lit his face and banished her fears, as he leaned down to give her *les bises*. There was his soapy scent and smooth cheeks, and she thought if she could just breathe it in, it would chase all her fears away. Did he never look unattractive? Her nerves eventually settled as he kept up a steady chatter, and he made her smile by saying that the bruise on her face had faded to a pretty yellow, and that not many girls could pull off such a color combination. Any potential hurt she might feel that he was making light of the event was erased by Victor's leaning over to mutter in her ear, "I wish I could hit him again for hurting you this way."

As April stepped on the train, she thought she saw the same black-haired figure—she recognized the scarf—stepping on the train several cars down, and her throat went dry. She craned her head to look, but he disappeared into the crowd. *No.* April shook her head. *Enough.* It was normal that her imagination would act up, and imagination was all it was.

"MISHOU, THIS IS APRIL." Victor stood to the side at his grand-mother's apartment and allowed April to be drawn in and kissed on both cheeks. His grandmother tugged his hand at the same time, so they were both held and kissed at once. Mishou had a way of breaking through ceremony.

"I'm so delighted to meet you," April said. She spoke French in her horrible American accent, but his grandmother did not appear to notice, and Victor was charmed that April was trying.

"For me, it's the same," Mishou said and, patting Victor's cheek, added, "I've long waited for Victor to bring home a nice girl, and he finally has." Victor's face heated up, and he hoped April didn't understand everything. He didn't want her to think this had any special significance attached to it, never mind that it felt like it did.

Apparently, April had understood perfectly. "*Il n'a pas ramené Margaux?*" she asked, with a crease in her brows. It was difficult to make out what she was saying, but her grandmother grasped the name at least.

"Margaux." Mishou puffed her cheeks as she blew out the air, firing off in rapid French, "What do we want with Margaux? That story is finished."

April's brow creased further. "*Margaux. Sa fiancée.*" She pointed to Victor, then smiled at his grandmother. "*Leur bébé?*"

Now he hoped it was his grandmother who hadn't understood. He hadn't quite found time to tell her about Matthias yet. Or, perhaps it was the courage that was lacking. His grandmother missed nothing, however. "Victor, why don't you come give me a hand in the kitchen. You—" She steered April toward the living room sofa, and in English said, "Sit here."

In the kitchen, Mishou turned on Victor. "What is this story about a baby? And about Margaux? Last news, Margaux was in Monaco. And there was no engagement. And there was no baby. Is there something you should be telling me?"

Victor sighed. "I'm sorry, Mishou. I haven't had the chance to tell you yet. Margaux came back from Monaco a couple weeks ago, and she got back in touch with me. When we met for the first time, she brought a three-month old baby. He's mine."

His grandmother turned to the counter and began unwrapping the cheese to put on the cheese board, her hands trembling more than usual. "And the part about her being your fiancée? I hope you're not going to make that mistake. She is wrong for you."

"I had offered to marry her before, and she said no. After I found out we had the baby together, I felt it was the right thing to do and I offered again. She still refused. But now...well, I think she's changed her mind and wants to get married. So we're working on setting a date."

"It's a mistake," Mishou repeated. For a couple of moments, silence reigned in the kitchen as she took the empty salad bowl and mixed the vinaigrette at the bottom, then dumped the torn lettuce from the salad spinner on top of the sauce. She handed the bowl to Victor. "And that girl in there? April?"

"What of her?"

"That is precisely what you need to figure out," she said, and turned to walk into the living room.

Mishou smiled at April to let her know all was well and prattled off some simple phrases meant to put her at ease, but when she turned her back, April mouthed to Victor, *Sorry*.

Oh mon Dieu. It wasn't her fault. He just realized how little he had wanted to tell Mishou. Deep inside, he knew this would be the reaction.

Lunch was onion tart and salad. April dug into it with relish, and that made both Victor and his grandmother smile. He ended up acting as translator for April and his grandmother since she had pretty much exhausted her knowledge of French. Mishou ordered him to ask if there had been any headway into the search for Lucas, but Victor already knew the answer to that. He briefly translated the question then answered in French. "No one knows where he's gone. Honestly, I didn't think he could be that resourceful."

Mishou nodded her head at April. "Is she in any danger?"

This one, Victor wasn't sure how to answer, so he asked April. "Do you feel like you're in any danger?"

April took a minute before responding, but finally shrugged her shoulders. "I'm not sure. I don't think he knows where I go to school, and I'm no longer staying in the building. I don't think it would be very easy for him to find me."

Victor translated that. He agreed, but felt her unease all the same. Mishou then asked what she was going to do about the paintings. When Victor translated this, April's eyes filled with tears.

"The paintings...nothing can be done. They're lost forever. Except for the earliest two—the dock in Chile. He painted this lonely dock in Valparaiso. It was before he and my mom had me. They were visiting the country, and he took the time to paint one of the local fishing wharves. Except for that one, and the one of me as a child running through wildflowers, I watched him paint every one. I was with him when he worked on them, and I saw the paintings come to life. It's not just the money—they were promised to be auctioned off. It's the sentimental value, to know that they're no longer in this world making someone's home more beautiful. To know he lost this legacy..." April paused, her mouth quivering.

Victor translated all that, his eyes not leaving April's face. He had known she was upset by the loss, but now he saw that she was haunted by it. And he couldn't find any words to bring her comfort.

Mishou took April's hands in hers. "You, *ma chérie. You* are his legacy."

April looked at Mishou in silence, then nodded.

Mishou held on to her hand. "You need to stay here. I would like for you to stay here." She indicated for Victor to translate it, and when she saw that April meant to protest, she said, "I will consider it an insult if you prefer struggling to find some place to stay rather than accepting the invitation of an old woman."

When Victor translated that, April laughed as, he was sure, his grandmother had meant for her to do.

"Well, okay then," April said at last. "How can I refuse?"

Chapter Sixteen

April moved in the next day. She was increasingly glad to leave Penelope's home, as she could feel the tension between Penelope's parents that flowed as an undercurrent in all their conversations. As she was packing her things, April paused and turned to Penelope.

"I wanted to let you know how grateful I am for your friendship, and for getting my security deposit back, and for taking me in even though things weren't easy at home." She stopped short, her eyes filling with tears.

Penelope was sitting on the bed, putting on lipstick in front of a hand mirror and looking very much like her usual self, which was to say, completely on top of a well-ordered life. April was reminded of the one time Penelope had shown a different side. "If you don't mind me asking, was your parents' fighting the reason you were crying that time I saw you in the studio? The day I came to have dinner with your friends?"

Penelope continued to blot the lipstick with her finger until April was sure she wouldn't answer. Finally, she looked up. "*Les gars*. That's what we call ourselves." It sounded like *lay gah*. "It means the folks," Penelope explained. "We all come from pretty well-off families, but we're just normal folk to each other since we've been friends since elementary school. Anyway, we all decided we would like both you and Victor to join us for our next dinner."

April gave a startled glance at Penelope's grin that accompanied these words. "Are you sure? I mean, yes. Absolutely. But Victor too? I would be glad for his sake. Honestly, I don't get the impression he has a lot of friends. But you know, we're not..." She chewed her lip. "He has a fiancée and everything."

"The *célèbre* Margaux? Are you sure you'd only be glad for his sake?" Penelope leveled her a questioning gaze that April couldn't meet. She would be unable to lie and deny it, but she didn't want to advertise it either. It was true that watching her friendship develop with Victor, and knowing nothing could ever come of it, was beginning to be a trial to her. A bittersweet trial, though, since she couldn't imagine giving up the friendship.

"I'm sure," she answered, more firmly than she felt.

Penelope let out a huff and grabbed a pillow and threw it at her. "All right. He can invite Margaux to our dinner, too. That will make us a perfectly uneven number, and we'll have to take out another leaf in the table, but Victor is an honorable guy, so we'll make this concession."

April smiled. It would be easier anyway for April to remember he was engaged—*engaged!*—if she saw more of Margaux and his baby. She wondered if he would bring Matthias.

"It'll be at Guillaume's place again," Penelope said. "I'll give you the address so you can pass it on to Victor...and Margaux. Is he going to help you move into his grandmother's apartment?"

"No. He has a business meeting he can't avoid. He said he would stop by later, though."

Penelope capped the tube of mascara she had just applied and swiveled on the bed to face April. "Tomorrow is our longest day at the studio. Where is your painting being held? I didn't see it with the others."

"Which painting?" April asked, wondering if Penelope simply hadn't recognized her painting, now that she'd mapped out the color in the sketches.

"The one you called *April à Paris*. It wasn't lined up with the other paintings when I was there yesterday."

"What?" April felt a twinge of panic. "I don't know. It should be there. Last I knew, it was on the rail in the back."

"Well, I might have missed it. Don't worry," Penelope soothed. "I'm sure it will turn up. Or someone placed another painting in front of it."

When she saw April's frown, Penelope stood and began pulling the sheets off the air mattress. "I was not crying because of my parents that day."

It took April a minute to realize Penelope was answering her question from earlier.

Penelope's lip stiffened. "Although that didn't help, of course. I'm worried about them, but they were happy when I was growing up, and I'm hoping this is just something they need to work through. Not the thing that will end them." She wadded the sheets in a ball and threw them in the corner, picking up the pillow next.

"It's Arthur. I...had feelings for him." Penelope licked her lip and darted a glance at April. "I've never told anyone that, except Guillaume and now you. No one knows." April didn't have the heart to tell Penelope she'd guessed it in an instant. "Anyway, he'd just told me he met a girl he really likes. She's an art student in Mr. Chambourd's studio, so of course she will be more talented than I am. He introduced me once, before I knew there was anything between them, and she's a tall, gorgeous model-like thing. Not a gnome like me."

Penelope's face was hard, and there was no trace of tears now. April sensed anger instead. She wouldn't offer any platitudes for what was clearly very painful for Penelope. "How long have you liked him?"

"Since I first met him two years ago," Penelope said. "I brought him into our group, and I always thought we'd get together because we were the two artists in a group of professionals. We were the only ones who weren't worried about pleasing our parents by getting married and beginning a life of *métro, boulot, dodo*."

"What..?" April pinched her brows in confusion.

"You know. The routine." Penelope waited for the light to dawn, and when it didn't, said, "You take the métro in the morning. Then you go to the *boulot*. Your job. Then you go home and *dormir*. You go to sleep. *Dodo*."

"*Métro, boulot, dodo*," April repeated, smiling. "I know nothing of that expression—or that routine. I'm not sure I ever will." She thought about Guillaume, wondering if she should say what she had observed. *No*, she thought. That one's up to him.

Instead she said, "I hope Arthur will change his mind, but... you know sometimes opposites attracting can be a good thing. Getting together with someone who has a *métro, boulot, dodo* lifestyle brings more order to your existence, whereas you bring more passion to his. It can be a good thing. I mean..." Her voice trailed away when she saw Penelope's obdurate expression. *Okay. Not open to hearing this right now.*

"I'll be happy to come to dinner and I'll give the news to Victor. Thank you for confiding in me," April said as Penelope picked up her suitcase, prepared to carry it downstairs.

They went to the front door, and Penelope rolled the suitcase in front of her and kissed April on both cheeks. "You both will fit right into our group. I can usually tell about people, and I'm rarely wrong," she said. With a sad shake of the head, she added, "Only Arthur."

MISHOU OPENED the front door wide to welcome April in with a rush of words that she only understood the half of. "Victor...come tomorrow...*rendez-vous*..." Mishou announced. And then April thought she said she felt young having a roommate. She was afraid that trying to capture every word would result in her having a headache, but she had to try to make the most of it for Mishou's sake, and for her own. April allowed Mishou to kiss her on the cheeks, the one language they could both understand, and smiled warmly at her.

The room set out for April was small and dim with white nylon curtains and a wooden armoire in the corner. The bed was a little lumpy, but she had the space needed for her stuff. It was an odd sensation, for all that she was moving into someone else's apartment, and a plain one at that, but April felt like she had come home. The bathroom contained a sink, bidet and bath in blue porcelain, with yellow and white flowered tiles covering the walls. The toilet was in a separate room, between her room and Mishou's master bedroom.

When April had unpacked her things, she wondered if she was supposed to stay in her room or if Mishou would expect her to keep company. She wasn't used to living with anyone, so this was unchartered territory, but surely she could make an attempt to spend time with Mishou and make the older woman's life less lonely. What would they talk about with the language barrier?

She needn't have worried. Upon exiting her room, Mishou called to her and brought her into the kitchen. She had laid out the flour, large grain sea salt, and butter. "*Viens. On va faire une tarte*," she said.

April looked at the kitchen counter and saw a quiche pan and the rolling pin, and it dawned on her. Mishou was giving her cooking lessons. April looked at her in wide-eyed delight. "*Oui!*"

"VICTOR, YOU'VE BEEN DISTRACTED LATELY." Margaux's sharp voice caused him to pull the phone away from his ear. "We really need to get started with the wedding if we're going to actually *have* one in six months. That's a really short timeframe under the best of circumstances. But if you don't start committing to some of the details, we'll never make it."

Victor loosened his tie. The business meeting with Brunex Consulting had gone really well. He was taking his grandmother's advice to heart and was actually considering putting a pause on his own M&A business. Instead he would attempt to manage one of the smaller boutiques they were planning to buy as a subsidiary to a larger acquisition. Yes, directing Brunex would have been a mistake. But directing one of the subsidiaries would be just the challenge he needed, and he'd probably be too far under his father's notice to suffer much from his scrutiny. Brunex Consulting was located in Dubai, but this particular boutique firm was based in Paris, which meant he could take the risk without uprooting himself from everything that was familiar. April had been right, though. It wasn't just about money. It was about finding satisfaction in the process.

It was hard to shift from his world to Margaux's, but when she cleared her throat, he snapped to attention.

"When does your dad want to meet?" he asked.

"This weekend. You haven't even approved the guest list, and how can we reserve anything without knowing what the final numbers will be?" He heard a tapping noise and figured it was her pen. She did that when she was nervous. "I suggest you come to the meeting prepared."

Victor couldn't keep the irritation out of his voice. He hated when she treated him like a little boy. "Tell your dad I'll come Saturday night. I'll have the list approved. Is that all?" he asked.

"Well..." Margaux seemed to hesitate. "You haven't told me lately that you loved me. Not since I've been back." Victor gripped the phone with his right hand and rubbed his forehead with his left. She wanted him to say that now? He had said it, and more. However, the fact that she *wanted* him to say it gave him the tiniest glimmer of hope. Perhaps the wedding would not be a mistake after all. If he could just remember what it felt like to be in love with her before. The completeness he felt when she loved him, too—or at least he thought she loved him—when he was with her family. Everything had felt right back then. And now they had Matthias. Maybe everything would turn out all right in the end.

When Victor remained silent, Margaux said, "My parents are beginning to wonder if this wedding is going to happen or not."

Ugh. She had managed to utter the one thing that was sure to douse him in cold reality. She just cared about what her parents thought, not about him. But then there was the baby. He was not going to let his baby grow up in a broken home if he had any say in it. "I'll come Saturday at eight," he said. "And I'll make an effort to be more involved in the planning. Your parents will not need to worry."

Victor hung up the phone with Margaux and grabbed his briefcase. He had held the meeting at his office, but now he rushed to April's art school. He wanted to be there on time since he had told Mishou to tell her he was coming. He arrived just as she was exiting the school.

"Victor. I didn't expect to see you here," she said. He looked to her left, and the sight of Ben brought on a surge of jealousy—completely unreasonable since Victor was not available.

"Bonjour," he said, offering his hand. Ben shook it, and Victor leaned over to kiss April. "Did my grandmother not tell you I'd be coming here today?"

"Oh, she said many things that I didn't understand."

He laughed. "I hadn't thought about the communication issue. I thought we could go together to her place so I could see how you settled in."

"Great," April said. "I'm actually free earlier than expected because the studio was closed for spring break. Our teacher is sick, and the director has already left for the week, so there was no one to open it for us." She turned to Ben. "Let's get lunch another time, okay?"

Victor saw his scowl before he turned away, but April hadn't noticed. "Your grandmother taught me how to make a *tarte à la moutarde*. Do you know what that is?"

"Of course I know what that is," he said, feigning insult. "It's only her very best dish. The one everyone begs a piece of whenever there's a neighborhood party. Did you do a good job?" he asked. "Are you pleased with the result?"

"It tasted so scrumptious," she said, looking up at him with shiny eyes. "And the thing is, I think I can reproduce it. I'm going to bring it for when we have the next dinner with Penelope Duprey and her friends."

"Oh, you're going to get together with them again? When?"

"Next Friday night," April said. "And I'm to invite you. And Margaux, if you think she'll come."

"Penelope invited me—and Margaux, too? Why?" Victor reached over to take her unwieldy portfolio that kept banging against the ground as she walked.

"Why not?" April looked at him in surprise. "Of course she would invite your fiancée if she's going to invite you."

His brows furrowed. "But that she would even invite me is not a very French thing to do. I mean, we've only met each other once."

"I think she invited you because she thinks you're a great guy for coming to my rescue." April smiled at him, daring him to deny it. It took everything in him to accept the compliment and not try to deflect it.

"All right. When you put it like that. I'm having dinner with Margaux's family on Saturday night, and I'll see if she's free to come." He pressed the button at the crosswalk.

"That's great," April said. Her voice sounded faint.

Chapter Seventeen

Victor rang the doorbell, dressed in khaki pants and a navy blue blazer. He had debated on, and finally rejected, the tie. Margaux's father opened the door, stepping back to allow Victor to enter before reaching for his hand.

"Well, Victor," he said, his voice a mix of what sounded like severity and affection. "It's good of you to come. We've gone as far as we can without your input on planning the wedding."

Taken aback by the softened greeting when Margaux's father was usually aloof, Victor returned the handshake. "I'm glad to be here, sir. I'm sorry I didn't make more of an effort before."

"Well," Mr. De Bonneville said gruffly, "the important thing is that we're doing this now. Let me take the time to address this while Margaux is upstairs with her mother and the baby. What did you get her in the way of rings?"

"Rings?" Victor swallowed, feeling his heart plunge.

"Yes. I imagined that, being the resourceful fellow you are, you would've already gotten the engagement ring and wedding band. When I asked Margaux about it, she didn't seem to know. I appreciate this kind of thoughtfulness." Mr. de Bonneville took Victor by the elbow and steered him toward the living room. "I don't hold with these modern notions of bringing the fiancée to look at the rings. A man needs to know what he wants, and he needs to understand the lady enough not to make a mess of it."

He sat, indicating the other chair for Victor. The armchair to his side, rather than the hard-backed sofa across the room. Mr. De Bonneville poured two scotches on the rocks and handed one to Victor, whose mind was now racing.

"Sir, I just want to warn you that I didn't come prepared to do an engagement ceremony tonight. I have the ring—" *Liar,* he thought. "—and was planning to give it to her when it's just the two of us." He had to stop himself from begging for her father's approval. No. Better to state it as if that were his intention all along. *Where am I going to get a ring? The same place as before, I suppose. But what does she want? Do I get her the same style as last time? She said* no *last time, you idiot.*

"—prepared to give a generous sum for a lavish wedding. You need only pay for the civil ceremony celebration and the honeymoon. My baby will have everything she wants, even if we have to pay extra to have it done on short notice."

Victor struggled to catch up. "That's good of you, sir."

"Where are you taking her on the honeymoon? If Matthias is weaned by then you can leave the baby here, and we'll hire a nurse to help us. I remember hearing you wanted to go to Singapore." Margaux's father leaned back and sipped his scotch.

"Yes, I had thought that perhaps..."

"I think Margaux is not opposed to traveling to other places, now that she's gone off to Monaco. It was her first time leaving the Paris area, you know, except for her yearly trips to her grandmother's country house. It did her a world of good, because she's finally ready to grow up and settle down."

Victor didn't know how to answer that, so he just said, "Yes, sir."

It seemed an eternity before Margaux joined them. Madame de Bonneville arrived first, saying in that wispy voice of hers that made you doubt she had ever once raised it, "Margaux is just finishing up bathing Matthias and she'll be right down." After greeting Victor, she tucked her skirt under her legs and sat on the hard sofa. She looked at the two men, then at her lap, not seeming to feel any pressure to advance the conversation.

Victor heralded Margaux's arrival with relief. She entered the room wearing royal blue pants and a white flowing top with a matching blue scarf in her hair. It was a lot of color for her—a step away from her usual fashion. Matthias was awake, for once, and cradled against her shoulder, looking around and trying to find his fist to shove in his mouth. When Victor rose to his feet and walked over, Matthias studied him gravely. Feeling foolish, Victor took Matthias's hand with two fingers and shook it. Matthias continued to examine him.

Margaux turned her cheeks to be kissed, and Victor felt the first softening toward her since she'd reappeared in his life. Here she was looking pretty and dainty and holding their baby. He couldn't imagine her giving birth, that she could be anything but perfectly put together all the time. She seemed approachable like this. Victor remembered how it was when they first went out, when she somehow appeared to choose him over all the men vying for her attention at the select party Victor had been invited to. He had fallen hard.

"Shall we go into dinner, Papa?" she asked. "Can you carry the bouncing seat, Victor? We might be lucky enough to have dinner peacefully without Matthias needing to be held."

Victor picked up the seat, dutifully, and set it next to her chair. Then, upon second thought, he put the baby seat between his chair and Margaux's. He may as well begin to get to know his son.

"I had our cook prepare mussels and French fries, knowing how much you like them," Mr. de Bonneville said. "Pierrette, why don't you go see about bringing in the entrées."

His faded wife hurried toward the kitchen while Margaux's

dad sat. Victor waited until Margaux had settled Matthias in his seat, and was seated herself, before taking his own place.

"Victor and I have not made much headway discussing the marriage," Mr. de Bonneville told his daughter. "We haven't gotten to particulars, but he's figuring everything out. The ring, the honeymoon—everything. I think we'll set you up in an apartment in the 16th. A *quatre-pièce* ought to be good enough for a starter apartment since you won't want more than the two bedrooms for now."

"Sir, I don't want to be far from my grandmother. I thought we could stay in my apartment." Victor leaned back so Margaux's mother could set the cucumber gelatin appetizer in front of him.

"Nonsense," Mr. de Bonneville replied. "She will understand that young people need to start out fresh. It's all about looking forward."

"*She* would understand it, sir. But I don't want to do that. My grandmother is the most important person in my life."

"Young people need to start out properly with their own place. The one they've built together," Mr. de Bonneville insisted, and Victor felt his blood rise. He'd almost forgotten how high-handed her dad could be.

Margaux, always the one to soothe tensions—more, he suspected, from an aversion to conflict than a real desire for peace —cut her father's imminent tirade with a few quiet words. "We'll worry about that later, Papa. Let's start talking about the marriage ceremony."

As if tamed, her dad shifted gears immediately. "I've spoken to the priest at the Madeleine, and he said he has very few dates open in the timeline we want. He's looking at nine months from now and said you may want to consider baptizing Matthias first. He also said Victor will need to take classes since he's not Catholic." He shook his head. "With all these impediments, we're not going to be ready in the six months we were shooting for."

"I don't have to be married in the Madeleine," Margaux said, pushing the cucumbers around on her plate.

The baby started cooing at Victor's side, and he longed to reach over and pick him up, but he didn't dare. Margaux and her father continued to weigh the benefits of being married in the best church in Paris versus having a speedier option, with her father, surprisingly, opting for waiting. Victor had been certain it was her dad who was pushing for a quick wedding, but now he was not so sure.

Madame de Bonneville brought the mussels to the table, and Victor listened to Margaux and her father discussing the merits of having a reception right in Paris in one of the restaurants overlooking the Seine versus borrowing the chateau of one of their family's friends. The guests would have to drive an hour and a half after the ceremony, but they could see about putting the more important guests in the chateau itself and finding bed-and-breakfast rooms for the rest of the guests nearby. Victor thought a chateau might be more charming, but no one asked him. The longer they talked without asking him anything, the more perverse his desire was to see how much they would actually plan without his input they had so insisted upon.

He looked over at Margaux's mother, who was picking the meat out of each mussel shell, not using the empty shell as clamps as his grandmother had taught him, but with an escargot fork. She was quiet as she ate, and looking for all appearances to have no other thought in her head than what she was eating. He wondered what would happen if he pushed his chair back, walked over to her, and shook her by the shoulders. Would she set her mussel down and pick up another?

Victor's thoughts bounced along in this manner throughout the dinner, the salad, the cheese platter, the macarons and the *digestif*. Amazingly, Margaux and her father did not solicit his opinion once, except to ask how many people he planned to invite. He had prepared that list, at least. It was not extensive. His grandmother. His father and whoever his father's plus one would be in six—or nine—months' time, depending on whether they waited for the Madeleine to be available, a few former colleagues from the time before he began training under his father...and he would invite his high school friend, though he had indeed run off with Victor's girlfriend at the time. The humiliation had lessened now that he had Margaux to show for it. A somewhat hollow victory, on second thought.

After dinner, with Matthias making happy noises in his bouncy seat, the four of them sat in the living room for one round of cards, after which Mr. de Bonneville rose and indicated for his wife to do the same. "I will leave you two lovebirds to spend some time alone together. I'm sure you have much to discuss."

"Thank you." Victor stood and grasped the older man's hand. "*Bonne soirée*, Mr. de Bonneville."

"You may call me Baudouin," Margaux's father replied. "You're marrying my daughter."

Victor almost fell over in shock. He thought her father would remain Mr. de Bonneville until the day he died. "Well. Goodnight then, Baudouin."

Mrs. de Bonneville faded away behind her husband, and he and Margaux were left alone with the baby, who started to fuss. Margaux picked Matthias up and leaned over to hand him to Victor. "Here. You'd best get used to this, I think."

Victor took the baby by his soft, pliable torso, terrified that he would drop him. He held the baby aloft in front of him, the baby's eyes level with his. He watched as Matthias put his fingers in his mouth, his unblinking stare on Victor.

"*Bonjour, bébé*," he said in a silly voice, feeling for all the world like a fool. The baby continued to examine him, and Victor settled him more comfortably on his lap, leaning the baby in the crook of his arm and staring at him. Margaux watched them quietly. "*Mah-tee-yas*," Victor said, enunciating each syllable of the baby's name. "Mah-tee-yas." He forgot Margaux was there, lost in the expressive eyes of his son.

Then Victor's world shifted. Matthias gurgled and gave a wide, toothless grin. Stunned, Victor wondered if the smile could be meant for him. "Mah-tee-yaaaaas," he said again, drunk with the victory of making the baby smile. Matthias's gurgle turned into a shriek of laughter, and he kicked his legs. Victor was so surprised he stopped making faces and peered at the baby.

"He's laughing?" he said. "He can laugh?"

Margaux shook her head with a smile of her own. "He's laughing. And yes, you did it."

Having expended the energy, Matthias appeared sleepy and lifted his fingers to his mouth again. Victor guided the baby's hands to help him along. "He's really cute," he said.

"We should spend more time together," Margaux said. "We've not had much of it between you taking care of April and me planning the wedding. But if we're going to get married, we need to make up for the lost time. Are you working a lot this week? Any new deals?"

Victor shifted the baby when he started to fuss again, then gave up and handed him back to Margaux, who soothed the infant with automatic movements. "Actually, I may as well tell you. I'm talking with the owners of Martin *et cie*—a subsidiary of Brunex. We're discussing my coming on as a manager for the business when they give up full control."

"Manager? What do you mean? When would you find time to do that? I mean, I can understand taking on more work than what you currently have, but how many hours a week would you have to put into it?"

"See, that's the thing." Victor exhaled, unsure of how much to share of this quiet dream of his. He supposed if they were going to be married he should be forthright. "I'm thinking of taking a year's sabbatical from turning companies to try to manage one. I think I would be good at it, and I might even take it further than if I just sold it as is—"

"That's a crazy idea," Margaux said. "What would we live on?"

"I do have savings…"

"Yes, but they'd get eaten up before we can blink. I have a *baby* now. It's not about just the two of us." Margaux bounced Matthias in her arms in short jerking motions.

We have a baby now, Victor thought, but he was too tired to argue. "Well, it was just a thought."

Margaux remained silent, as she put Matthias back in the bouncing seat and turned on a gentle rocking motion. "Shall we plan to go out and do something together soon? I don't know, dinner or dancing? Like I said, I think we should be spending more time together."

"We've been invited to dinner. I've been meaning to tell you. It's hosted by one of April's friends from the art studio, and she made sure to say that both you and I are invited. We don't have a lot of friends in common, so why don't we go?"

"April again." Margaux's eyes snapped. "She appears a lot in our conversations."

"April is my friend, nothing more." Anxious to change the subject, Victor added, "Her friend, Penelope Duprey, is really nice. I think you'll like her."

"Penelope Duprey?" Margaux shot him a look of surprise. "I think I know her. We might have gone to school together. How old is she?"

Victor shrugged. "She looks about our age, I guess."

Margaux smoothed the embroidered velvet on the arm of her chair, and Victor found himself holding his breath, hoping she would agree to the plan. He couldn't explain to himself precisely why he wanted to go.

Finally, Margaux looked up, apparently decided. "I haven't seen her in years. When is it?"

Victor quietly exhaled. "Friday next week."

"All right," Margaux said. "Because it's Penelope, I'll go."

Chapter Eighteen

The studio opened up again a week later, and by now, April's fear that her painting was missing had reached a fevered pitch. She hadn't told anyone about it, hoping that Penelope had just overlooked it among the other paintings. Penelope arrived five minutes later and came to stand beside April as she pulled the paintings, one by one, out of the stock. When April reached the last one, she swallowed in fear and disappointment. "It's not here. Do you think Françoise might have moved it?"

"We'll ask her when she gets in," Penelope replied, troubled. "It's got to be here somewhere. Who would have taken it?"

April turned to look at her. "I'll be honest. I'm afraid Lucas figured out where I study, and that he broke in and stole it. He knows which painting is mine since he watched me work on it."

Penelope shook her head. "I don't think so. We would've heard something if there was a break-in. Does Ben know it's missing?"

"I haven't seen him all week, although he called a couple of times, and I haven't had a chance to call him back. I'm not sure what's going on with him, though. He's been weird around me lately, and even before the break, he was skipping some of the classes. It's like he's lost interest in studying or something."

"Maybe he thinks you lost interest in him, so painting is less fun now."

"I was never interested in Ben, you know."

"Oh yes, *I* know."

April decided not to ask what that tone of voice was meant to imply and carried her other painting to the easel in the corner where she could work undisturbed. She couldn't do anything about her lost painting until she'd spoken to Françoise, but she could work on completing this one, and maybe sort through how she was feeling about everything. She just needed a little time alone to think and paint. Penelope didn't seem to pick up on her need for solitude, though, because she eventually came to where April was and stood over her canvas.

"How are your cooking lessons with Mishou going?"

April finished filling in the edge of the green shrub, then looked up. Penelope had put her canvas on the easel next to April's and was smiling at her. April felt a rush of affection. Solitude could be overrated at times, and she was glad to have Penelope for a friend. "Good. I've learned two dishes, and I'll be bringing a *tarte à la moutarde* on Saturday night."

"Bravo. I'll tell the others. Can't wait to try it." Penelope leaned in to study April's work more closely. "You chose your location well on this painting. Don't worry too much about the other one yet. I'm sure one of these is going to be chosen, and I'm not giving up hope that we find the other."

In a swift change of subject, she said, "Victor called me and said they're coming on Saturday. You gave him my number?" April nodded. "He said Margaux might know me, and I'm sure he's right. I went to school with a Margaux de Bonneville."

April looked at her in surprise. "He didn't tell me that. What's she like?"

"Oh..." Penelope looked down at her palette. She hadn't

started mixing the paints yet. "She was like all the girls in our school. Privileged. I never got to know her very well, though we have many acquaintances in common."

"If that's what everyone was like, you're lucky to have found your group," April said. "They're good friends. *Real* friends."

"Yes, it's true. I'll be curious to see Margaux with Victor. I can't really picture them together."

"Really?" April toyed with the end of her brush, feeling strangely empty. "I would think they'd be perfect together. I mean, I know this is judging on appearances alone, but they seem to come from the same world. They both have money, they're both super good-looking—"

"Oh, so you think Victor is good-looking, do you?" Penelope teased.

"Come on." April rolled her eyes. "Who doesn't?"

"Hmm." Penelope wore a smile that April chose to ignore. "Anyway. Apparently Margaux is not bringing the baby. They're going to have her parents watch him, so we'll get to see them together. See if they're a good fit." Penelope squeezed white paint on her palette and reached for the ochre. "They're not really from the same world, you know."

April looked up from her painting. "What do you mean?"

"Well, Margaux is from old money." Penelope shrugged. "Victor is *nouveau riche*."

"I don't really know what that means."

"It just means that Margaux comes from a family with an old aristocratic name and property—an apartment in Paris, land and a house in the countryside. A heritage passed down from one generation to the next. Victor wasn't born to money, but he has a father who is very successful." Penelope smiled at April's look of confusion. "Don't ask me how I know. I just do. If I didn't know Victor at all, I would say that *that* was what attracted him to Margaux in the beginning. The privilege that you can only get from birth. But since I've seen how he is with you, I'm willing to bet any feelings he once had for Margaux are over. He's staying with her because of the baby."

April rinsed her brush in a swift motion. "That doesn't help at all."

"Because he's not available?" Penelope grabbed the nearby stool and sat so she could be level with April.

"Yeah. Totally unavailable, and he's doing the right thing by being with the mother of his child." April met Penelope's gaze and shook her head. "Don't encourage me about him. I need to focus on being a good friend to him because that's all it will ever be."

Penelope breathed in. "Got it." She picked up a dab of ochre with her palette knife and swirled it into the white. "I had better get started on my own painting. I don't have high hopes of its being included, but I need to give it my best shot."

April went back to her canvas, the weight of despondency settling over her again. Everything she'd told Penelope was true. Victor *should* be with Margaux. It was not April's style to try to pull a man away from another woman, and that was doubly true if they'd already started a family together. She would not allow any thoughts of crushes, or feelings, or anything of that nature to turn her from doing what she felt was right.

She couldn't help her thoughts, though. They drifted to Victor and the way he'd defended her, punching Lucas after he pulled him off her, the way he leaned in to kiss her cheeks. She wished...

"Haven't seen you in a while."

April jumped as the stool scraped at her side. Ben had finally showed up. She looked at her painting, which now had an errant brushstroke across the canvas. "Oh shoot." She examined it. No, it wasn't a staining pigment, so she could wipe it off with the soft cotton rag. "Hi, Ben," she said, absentmindedly.

"Are you avoiding me now?" Ben was studying her face, his own a mask of irritation, or of hurt. She couldn't tell.

"No, Ben. I had to settle in after the move. I'm sorry I didn't get a chance to call you back." She didn't meet his gaze, not wishing to see what else he was trying to communicate to her. "It's not been easy for me."

"I wish you'd let me help." Ben reached over and put his hand on her knee. April, startled, looked to see if Penelope was still there, but she had gone to get some water. It was time to redirect Ben's thoughts.

"Do you have any idea what happened to my painting? The surrealist one with the apartment building and my face?"

He took his hand off her knee. "No. It's missing? You looked behind all the paintings on the wall? And in the back?"

"Yes. I've looked everywhere. My one hope is that Françoise put it somewhere, though why she would is beyond my guess."

"I'm sorry, April. I hope you find it." Ben stood. "I'd better get my painting started. Did you know Mr. Chambourd is going to make his decision by this weekend?"

"Yes." April gave him a look. "Get to work. You still have all the pipes to fill in on the Georges Pompidou center. And Ben?" He looked back at her. "We're still friends. We can go out for lunch later this week, or at least for coffee, depending on how much more we need to get done before the paintings are judged."

"All right. " Ben nodded and went to his painting on the wall. He was a good guy, and she didn't want to burn any bridges.

Françoise came in then. There was to be more free painting than class hours as everyone got ready for the exhibit, and Françoise had adjusted her hours, using class time, and staying late, to help whoever needed it. April decided to go to her before others claimed her attention.

"Bonjour, Françoise." Their teacher required all her students to use proper French greetings, insisting it was something everyone should know how to do since they were living in France. A *bonjour* for the day, a *bonsoir* for the evening, and never, ever start a conversation without first greeting the person in front of you if you didn't want to be written off as having no manners.

When April had her teacher's full attention, she asked, "Have you moved my painting somewhere? The one you said Mr. Chambourd noticed? I thought perhaps you put it in a room to ready it for the competition."

Françoise shook her head, and frowned. "No..." Then she shot her head up with a look of alarm. "Two weeks ago, though, the lock was broken to this room. We were panicked until we saw that nothing had been tampered with and nothing was missing. At least...I thought nothing was missing. I didn't think to check each painting. Yours is gone?"

April nodded her head, miserable. "There aren't surveillance cameras in the room?"

Françoise said, "Not in the room. There are on the east corner. If the person passed by there, the cameras will have caught him, but that's a small chance. Maybe it was one of the students. Someone who was jealous that you were singled out that way." She let her breath out in a huff. "Stupid of me, really, to say which painting was noticed. I'll have to do better in the future. But I hate to think of anyone here..." She looked around at the classroom, which was now nearly full, with students working assiduously.

"I don't think it's anyone here," April said. "Do you remember how I told you I was attacked? And that's how I got the bruise?"

Françoise nodded, concerned. "You think it's the same person?"

"Yes. I told you he destroyed my father's paintings? Well, I'm afraid that was not enough for him, and he wants to keep going and destroy..." April threw her arms out, "...everything." Her eyes filled with tears and she swiped at them angrily. That Lucas could make her cry, that he would have any power over her at all, made her want to scream.

Penelope had come up to stand by her, and Ben was watching them from his easel. Françoise said, "You're going to need accompaniment everywhere until we find him. I'll check with the local police to see if they can examine the street camera. Penelope, you're friends with April, right? Do you think you can arrange to see her home safely from here?"

"Sure." Penelope put her arm around April. "So the painting is really missing? I can't believe it."

"I didn't know he even knew where I went to school." April was trying hard not to cry, and her throat ached from the effort. "I'll be fine. You don't have to accompany me everywhere. I'll just be careful not to go out where there aren't a lot of people."

"Let's take one day at a time." Penelope exchanged a glance with Françoise. "I'll come to your new apartment with you today. Then we'll see about the future. I agree, though. No going out alone, especially at night. This Lucas guy seems to be more capable than any of us gave him credit for. So far, he's eluded getting caught, he's tracked where you go to school, he's managed to destroy your things in two different places. From what you've told me of him, I didn't think he had it in him."

"Honestly," April said, "I think he has nothing else to lose."

"And those are the most dangerous ones," Françoise said. "I want you to focus on your work now. We've replaced the lock to this room with a better one, and I'll be keeping this painting in the back storage area just in case."

"He hasn't seen this one, so there's probably not a risk. But thank you. And thanks, Penelope. I'll be glad for your company today, at least." To her teacher, April said, "Would you mind coming over to look at what I've been working on to see if there are any improvements I should make? I really hope Mr. Chambourd will like this one as well."

"Sure," Françoise said. "I think we need to work on the couple outside the umbrella shop. That's the touch of whimsy in this painting, and it's missing something."

Chapter Nineteen

Victor held the elevator door for Margaux and let it shut behind them as they went up to the apartment where the dinner with Penelope was being held. She leaned into him in an old familiar way, and said, "It's weird without Matthias. I'm not used to being without him."

"He's taking the bottle now?" Victor asked. "In case he gets hungry?"

"He's always had mixed from birth," she said. "I didn't have a lot of milk at first, so he needed formula, and I liked the freedom of being able to go out."

"Is that what you used to do in Monaco? Go out?" Victor asked, and when she shot him a look, he protested. "You never told me what you were doing there."

"I was visiting my cousin—"

"Yes, your cousin," Victor said. "But really? For a year? What were you doing all that time, and why didn't you come home before the birth? You didn't even tell your parents." *Why am I bringing this up now?* he thought. *What's the point?* But he couldn't help the surge of anger that had seemed to spring up from nowhere.

Margaux clucked her teeth in impatience as the elevator door opened. "I told you I couldn't tell my parents, or they'd make me come home."

They walked into the corridor, and Victor turned and stopped her in her tracks. "Why didn't you want to come home?" Victor knew he had chosen the worst possible moment for the conversation, but the frustration that had been building in him just wouldn't stay put anymore. "Was there someone there you wanted to see?" *Whoa. Where did that come from?* Suddenly, Victor knew what had been bothering him ever since Margaux had come back. He didn't know what had brought her to Monaco, and he didn't know what had kept her there. This was too vital a piece of information to shove under the rug if they were going to be married, even if Matthias was involved.

"Victor..." Margaux's voice had gone soft, though there was a tinge of frustration there. "All that doesn't matter now—"

The door to the modern elevator pinged behind them, and April stepped onto the corridor, carrying a quiche pan. "Oh." Her eyes opened wide when she saw them. She was wearing jeans and a soft pink shirt, cropped short in the front and lower in the back. Her hair was down over her shoulders—the first time Victor had seen it like that—and the skin around her eyes had returned to a porcelain white, which made the blue of her eyes stand out. He suffered a pang of longing for what would not be. "Bonsoir, Margaux," she said.

She smiled at both him and Margaux in her welcome but seemed to sense the tension, because she held back from saying more. Victor hadn't seen April all week, and his first glimpse of her was like a buzz. Then he came to his senses. "Hi, April." He reached over to kiss her cheeks. She smelled so good, he wanted to throw his arms around her and pull her close, but there was the quiche pan in the way. And, of course, there was Margaux.

"Are you coming in?" she asked, looking at each of them in turn.

"Yes." Margaux moved toward the door. It was only one word, but it was the first Victor had ever heard her utter in English. It was as if she wanted to show him that she, too, could speak another language.

Penelope opened the door. "Bonsoir, Margaux," she said, casually, as if they had seen each other only a few days ago.

"Bonsoir, Penelope," she replied, giving her *the bises* and following her into the living room. Then it continued like that. Every person in the room, except Arthur, knew Margaux and greeted her in a relaxed, unsurprised manner, although Victor sensed a bit of reserve in their welcome.

He hung back with April. "Seems like they all know each other, huh?"

"Uh huh," she said with a smile. "So we're the odd men out."

"April, I heard you brought us a sample of your culinary delight," Guillaume called out from the kitchen.

"Yes, a *tarte*," she called back, but didn't move forward just yet. It was as if she wanted to stay in the entryway with Victor. He hoped that was the case because it was exactly what he was feeling. Suddenly he remembered. He was *not* available. The realization must have shown on his face because she took a step toward the living room where the others were.

"Are you coming then?" Guillaume asked. "Let me meet your friend."

"Coming," April said. Then she whispered, "Everything okay with Margaux and the baby?"

Victor pressed his lips together and muttered, "Perfect."

THIS DINNER WAS like the last one April attended, except Margaux seemed to throw a blanket of reserve over everyone. There was less laughter and teasing as the group sat around the table peeling cucumbers and cutting crosses into the radishes so they could stuff pats of butter inside. Victor immediately grabbed a knife and began helping with the radishes, but Margaux sat, primly, hands on her crossed knees, watching everyone work.

"Would you like a glass of wine?" Arthur came over to Margaux, holding the bottle of rosé.

"Just a Schweppes, please," she said. "I'm still breast-feeding."

"A Schweppes it is," he said, then called out to Guillaume. "*T'as du Schweppes?*"

"In the pantry," Guillaume called back. "April, bring your *tarte* here so I can take a look."

"I want to see it too." Victor dropped the knife on the cutting board and walked to her side, and April noticed Margaux's head shoot up as she watched him walk over.

"Pressure," April murmured, with a little smile, as she removed the clean cloth that was covering the dish and set it to the side. She was proud of herself. The tomatoes were cut in thin slices and scalloped around the top of the *tarte* over the Dijon mustard and grated Emmental cheese. She had sprinkled fresh chopped basil and pepper, and had drizzled olive oil over the top just as Mishou had showed her.

"It's magnificent," Penelope said, peeking around Guillaume's shoulder, and he leaned back into her. "I told you it was a good idea for you to stay with Victor's grandmother."

"There's no one like her for cooking," Victor confirmed. "Are you going to serve it like that or warm it up?"

"I think warm it," April said, biting her lip. "I mean, right? Wouldn't it be better?"

Guillaume stood straight as Penelope pulled away, *releasing him from his spell*, April thought, and she didn't think she was imagining things. "Guillaume is the best chef here. So do whatever he thinks."

"We'll warm it at a hundred and fifty degrees," he said with a smile. "A slice for everyone with some salad for our entrée, and I'll put the filet mignon in while we eat that. Victor, want to give me a hand with the potatoes?"

They spent another hour preparing the dinner while they munched on smoked salmon toasts and buttered radishes, then finally sat to sample the entrée. Margaux seemed to relax and fall into conversation with everyone, even reminiscing about their high school days. "How many years younger were you?" she asked Aimée.

"I was in the class just behind," Aimée said. "So not a big age difference."

"Yes, I remember you. You look familiar."

Morgane said, "You weren't in the science track with the rest of us, but we did have history together. I don't know if you remember."

Margaux nodded. "I remember. Madame Cheval."

"And she looked like a horse, didn't she," Théo said with a snort.

"Come on, she was nice." Auriane batted him on the arm.

April's French had improved, and she was starting to catch most of the banter between everyone. She darted glances at Victor. He must have been happy that Margaux was participating in the conversation. Penelope kept drawing him into a separate conversation, and April wondered why. She wasn't jealous, but it was as if Penelope wanted to get to know him better. To take his measure? She couldn't be sure. Guillaume threw his napkin on the table and got up to fetch the next course.

Arthur asked Margaux what she'd been doing after school, and she replied that she went to *Science Po* for university. Arthur had also gone there before deciding to abandon politics to study art, and they began to compare notes on teachers and classes. Penelope had just started to ask Victor another question when she overheard Margaux say that she'd gone to Monaco for a year and had only come back recently.

"Franck Duboise is there," Penelope said. "Did you guys meet up? It's a small place, so I'm sure you would have run into each other if you were in Monaco a whole year."

"Oh, I..." Margaux turned bright red, surprising April, who would have thought her capable of hiding any emotion she might not wish to be made public. Victor had turned to Margaux, and his jaw dropped.

Penelope continued as if Margaux had not shown any embarrassment. "He's running the family hotel there. His parents have decided to sell their apartment in the sixteenth and settle in Monaco permanently."

Margaux looked down and fiddled with her knife. "Yes," she replied. "We did run into each other a few times. He doesn't live that far from my cousin, so we would see each other at the market and sometimes when we went out."

"Is he friends with your cousin?" Penelope probed. "Martin, can you pass the carafe of water, please?"

Margaux didn't answer right away, but when she saw that Penelope was still waiting for her reply, said, "They seemed to know each other pretty well. As you said, it's a small city so everyone knows each other." Her words fizzled, and silence settled over the table.

"This filet mignon is delicious," Penelope said, with a bright smile. "I like the pepper crust this time."

April wanted to help clear the air, so she added, in English, "Me too. Guillaume, you are really a star in the kitchen."

He laughed. "Don't let Penelope's false humility fool you. The pepper crust was her idea."

Penelope jerked her chin, hiding a smile. "It was good, *non?*" She popped a bite in her mouth.

Penelope turned to Théo, who was on her left-hand side, leaving Victor free to speak to Margaux if he wished. April watched them, wondering if he'd noticed how uncomfortable Margaux had been when Penelope mentioned Franck's name. Of course he'd noticed. How could he not? She wondered if Margaux had been in love with Franck while she was there. Nothing could come of it if she were pregnant, but perhaps she couldn't help her feelings. Maybe that was why she stayed in Monaco as long as she did, unable to break away from a relationship. April hoped she'd given that up and was fully committed to Victor now. He deserved no less than complete fidelity. The baby deserved it too.

After dinner, April went to get a flyer from her bag that she thought might interest Penelope, and Victor met her in the hallway lined with glass-enclosed bookshelves. "Penelope told me your painting was stolen?"

"Yes," April said, turning toward him.

"April, you should tell me these things. We're friends." He folded his arms and leaned against the glass.

She looked at her feet. *He's not available*, she told herself. "I don't have all the details yet. Françoise—my art teacher—was going to ask the police if they were able to catch anything on camera, and I wanted to see if she had any news for me before I said anything."

"You need to tell me everything right away," he insisted. "Don't wait to have all the answers before you say something. Let me help."

April crossed her arms, imitating his posture. "How are the wedding plans going?"

Victor looked away.

"She seemed uncomfortable—" April dropped her voice to a whisper. "Margaux seemed uncomfortable when Penelope asked her about that Franck person."

Victor took a breath. "Yeah, well, that could be anything. She's always had a lot of secrets. He could've been rude to her once, or they could've had an affair. I'll never know."

"Don't you think you should have the right to know these things before you get married?" April knew she was treading on thin ice. She was questioning the wisdom of his marriage to Margaux, and her motivation was not, in the least bit, pure. She had feelings—sometimes overwhelming feelings—for him, herself. She needed to stop, but couldn't seem to help herself.

"I just know Matthias deserves for his father to be involved," Victor said. "He deserves an unbroken home. I always promised myself I'd give my children better than I had. Better than my father gave me."

April felt her heart sink. He was perfectly right. "You're a good guy," she said. Then, drawing on an inner strength—determined to let him be free to do what was right, even if it meant she would lose him—she asked, "How is Matthias, anyway?"

"Matthias smiled at me," Victor said. He grinned at the memory. "I made him smile. He's really cute."

April laughed. "I told you you were a great dad."

Penelope peeked into the hallway. "We're about to play poker. Who wants in?"

"Me," April said. "But I need a refresher for the rules. It's not for money, right?"

"No, just for chips. Hey, Victor," Penelope said, "are you able to take April back to your grandmother's apartment tonight after you bring Margaux home? She probably won't ask for help, but we're afraid Lucas is following her, and we want to make sure she doesn't get stalked."

"Sure." Victor turned to her in consternation. "Another thing you're not telling me, April. Please tell me these things."

A flash of anger came over April, and she replied without thinking. "Don't expect me to tell you everything. It's not like I'm your girlfriend. I don't owe you explanations, or details, or anything."

"Er...let me see how the game is going." Penelope turned, whisking away a smile.

"What are you talking about, April? We're friends. Friends talk."

"Victor," April hissed. "It's like you expect things from me you don't even expect of your own fiancée. You want me to come to you for help and tell you everything. But you don't even know what Margaux was doing that whole year in Monaco. You don't know what brought her back or...or whether the baby is even yours." *There. I said it.* April's pulse pounded in her temple.

"Victor doesn't ask me these things, because he already knows the answer." Margaux's cool voice came from where the living room joined the hallway. "And, since *he* is satisfied, I don't see what business it is of yours." Margaux managed to communicate all her disdain in two sentences.

April's face was crimson. She could feel the heat of shame emanating from her. She'd let everyone know how she felt about Victor as plainly as if she'd announced she was in love with him at the dinner table. *It's not like I'm your girlfriend.* And what was even worse was that she was completely in the wrong attempting to sow seeds of doubt. She was not the type of person to try to break people up. She was not "the other woman." It was not her style. If a man wasn't free to love her, she had absolutely no interest in him.

So what had happened? How had she gone so wrong?

Victor's eyes were fixed on hers. He hadn't answered, but now he looked toward Margaux and the crowd that was gathering behind her. "Hey guys, could you give us a minute? Margaux, I'll be right there to take you home. I imagine the baby needs you."

Margaux folded her arms and planted her feet. So Victor took April's arm and pulled her into the first room he saw. It was the toilet, and they had only enough room to stand face-to-face. He fumbled for the light, and when it went on, April wouldn't look at him. He grabbed her by the arms.

"April, I need to say this fast so no one gets the wrong idea about us being in here together."

They were standing in a tiny cubicle, nose to nose, and his words brought on an insane desire to laugh. She needed to get a hold of her emotions. *He's not available.*

"I think one of the biggest regrets of my life," Victor said, "will end up being that I wasn't free to follow my feelings in this instance. But I'm not. I'm a father, and that comes first."

I am a great fool, April thought, and any wisp of humor over the situation fled. To complete her shame, her eyes filled with tears.

"If I could've followed my feelings..." He stopped short, looking at her eyes, her lips...They heard only the sound of their breathing.

Then Victor dropped his arms, turned in the tight space, and opened the bathroom door. "Margaux and I need to get going. Penelope, do you think one of you could see April home safely?"

"Sure," Penelope said. She handed the pack of cards to Auriane and slid past Victor to where April was. "You guys go ahead and play."

Chapter Twenty

"I'm so stupid," April said, tears streaming down her face as she walked toward the métro, Guillaume on one side of her and Penelope on the other. "I know he's not available, and it's not *me* to let my feelings go for someone I can't have. And I basically announced in front of a crowd of strangers *and his fiancée* that I was in love with him. I'm so stupid," she repeated.

"You're not stupid, and we're not strangers," Penelope said. "So stop that right now. Here. Let's not take this métro. Let's walk to the next one. It'll be a direct line and will give us a chance to talk." Guillaume silently obeyed Penelope, guiding April around the railing to continue on the sidewalk.

"Honestly, though," Penelope said, "It was pretty obvious you loved him even before you said anything. How could you not have feelings for him when he saved you?"

"Yes, but he's going to marry Margaux, and it's the most ridiculous thing in the world that I'd make a big scene about someone who's unavailable. And in front of his fiancée." A fresh wave of tears came over her.

"I'm not all that sure he's going to marry Margaux," Penelope said. "I know she doesn't love him, and she won't be good for him, trust me."

"You didn't hear him," April said. "He *is* going to marry her because of the baby."

"Sometimes everyone thinks two people are going to get together," Guillaume said, breaking his silence, "except that *you* know that someone is meant for you. And sometimes it turns out everyone else is wrong." April turned to look at him, and she caught Penelope's gaze. "Hypothetically speaking," he said.

The only sound for a few minutes was their feet on the pavement before Penelope spoke up again. "Like I said, I don't think he's going to marry Margaux. I just need to come up with a plan. In the meantime, I wanted to talk to you about something. Arthur told me that Mr. Chambourd is going to announce which paintings will be shown at the gallery just after class on Thursday. He can get us in to hear the announcement if you want to come with me. I'm sure Françoise will be there, but if you want to find out before the rest of our class, why not come with me?"

"All right." April fell behind them as the sidewalk narrowed, her eyes trained on the curb that lined the dark road. "May as well."

⁊❧

THE GALLERY in the *École des Beaux-Arts* was located on the first floor at the back of the building, a beautiful atelier that overlooked a cobblestone courtyard with an old mulberry tree right in the center. April followed Arthur and Penelope into the room where a crowd of mostly young people was already assembled, with Mr. Chambourd in conference at the front with Françoise and two other people.

April took in the room with interest and walked over to read the plaques on each of the statues. *Vénus au Collier.* The horse's head from the Parthenon, a caryatid statue, and more recent examples of art in its various stages from sketch to completion were displayed around the room. Her attention returned to the students, who looked as nervous as she felt.

"*Chers élèves, chers confrères, bonjour.*" And with a smile, Mr. Chambourd added, "And everyone else. I know you're excited to hear which paintings have been chosen for the art gallery. Let me introduce you to Monsieur Axel *et* Madame Provost, who assisted me in making the selection. As my collaborators in the showing, they have a special interest. They also have the knowledge of what will sell.

"I've assembled a team of six," Mr. Chambourd continued, indicating for them to come forward, "who will help me unveil the chosen paintings so you can see what they'll look like placed in a particular order. You will appreciate the harmonious effect when they're assembled together. *S'il vous plaît.*" He swept his hand up with a flourish.

At his cue, the men went into the corridor and rolled racks of paintings into the room, then turned the racks so they were facing the students. All of them were covered with black cloths. April counted the rolling easels as they were brought in, and there were eighteen of them.

"Without making you suffer too much from suspense, let me just say that the selection was difficult. There was a particular painting I'd meant to give the prime spot in the gallery, but in the end it was not presented for selection. Still. What we have here will bring my collaborators and me an interesting sum and will launch some of you as upcoming artists. Without further ado, please unveil the chosen paintings."

The first one that caught April's eye was the Pompidou center, with its celebrated pipes covered with foliage or water or sky. An element for each one. *Ben's painting was chosen. He was right. He got in.* Heart pounding in her chest, April quickly scanned the rest of the paintings, but she did not see her *Passage de l'Ancre.* Stunned that her hopes were dashed, she was not able to appreciate the harmony of Mr. Chambourd's exhibit.

Was that it then? No other paintings had been chosen? She looked around the rest of the room and on the sidelines to see if she'd missed something. Her gaze settled at last on Penelope, whose face had fallen. Then it hit April. *Her* painting had not been chosen either. Only Ben's was recognizable from their class.

"*Félicitations*, Arthur." Penelope kissed him on both cheeks. Apparently his painting had been included. April tried to put on a brave face, but she had to swallow and blink back tears. She hadn't realized how much hope she'd tied up in her painting getting accepted. It was the only way she knew of to earn some income so she could at least stay the rest of the semester.

She would have to go home. There was no other way around it. She'd completely run out of money with no promise of getting any more. April didn't want to stay and watch Victor marry his fiancée. She didn't want to be a target for Lucas, who'd apparently not stopped stalking her. Everything she had was lost.

"I'm going to go," she murmured to Penelope, who looked concerned, but who had her own disappointment to handle. She just gave a small wave in return.

April made it as far as the door when Françoise called out to her, stalling her from going any further. "I heard Mr. Chambourd's student was bringing some people from our class, but I didn't know it would be you."

"Penelope is friends with Arthur," April answered, just wanting to leave.

"April." Françoise put her hand on April's arm. "I just wanted to tell you that Mr. Chambourd would've included your other painting. He told me so. In fact, yours was the one he wanted to feature in the prime spot on the gallery's far end wall. He was disappointed when he learned that it had been stolen." April kept her gaze trained on the ground. "It's a small comfort, I know. But it shows you just how much talent you have."

"What was wrong with my *Passage de L'Ancre*?" April asked.

"Nothing. Nothing wrong. It just…didn't catch his eye in the same way. He said your other one had all the hope of a visitor discovering Paris, all the youth we long to hold on to. The painting provoked such strong emotions, and the message was that Paris brought them forth."

"Did you ever hear back from the police?"

"I did. They checked, and there was nothing on the camera. Either he knew it was there, or it was just pure luck that he went the other way."

"A week ago, I would've said it was dumb luck, but given the fact that he's managed to elude the police so far, I would say that Lucas has more connections in the underworld than I would've thought. How is it possible that they haven't found him yet?"

"Well," said Françoise. "Maybe the police aren't trying very hard, which, honestly, is a possibility. For one thing they have a whole series of protocol to follow if they want to bring someone in, and the crime usually has to be rather serious. For the moment, it's a big deal in your life, but not necessarily a huge misdemeanor in the eyes of the law. Not enough to put a lot of resources on the task. And for another thing, he does seem to be more resourceful than he first appeared."

"I need to leave," April said. "I think it's time I went home. At the very least, I'm sure I can get a job at the ice cream parlor where I used to work after I graduated. Just something to start off until I can get on my feet."

Françoise nodded. "I understand if you want to do that. But you've got a month left of school and you're very good. I'd be disappointed to lose you before it's time." She looked April in the eye. "Just take some time to think about it before you rush into anything. Do you have money to live on? Could you survive another month in Paris?"

April thought about it. She did, actually. Since Penelope was able to get her deposit back, she did have money. And she could survive until it was time to go. "I'll give it some more thought," she answered.

MISHOU WAS HOME when April arrived. "*Alors?*" Mishou asked. "I haven't seen you since you went to the dinner. Was your *tarte* a success? When she spoke slowly April was able to understand everything, but she had more trouble answering. The effort served to draw her attention away from her worries and disappointment.

"Everyone liked it," she said. "Thank you for teaching me."

"Oh." Mishou wore a pleased smile as she shrugged. "*C'est normal.* Now, we just have to think about what else I can teach you."

"I'd like that," April said. "I was thinking—"

She was interrupted by the doorbell. Mishou raised her eyebrows. "I'm not expecting anyone, are you?" April shook her head. When Mishou opened the door to reveal Victor, April felt like her heart was going to leap out of her chest.

"April," he said, then stopped, as if he suddenly remembered. "Bonjour, Mishou." He kissed his grandmother.

"Never did I think to have so many visits, Victor," his grandmother said with a mischievous smile. "I have something to do in my room, so I'll leave the two of you."

When Mishou left, carrying a cloud of some outdated fragrance with her, Victor and April eyed each other warily. Victor was the first to speak. "Penelope told me that your painting didn't get accepted."

It wasn't what April thought he was going to say, and the reminder did not go down easily a second time. "She called you already?"

"No, actually I called her. I wanted to make sure you got home all right last night."

"I'm fine," April said. "No need to worry."

"I do, though," Victor said. "I care about you a lot, April. If things were different..."

"Now that is about the least helpful thing you can admit," April said. "Things are not different and they won't be, and it doesn't do any good to dwell on the fact. Look. I'm sorry for putting you on the spot. I can't believe I even brought it up at all, because I have no interest in trying to put a wedge between couples. It won't happen again. We can move forward."

"If it weren't for Matthias," Victor said, "I would want something more."

April put her hands on her hips, her anger rising again. But she stopped, exhaled, and strove for a gentle tone. "See. This is not good for you either. You need to be all in, Victor. If you're going to marry Margaux, you need to stop speaking about it as if you have regrets already. We need to focus on friendship, and you on getting ready for a future with Margaux."

Victor didn't answer right away. Then, "You're not leaving, are you? Not yet?"

"No. I was going to, but I think I'm going to stay till the end of the semester. I'll have just enough for that with my deposit."

"Good," Victor said. He stood there, and just as she was about to ask if he wanted to sit, he said, "The police have a lead on Lucas."

"Do they?" The news made April's heart rate pick up. "Did they find him? Where is he?" If only she could get closure in this area.

"They didn't find him, but that's why I came today. I wanted to tell you they had a lead. Apparently they interviewed one of his friends, and he told them about someone Lucas hung out with, and when they went to his apartment, they found an attic hothouse for marijuana. His friend is probably spotting him some cash, and that would explain how he's managing to get around without using his credit card."

"But he wasn't there," April said.

"No. However, I think it's going to start getting hot for him. He's not going to be able to go back there, so I don't know where he will stay or how he'll get more cash. The police already apprehended his friend, and I'm guessing there's someone stationed there in case he's stupid enough to return."

"But if you know about it, then he probably does too."

"Maybe not. I went to the police station to find out if there was any news, and that's what I learned. The policeman told me to make sure you're careful. It seems Lucas has nothing to lose now. I wanted to see if I could walk you home from school on the days you have class."

April pressed her lips together, torn. She was touched by his attention, and truly scared by the idea of being stalked by Lucas. But to spend more time with Victor meant losing her heart to him even more. She just knew it. It was the stupidest idea. She would have to say no.

"Okay," she said. "I'd appreciate that."

Chapter Twenty-One

Victor sat on the bed in the guest room. The slashed paintings were lined up against the wall and the door. Though he was no judge of art, he could guess at their value before they'd been destroyed. He could see the beauty and skill that went into creating them. More than anything, though, he remembered April's tears at losing them.

April was...remarkable. Not one of her losses destroyed her. Not Lucas's attack on her person, not the destruction of her father's paintings, not the theft of her own painting, not the imminent threat that Lucas would attack again. Victor had already decided to install an alarm at his grandmother's place to protect them both.

April cried, but she got up again, and he was hard-pressed to think of anyone who would do as well as her under similar circumstances, himself included. He certainly couldn't imagine Margaux rising above the challenges, she who depended on her father for everything.

Victor stood and went over to the largest painting—April, as a toddler in the wildflowers—and tipped it to examine the back. The art restorer, whose shop was located under the Arches at the

Bastille, had promised the painting could be restored. It wouldn't sell for any value, but it would be good enough for April to hang in her home. And with the extra price Victor was willing to pay, the art restorer would put everything else on hold and focus just on this project. He could have all six paintings fixed in three weeks.

Victor wrapped them back up in linen and carried them to the front door to await the messenger, who was sent to collect them. It was a skilled carrier, who'd know just how they should be transported. Victor had planned the pickup before he was to meet Margaux in a couple of hours, then April later that night. He supposed he shouldn't overly tempt himself by spending so much time with April, but he couldn't leave her alone knowing there might be a threat. She'd been invited to Guillaume's again, but this time without the crowd. Only Penelope would be there, and she'd extended the invitation to Victor, asking him to escort April since they weren't able to pick her up.

The doorbell rang, and Victor buzzed the messenger in, placing the paintings in such a way that they'd be easy to collect. The exchange was done quickly with a rack to carry the paintings, an efficient carrier used to handling priceless things, and a quick signature to accept the change of hands. Victor had already had them insured, though they were effectively worthless to anyone but April.

MARGAUX WAS at the corner café, waiting for Victor. As she rocked the stroller back and forth, smiling as he came in, it dawned on him how little he'd seen her content since she returned to Paris. The smile softened her. It changed her expression into something akin to warmth, and he remembered how crazy he'd been about her before.

When he went to kiss Margaux on the cheek, she turned so that their mouths grazed, and he pulled back in surprise.

"I just thought we should..." Margaux started. "Well...it's been a while."

"Yes. True." Victor sat, not knowing what to add. The kiss had been familiar, but not, if he were being honest with himself, completely welcome. In fact, it was a shock to realize he'd not thought of her at all that way, though they were getting married. He'd been so focused on the baby and the change the status would bring in his own life. Stable. Serious. He'd have a sense of belonging. *I won't end up like my father*. He'd not thought about Margaux's role in it all.

"How's Matthias today?" Victor reached over and pulled the blanket aside so he could see his son's face.

"No, don't do that. He likes the blanket on his face when he sleeps. It comforts him." Victor picked up the menu, and Margaux added, "He's doing well, though. He's starting to drool so he might be getting teeth soon."

Victor tried to picture Matthias with teeth, but he couldn't imagine it. He really liked his son's toothless grin. As if on cue, Matthias began to stir and raise his hands to stretch. They only went as far as the top of his head, and Victor thought how cute that was too. His son was perfect.

The reflection suddenly made him frown. He opened his mouth to speak when the waiter came over.

"*Vous avez choisi?*"

Margaux ordered a *salade niçoise* and a carafe of water, and Victor closed the menu and handed it to the waiter.

"*Un steak-frites.*"

They were alone again. "Margaux," he said. "We need to talk seriously. Who is Franck Duboise? You were clearly affected when Penelope mentioned his name. If we're really going to get married, we need to have all the cards on the table."

Margaux sighed. "I knew you were going to ask me about him. It's so stupid though. They just caught me off-guard, which is why I reacted that way. Franck is nobody, except that I was in love with him in high school, and just about everyone knew it. It was embarrassing."

"Did you see him here in Paris before you ran off to Monaco?" Victor asked. "Were you really there to see your cousin?"

Margaux sat up straighter. "I'd planned on visiting my cousin for months. Ever since Christmas I'd planned to go, and you knew about that. We talked about it."

"Yes, but you were going to come back. You were only supposed to go for two weeks. Then, suddenly you're breaking things off with me, and you disappear for a whole year. And then you come back, expecting to pick up where we left off. What's going on?"

"You were ready to marry me at any price," Margaux said, her lips thinning out. "You practically said so. You wanted to marry into my family as much as you wanted to marry me. So why now does it suddenly matter how long I stayed in Monaco and why I didn't tell you about anything that was going on, including Matthias?"

The idea of marrying into Margaux's family *had* appealed to him as much as the idea of marrying Margaux. *Was I that transparent?* Victor realized with a shock. "Yes, but...I wasn't willing to marry you if you were cheating on me, or if you didn't love me back. You misunderstood me."

"I wasn't cheating on you," Margaux said. "I just needed to get away. I needed to get away from everyone's expectations of me. Monaco was the perfect place to do that. A year without any major worries except what beach we were going to go to and what parties at night. Yes, things got weird when I found out I was pregnant, and I wasn't able to do as much. But I had a good doctor there, and I got the break I needed. Now I'm ready to settle down." She looked him in the eye, her hand reaching out to rock Matthias's stroller. "I'm ready to settle down with *you*."

"Is the baby mine?" Victor hadn't intended to ask it, but the question had been brewing and festering even before April brought it up. He wanted to give Margaux the benefit of the doubt because, for all that she was reserved—giving up her innermost thoughts like an oyster would give up its pearl—she'd never been a liar.

Margaux looked out the window. "I can't believe you have to ask me that question," she said, sounding resigned. "It's that girl, April, who put it in your head. Maybe I should be asking *you*. Do you have feelings for her?"

Victor couldn't answer that, at least not in any honest way. "We need to be honest with each other if we're going to build a marriage on something solid. So please answer me truthfully. Is the baby mine, and do you love me enough to marry me? Do you love me enough to stay married? Because as much as I want to provide a healthy family if the baby is mine, I'm not interested in getting married only to get divorced five years later."

"Stop asking about the baby. He's yours," Margaux snapped. Neither of them had noticed the waiter return with the carafe of water hooked between his fingers and two plates balanced in his hands. Margaux turned as red as Victor felt.

"*Une salade niçoise et un steak-frites*," the waiter announced as if he'd heard nothing out of the ordinary. "I'll be back with the bread."

After he left, each was silent. Victor picked up his fork and knife and began to cut the steak. Finally, he said, "It was a fair question."

Margaux didn't answer right away but just speared the lettuce and began chewing. "There comes a point when you have to trust me. I think we need to stop having these conversations—stop fighting all the time about the same things—and just start planning the wedding and assume everything is going to be okay."

Victor wasn't sure if that logic equated to burying one's head in the sand, but he nodded. The idea of a paternity test was repugnant to him. He disliked what it said about his relationship with Margaux, and the baby would only end up being caught in the crossfire. Matthias deserved more than that. The baby began to fuss, and Victor reached over to take him out of the stroller. "*Salut toi*," he said, tickling his toes. Margaux smiled at them, and he met her gaze and held it. Matthias giggled and kicked his feet, causing Victor to look down again. Yes. They needed to make this work. This baby would make it worth it.

❧

MISHOU'S APARTMENT was lit up, though it was not yet dark. Even the guest room had a light on, and from the street, the place looked lived in. Victor punched in the code and went up the stairs. His heart started to lift the closer he got to seeing April, but that only confused him more. It was time he let go of this particular desire. He needed to be serious now and start looking forward and building his family. These were lofty thoughts, but they didn't bring Victor any comfort when he thought about relegating April to a role of friend and nothing more. For once, however, he needed to do the right thing.

"*Bonsoir*, Victor." Mishou opened the door wide. "Perhaps the best thing I did was to invite April to stay, since I see you all the time now."

"*Coucou*." Victor stooped to kiss his grandmother, his determination wavering. He had to tell her. "I had lunch with Margaux today, and I will be marrying her. I just thought you should know that. So you don't get any false hopes about April."

Mishou fixed her eyes on him for a long moment, then turned to lead the way into the living room. "I like April, you know."

"How could anyone not like her?" Victor asked.

"No. What I mean is—April is the girl for you." Mishou changed course and went into the kitchen. She pulled the step stool over to the cupboard, but Victor stayed her with a hand.

"What do you need? I'll get it."

"The pistachio nuts," she said. "It's a noble sentiment to want to marry that woman because you have a baby together. I'm proud of you for thinking that way. There are too few young men willing to step up and take responsibility, and that is precisely what you are doing." She took the nuts from his hands, set them on the counter and patted his cheeks.

"But she is the wrong woman for you. Margaux never did fill that void you had when you started dating her. And—*mon chéri*— you haven't noticed this, but that void has been long filled. You filled it. You forged your own path. You realized your own worth. You don't need Margaux anymore."

"But the baby needs *me*," Victor said, his eyes on his grandmother, who was bustling about taking bowls, cocktail napkins and glasses to set on a tray.

"I agree. The baby needs you. So be there for him. But marriage is irrevocable. Even if you end things, which I fear you will, or stay and end up a shell of your former self, a part of you will be destroyed. That baby was made without your knowledge and without your participation."

"Well, not completely," Victor said with a laugh.

"Naughty boy. You know what I mean. She certainly didn't come to you for help until she'd decided it was time to provide a traditional upbringing for the baby. Where was your input all along? She has called all the shots. It's wrong. It's *wrong*." Mishou dumped the pistachio nuts into the bowl and set the bag on the counter with force.

"Mishou." Victor took his grandmother's hands in his own. He hadn't seen her this upset since he ran away from her at the park when he was five. "So you're telling me I should dump Margaux, despite our history and our baby together, and...do what precisely?"

"Marry April," Mishou said, looking up at him.

Her words pierced him with longing. *Marry April*. If only that were a possibility. It wasn't. It just wasn't. He wouldn't think about it.

Victor couldn't stop the next word from spilling out of his mouth. "Why?"

"I've heard you talk about your girls over the years. I've met one or two. I spent enough time with Margaux to last a lifetime. Before April, I'd never seen anyone who makes you better, who loves you for who you are, and who brings out the very best in you. Certainly not Margaux."

"Do you think April loves me?" Victor knew he shouldn't ask. He couldn't help himself.

"She only understands half of what I say in French. And I only understand half of what she says in English. But I do understand the word *Victor,* and she must've uttered that word a half-dozen times when I was giving her a cooking lesson, and at every conversation we've had since." Mishou opened the refrigerator. "A beer?"

Victor looked around, suddenly realizing what he was doing here. And where was April? He and Mishou had been having this personal conversation about April, and he didn't even know if she could hear what they were saying. "Is April here?"

"She said she was going to step out to go to the grocery store. Apparently you two are going to dinner together, and she said she needed to bring something. She was going to get flowers."

"Yes, but—" Victor stood, frozen. "When did she leave?"

"She left an hour before you arrived. In fact, she should be back by now, but I'm glad we had this time to talk. I've been wanting to say these things to you, but every time you're here, so is she, and I can't very well tell you she loves you with her standing right there." Mishou shrugged. "Then again, I suppose I could have. The two of you remind me of me and Papi. Except we were a lot smarter than you children. We knew right away that what we had was special. You two are going to miss out if you don't open your eyes."

Victor's mind was whirling. "Do you know which way she went?"

"Well, I told her the *floriste* two streets over would be open until eight since she would probably miss out on the grocery store. I suppose she went there. April should be back any minute though. She told me she wanted to have time to change before you came to get her."

Victor started for the door. "Mishou, I have to go. I'm guessing she didn't tell you, but she might be in danger. We think Lucas—the one who hurt her—is following her. She wasn't supposed to leave the apartment until I came to get her." He yanked the door open. "I'll be back."

Victor took the steps two at a time, and only his grip on the railing kept him from falling down the stairs. April was in trouble. He could feel it in his bones.

Chapter Twenty-Two

It was supposed to be a quick outing. She and Victor couldn't show up empty-handed at Penelope's house, and the florist might close by the time Victor arrived. In any case, they were in *Châtelet-les-Halles*, which was teeming with people. Nothing could happen.

April stepped outside the apartment and walked across the intersection of cobblestone roads toward the main street. A smell of grease assaulted her from one of the gyro shops on the way, and it mingled with the scent of cigarettes, and some other unidentifiable smoke from a group of teens who appeared to have nothing better to do. She left the cobblestones and crossed at the light to reach Marcel Floriste.

A tinkling bell heralded her arrival, and she was enveloped in the warm humidity of plant life as soon as the door closed behind her. Calla lilies were perched in long buckets of water to her right, and the roses, hydrangeas, daffodils, and narcissuses flanked her on all sides. The florist was wrapping a large, mixed bouquet with deft fingers—first the green tissue paper, then the clear plastic to create a well for the water on the bottom. A ribbon to tie it, another to loop and seal in place with a sticker, and the bouquet was ready. He turned his attention to her.

"*Bonsoir, mademoiselle*. How may I help you?"

"*Bonsoir, monsieur*." She struggled to remember how to say potted plant in French. "*Fleurs dans un pot, s'il vous plaît*."

A potted plant was better, she'd decided. It would last longer. She pointed to the pastel blue hydrangeas, which were such a cheerful blossom, and Guillaume had just the spot to put them. There was empty floor space to the right of his window, and he could replant them in a bigger pot if necessary.

"*Les hortensia*," the florist said, as he set the hydrangea on the counter with a flourish. So that was how to say them in French. Then she made out something along the lines of "just the thing" as she watched him wrap them in the same tissue and plastic and put them in a shiny black paper bag with the logo. It would be a beautiful gift to offer Guillaume—and Penelope, eventually, if her hunch about them ending up together proved correct. At forty euros, it didn't come cheap, but Guillaume always opened his home to everyone, and he'd been so welcoming to her in particular. She thanked God for the day she and Penelope became friends and suspected it would be for life.

April left the florist with her purchase and decided to cut through a park that would lead back to the cobblestone streets of Châtelet-les-Halles. The weather was balmy, and the fenced-in pockets of flowers that seemed to be in profusion all over Paris sent wafts of fragrance into the dirt path. She had not yet walked halfway through the garden when she began to feel ill at ease. It was more deserted than she'd thought it would be, and she began to remember Victor's warning, and Penelope's request that she not go anywhere unless accompanied by other people. April paused, wondering if she should turn back and go through the main street, or whether it would be faster and safer to continue through to the other side.

Three youths angled toward her, eyeing her in a way that made her nervous. All three wore hooded sweatshirts, and they were smoking and laughing. One was drinking a beer. The group fell silent as they drew near and she tensed, wondering if she screamed whether anyone would hear. It had been a stupid split-second decision to enter the park when she knew she was at risk of Lucas following her. It never occurred to her that she might meet danger from someone else on the street.

"*Oye, la miss*! You shouldn't be here alone, you know. It's not a good place to be."

"Ah. Okay, *merci*," she answered with a trembling smile. *If I treat them with respect, they won't know I'm afraid of them.*

"*T'es Américaine*," the same one said in surprise.

"*Allô*," another one said.

They began laughing and elbowing each other, and the third one swaggered toward her. "Do you 'ave New York?"

They didn't make sense at all, but she smiled more naturally now, nearly certain these three meant no harm. "I'm from Seattle," she said in English just to give them something to puzzle over. They laughed again and shifted into some street slang she had no hope of deciphering. April relaxed as they lost interest and continued on their path. The other end of the park was only a few meters away.

A movement from the hedges on the right, which hid a parallel path, caught her eye and she jumped, suddenly alert. Her eyes scanned the opening to the street, but there was no one there. She looked again at the hedges as her worst fear materialized. Lucas.

"They were right, those scum," Lucas said, advancing upon her. To her mounting terror, she saw a knife in his hand. April calculated the distance to the street, but she wouldn't have time to run there without him doing her some serious damage first. "You shouldn't be here alone."

"Lucas. They will find you," April said, and finding her voice steady, risked more words. "Don't add to the list of things they'll take you in for."

"I haven't decided yet what I'm going to do," he said, and sucked air in through his nostrils. "All I know is that you've ruined my life, and you're going to pay for it."

She didn't try to reason with him. This creep was beyond reason. But anger grew inside of her. *She* ruined *his* life? What about her father's paintings? What about her own stolen painting? What about walking around in fear for the last couple of weeks?

"What did you do with my painting?" she asked.

"Your father's paintings, you mean?" Lucas gave an ugly laugh. "Not worth much now, are they? You should've let me sell them. Then you would've still gotten a good price for them, and I would've left them alone."

"Yes, my father's paintings. But what about mine? You went into my art school and stole it. Where is it?"

"Your painting? What painting? That thing you were working on in the courtyard? That one's not worth the trouble."

April didn't have time to think about what his words might mean. Whether Lucas was lying or not. She had distracted him with her questions, but now she craned behind him to see if the three teenagers were still there—or if anyone was there—and he whirled to look. When he saw nothing but the empty passageway, he turned back.

She saw when he was about to act. The look in his eyes changed. In three strides he was upon her, and she swung her arm back to gain momentum. Just as he lunged forward to grab her with his free hand, she struck out at him with the flowerpot to block his movement. It was an ineffective swing, and the pot only banged his head, but didn't stop him. Furious, Lucas closed the distance and grabbed her, raising the knife.

"Help!" she shrieked.

The sound of shouts came from the entrance ahead. She couldn't see who it was, but Lucas dropped her arm and turned to face them. Whoever it was posed enough of a threat to him to let her go.

The same three teenagers materialized at the park entrance. They'd simply done a full circle and had come back into the park a second time. This time their laughter held some menace, but it was not for her.

"Picking on girls, are you?" the leader said.

Lucas shifted the knife from hand to hand, looking nervous now. "I don't have a problem with you."

"Yes, but we like this American."

"And it's been a while since we've had a good fight." The one who said this took the last swig of his beer, then shattered the bottom of the bottle on the cement gatepost. April gasped at the noise.

The largest of the teenagers shifted to the right where Lucas held the knife, and the one with the broken beer bottle came on his left. Lucas made a desperate lunge with his right hand, but the teenager on his right grabbed his arm with ease and held the knife captive. The leader of the group punched Lucas in the stomach with a sickening thud and when Lucas doubled over, he gave him an uppercut. Lucas dropped the knife.

The teenager picked up the knife and deposited it in his pocket, then looked at April and jerked his head toward the exit. "*Vas-y.*"

April didn't waste any time in obeying. She hurried to the exit, trembling, and rushed into the street. In a half jog, she hurried down the sidewalk toward her apartment, choking back sobs. Rushing forward, April came up against something solid, and two arms wrapped around her, cutting off her vision. She screamed.

"April."

Blinded by tears and terrified, she nearly screamed again when the familiar scent of Victor pervaded her senses. She looked up, panting. "Victor. How did you find me?"

Victor didn't answer right away, he just pulled her into another hug. "You're safe," he whispered into her hair. "I was so worried. Mishou said you went out to get flowers, but by the time I got to the store, it was closed. I didn't know where you were. I was afraid Lucas had gotten to you."

"He did." Her voice was muffled from leaning into Victor's shirt. She didn't want him to let go.

"What did you say?"

She pulled back this time and said, "He did reach me. He found me. He came at me with a knife in the garden there." April pointed to the entrance to the park. "But there were some teenagers who helped me. I think they're still with him." She hesitated. "They were beating him pretty badly."

"Good," Victor said, fiercely, between clenched teeth. He was shaking, she noticed, and she thought it might be from anger. He stared at her, his thumbs on her cheeks and his fingers in her hair, and she thought...she thought he was going to kiss her. For a crazy instant, her mind fled the situation and she mused that it would be her first kiss, if you didn't count Michael Grant's fumbling attempt in the ninth grade. Forgetting about whether Victor was free or whether it would be the *right* thing to do, April waited.

Victor pulled her back into a hug and let go just as quickly. "I need to call the police. I should also check on what those boys are doing to Lucas. As much as I could kill him myself for everything he did to you, I don't want them to get caught for murder. And I suppose I don't really want anyone to die."

April gave a trembling smile at that. "No." Her belly was hollow, her heart an echoing chamber. She accompanied Victor to the entrance of the park, but they couldn't see the fight from there. There weren't any sounds either.

"Stay here at the entrance where I can see you. I'm going in further to look." Victor didn't wait for an answer but turned and walked toward the place where she'd been accosted.

She took a couple more steps into the park so she could see him and waited for his report. In any case, it was clear the boys weren't coming back. After a minute, Victor called out. "He's here, and he's unconscious. I'm going to call the police, and I want you to stay right there. I want to be able to see you, but I don't want you to get too close." Victor pulled his phone out of his pocket, waited while it rang then spoke, explaining the situation and giving directions to where he was.

April leaned against the short fence, her back on the round bronze knob of the gate. To her left, she saw a green, painted park bench and she walked over and sank down into it, waiting for Victor to finish up the conversation. From here, she could see Lucas's form on the ground. There was blood, and she shuddered. That could have been hers.

"That's good," Victor said, when he saw where she was sitting. "Stay there and rest. I'm not leaving him. And this time I have my shoes on, so he's not getting away." He looked down again, adding, "Not that he could. He's going to need the hospital."

BY THE TIME the police arrived, Lucas was still unconscious. April got a glimpse of his purple, swollen face that had a jagged cut down the side. He was still breathing, however, and when the police asked her for a description of the teenagers who saved her, she couldn't remember too many details. "They had hoods," she said. "One was tall and one was short and stocky. The other didn't leave much of an impression." The truth was, she didn't want to try too hard to identify them. The lieutenant seemed to sense that, studying her as she answered, and didn't push her for more.

She still had to go in to the police station and give a statement. By the time they were done, it was too late to go to Guillaume's apartment, and April thought to check her telephone. There were four messages.

"Penelope, it's me," April said when her friend picked up. "Everything is okay. Lucas found me, but it's all over. He's in custody. I'll tell you all about it next time we see each other. No, no. I'm too tired to tell you everything now. Victor is with me." She handed the phone to him. "She wants to talk to you."

"*Oui, allô.*" Victor listened. "She's exhausted. She'd gone out on her own to get some flowers—"

April clapped her hand to her head. "The flowers!"

"—and he followed her. Some teenagers beat him up and I found April as she was coming out of the park where it happened. We can fill you in on the rest when we see you." He listened some more, his eyes on April, and he finished with, "*Ça marche,*" before hanging up. "She wants us to come tomorrow. She also wanted to know if the police found your painting where Lucas was staying."

April shook her head. "He said he didn't have it. Of course, we can't believe anything he says. But the police didn't see it when they went to the friend's house where he was staying, did they?" Victor shook his head.

"I don't know. I sort of believe him," April said. "He seemed surprised when I asked him about it. He said it wasn't good enough for him to go after it."

"You don't believe *that*, do you?" Victor looked sideways at her. They'd begun walking toward the apartment, but slowly. April felt too shaky to take big steps.

"No. Mr. Chambourd thought it was good, and he knows more about art than Lucas does." April gave a weak grin. "But honestly. If he doesn't have it, where the heck could it be?"

Victor put an arm around her waist. "I don't know, but I'll help you find it, no matter what it takes."

"Well," she said, accepting his arm, even leaning into him, though she knew it was wrong. "In the end, I'll go home in a month. If we find it, we find it. If we don't, we don't. Either way, all my dreams—everything my father wanted me to do—it's all come to nothing. And I'm going to need to figure out how to rebuild all that and get a new dream."

Victor held her for a little longer as they walked, then pulled his arm away. Perhaps he, too, felt it was wrong. Or perhaps he was steeling himself like she was. With him marrying Margaux, she didn't see how their friendship could last.

Chapter Twenty-Three

The studio was empty except for Ben. April wove her way around the easels to where he was bent over his work. "Ben, you're here. I haven't seen you around lately. Congratulations on getting your artwork accepted." Her smile fell when he turned to her with a haggard look on his face. His gaze shifted back to his painting.

"What is it?"

When he didn't answer, April sat beside him and stared at his profile, willing him to turn. "All right, Ben. We know each other pretty well, so I think you can tell me what's going on. Whatever it is, I can handle it. Perhaps I can even help."

"It's nothing," he said. "How's your roommate situation going?" His voice sounded bitter.

April leaned back, puzzled. "Good. I'm grateful to be able to live there. Mishou is great. She's teaching me how to cook, and my French is definitely improving."

"You must see Victor all the time now," he said.

Suddenly his bad attitude became a little clearer, and April's voice grew wary. "Yes, a little more. Is that what this is about?

Come on, Ben. You knew there was never going to be anything between us."

He shrugged but remained silent. Perhaps he hadn't known. Or hadn't wanted to know. April tried a different tack. "I have good news. Lucas was taken into custody."

"Who?" Ben flicked a glance her way between heavy brows.

"Lucas. The guy who attacked me. Honestly. It's no wonder nothing was ever going to happen between us. You're only concerned about yourself." April shot up and turned to leave. Two students entered the room, and when they saw Ben, they whispered to each other. Of course he would be getting lots of attention now that his painting was selected. So what in the world did he have to be all grouchy about?

April had taken two steps when Ben spoke in a low voice. "I took your painting."

Did I just hear him correctly? Turning slowly, April's gaze settled on the crimson flush on his neck. "What?"

"I took your painting. I knew yours was going to get selected, and I wanted my own to have a chance. You didn't want anything more to do with me anyway. So I took the painting from the studio and hid it in my apartment. It's still there." Ben slumped forward, a combination of defiance and misery, waiting for her reaction.

What...a...jerk. These and other words whirled through her mind, but she didn't voice them. She opened and closed her mouth twice before knowing how to respond. Her words came out through gritted teeth. "Ben, give the painting back, please. As soon as you can."

April turned and left the studio, walking with long strides down the corridor to the street. When she exited, she squinted into the sun, attempting to push down her anger in the warmth of its rays. The brown buildings were dappled with the shadows of leaves, and the street was almost void of pedestrians. A few cars drove by quietly, leaving her to wrestle with her thoughts.

Ben had been her friend. Not a close friend, but a friend. And now it turned out he was nothing more than a selfish, jealous, immature *traitor*. She stomped along with heaving breaths, refusing to waste any tears on him. Victor was a friend too, and he actually listened to her. He actually cared about her paintings, and her safety, and how she felt. But he was a completely *unavailable* friend, and that was what hurt the most. In her heart of hearts, she knew that if he didn't have the baby with Margaux, Victor would want to be with her. They were so comfortable together. Comfortable, with that added element of spark.

Not all that comfortable, after all.

April's phone rang, making her heart leap. Perhaps it was *him*.

"I called to get the latest on Lucas." Penelope's voice rang out, and April pulled the phone away from her ear. "Served him right, the jerk, that he'd get beat up by a bunch of *racaille*. And you, *ma chérie*, are completely safe now. You can live freely without looking over your shoulder."

"Yeah." April had stopped walking, and leaned against one of the trees that were planted in a square cut out in the sidewalk. Her melancholy must have shown in her voice.

"What's wrong?"

April's throat worked as she tried to get the words out. "Victor is going to marry Margaux." Then the tears started, and she began walking again, hoping no one would see her, hoping she could pull out her next words without sobbing.

"*Ma chérie*." Penelope's voice was full of tenderness. "What brought this about? Did you just see him?"

"No. I just saw Ben."

She sensed Penelope's confusion by the long pause on the other end of the phone line. April didn't have it in her to explain, so Penelope was forced to ask. "What does Ben have to do with Victor?"

"Ben stole my painting. Or not stole, exactly, but borrowed it. Well, he took it so it wouldn't get entered into the competition."

Penelope gasped. "That is *infamous*. How did you find out?"

April's voice was as melancholy as she felt. "He confessed. He feels bad about it."

"Oh, I'm sure he does. How could he have done something like that?"

April went on as if Penelope hadn't asked a question. She couldn't have answered in any case. "And his painting made it in anyway. He didn't have to go to all that trouble."

"Yes, but it might not have. They were limited in number, so someone's painting would've been left out. It might very well have been his." Penelope reflected for a moment. "Although, his was quite good. What a stupid thing to do, really. What a stupid man."

April exhaled and moved forward again, her phone clamped to her ear. "He did say something about being jealous. I think he's jealous of Victor."

"Ugh." She heard Penelope's snort. "All the more reason you would never have ended up with Ben. He just retaliated instead of trying to win you over. No wonder Victor is the one who won your heart."

"Please don't. His heart is not free." The tears threatened to fall again.

"Victor loves you. I know he does," Penelope said. "It's just the baby thing, right? The only thing that's holding him back?"

"Yes, but truthfully, it holds me back too. I wouldn't want him to do it any other way. I wouldn't want him to be different than he is. I *like* that he wants to stick around and be there for his baby, and I get that he wants to give Matthias a happy, safe family."

"Hmm," Penelope said. "Bet you anything the baby isn't even his."

"Maybe. Unfortunately, there's no way to be sure without a paternity test, and it's not up to me to insist. I think Victor is avoiding it through some misguided sense of honor. Anyway, it's useless to dwell on it." April took a deep breath. Her anger had left her, and in its wake there was just fatigue and a sense of futility. "All right, let me get going. I need to go home and see how Mishou is doing. She seemed tired before I left this morning."

"I'll talk to Arthur to see what we can do about getting your painting included in Mr. Chambourd's gallery. Does Ben realize he's losing his chance to have his own painting shown by this confession? I mean, he could probably go to jail."

"Honestly, I'm super mad at Ben, but I don't want him to go to jail. He looks like he hasn't slept in a week, and in some way I feel like the guilt was punishment enough. I do, however, want my own painting to be included, so I'd be grateful if you could talk to Arthur. Or even Françoise."

"You're a better woman than I am," Penelope said, "but all right. I'll let you know today what he says. We need to work fast because the showing is in two weeks. I'll call you later today with news. Oh, and save Thursday night for dinner at Guillaume's. I've got a surprise, and if it's as good as I think it will be, you'll be happy. *Bisous, ma chérie.*"

April couldn't imagine that anything could possibly make her happy. "*Bisous,*" she said, and hung up.

MISHOU WAS SEATED at the table, fanning herself slowly when April entered the apartment. "April, I haven't seen you all day. Are you recovered from yesterday's fright?" Mishou had stayed up the night before until Victor brought April home, and Victor had had to help his grandmother into her bed after all the excitement. Today, Mishou's listless attitude concerned April.

She came and sat at Mishou's side. "Are you all right? It's very warm in here." April went to open the window, but Mishou waved her away. "*Ça va, ça va.* It's not usually this hot in June, and it will probably cool down again."

"May I bring you some lemonade? I bought some yesterday, and I've kept it in the refrigerator."

A SWEETHEART IN PARIS

"That sounds nice." Mishou began to wave her fan again as April rushed to get her a glass of cold, sweet lemonade. She'd have to talk to Victor about getting some type of cooling system in his grandmother's apartment, although she wasn't sure air-conditioning was common in France.

After a few sips of lemonade, Mishou seemed to perk up. "It's a relief that horrible Lucas was put away and will not cause you any more trouble. Have they looked for your painting?"

"No need. I know where it is." April gave a weak smile. "My friend, Ben, took it."

"Some friend." Mishou blew out through her lips, the French expression of dismissal. "So what will happen now?"

"I'll ask the professor to consider including it. Maybe there's still a chance. If it sells, I sure could use the money." April went back into the kitchen to pour herself some lemonade too. The buzzer rang, and April hurried to answer it, but Mishou was already up.

"I wonder who that could be." Now that Mishou had had a few sips of lemonade, there was a decided pep in her walk, and her eyes sparkled. April wondered if the leap in her own heart showed on her face.

"I'm always here. I know, I know." April heard the amusement in his voice—a voice she was coming to love. She stood behind Mishou at the door, then stopped short. Victor was pushing a stroller into the apartment.

"Oh, now who is this?" Mishou leaned over the side of the stroller, her face alight, and all trace of lethargy gone.

"Mishou, meet Matthias." Victor positively beamed as he presented his son to his grandmother.

Matthias was sucking on his fingers and when Mishou, April, and Victor all peered into the stroller, the baby broke out into a toothless grin. "Aren't you just *un petit chou*," Mishou crooned, reaching for the baby. She started to lift him out, but Victor had to unhook the straps first. He picked him up and handed him to his grandmother, apparently not concerned that she was too weak to hold him.

April suddenly felt like an outsider. How foolish she'd been to think the baby wasn't his, or that she had any sort of future with him. Matthias was even starting to resemble his father, she thought, and Victor was practically beaming.

"So Margaux let you take him?" April strove for a normal tone over the lump in her throat.

"She practically insisted. She said I needed to get used to being his father, and that I should spend some time with him." Victor leaned over his grandmother and grinned at Matthias, and his son responded with a giggle. "Margaux is in full wedding-planning mode, so I think it'll do her some good to have free time."

With Matthias propped on her shoulder, Mishou walked to the sofa. "You're still going to marry that woman, hmm?"

Victor's gaze dropped to his feet, and all trace of enthusiasm disappeared. "How can you ask me that when you're holding my baby?" He darted a glance at April, and she thought she saw regret there. Misery. Longing? "It's the right thing to do," he said in a firm voice.

"*Bah.*" Mishou gave another sign of dismissal, and a ray of humor pierced April's own misery. Mishou certainly had ideas about how things should be run, and who was worth her grandson's time. At least April had made the cut.

"April."

Pulled out of her thoughts, she looked up, startled. Victor came to stand in front of her, an intimate gesture she struggled not to read too much into. "I went to the police station to ask if they've made any headway in interrogating Lucas about your painting, but they said he has no idea where it is. I think—"

"I know where it is. Ben took it. He was jealous." The words came rushing out, and she hoped it was the last time she would have to explain. "Penelope is going to talk to Arthur to see if it's too late to include my painting in the exhibit, and she said she'd let me know as soon as she had word."

Victor shook his head. "What? I can't believe he had the gall to do that. *Quel idiot*. It's so...*selfish*." He blew out his breath, looking at that instant very much like his grandmother. "Well. Perhaps we'll have something to toast to on Thursday night." Upon seeing April's look of confusion, he clarified. "At Guillaume's. I assume you're going?"

"Penelope told me about it. I'm glad they're including you in all the invitations, too. Now we're *all* friends, which is the best." April gave a small smile. "I assume Margaux is coming."

Victor's expression fell a little. "Yes." He looked at Mishou, but she was fully occupied with Matthias. He leaned toward April and whispered, "I'm more sorry than you will ever know that...we could never take our friendship to a deeper level. We've only known each other for a short time, but you are the best friend I've ever had—" He seemed to swallow nervously, and she suspected he was unaccustomed to revealing so much of his feelings. "—and you're my favorite person to spend time with."

Victor leaned down to kiss her on her cheek, but because she turned her face in surprise, it landed on her mouth. Their lips met in a gentle touch that lasted only a split second, but jolted straight to her heart. "I'm sorry," he said, when she gasped in surprise.

He stepped away, and she saw he was now red in the face, as he shoved his hands in his pocket.

"I'm sorry too," she said, softly.

Chapter Twenty-Four

Victor headed down the familiar street on his way to Margaux's apartment. He had walked this way so many times while they were dating, and his steps had always lightened the closer he got. Now, his gloom seemed to deepen. That kiss. He had kissed April, and he wanted more. His heart felt raw and filled with longing. How could he even think about getting married to someone else when he was feeling this way about April?

He'd been a fool to think it would be enough to marry into a stable family and provide the same for his son—that it could fill the hole that had been in him for as long as he could remember. No, it wasn't enough. The family would be stable, all right, with a father, a mother, and a son; but he wasn't sure there was any love. With blinding clarity, he saw that he had matured enough to take the next step in his life. He was ready for marriage. He had just offered it to the wrong person.

Even if Matthias was now in his life, he needed to make a decision that would be the best for all of them before it was too late. It was time to put an end to the madness and tell Margaux he could never marry her. He would simply be in her life as father to her child. Oh, but Matthias...for this kid he would do anything. He would be the best father this kid could possibly have.

Having reached the decision, his steps grew more determined, but a sense of wariness settled over him. He was now going to have to tell her, and Margaux was not someone he could simply dismiss. If he'd thought Christelle was bad...Margaux was capable of making him doubt decisions he had so firmly made on his own the instant he tried to communicate them to her. This time he would have to take a stand.

Victor arrived at the door and rang the bell, and Margaux's voice came over the intercom, announcing that she would be right down. Victor sat on the whitewashed ledge near the entrance, rehearsing how he was going to break the news to her. Now that he was decided, he needed to do it fast. Like ripping off a Band-Aid.

He saw her coming out of the elevator through the glass door of the entryway, but he couldn't open it for her since he had no key. She clicked the door open and allowed him to hold it while she pushed the stroller through. "You're bringing Matthias?" Victor peered into the stroller and saw his sleeping baby, and his heart filled with love. *No matter what I say to your mom*, he thought, *I will be there for you.*

"My parents couldn't watch him. I'm sure he won't cause any problems. He'll probably sleep through the whole dinner anyway." She allowed Victor to push the stroller as they stepped on the street toward the métro.

"What are your parents doing tonight?" he asked, trying to muster the courage to break things off.

"They're having dinner with the cleric at the Madeleine church to see if they can get around some of the restrictions on using it for the wedding." Margaux turned to face him as they walked. "They're really going all out for this wedding. I hope you appreciate it since your father hasn't offered to do anything."

Victor almost froze in his steps. He hadn't even told his father yet. This was the final straw, the harbinger that showed this wedding shouldn't take place. If he'd been serious about marrying Margaux, he would've told his father right away about setting the date, more from a sense of defiance than affection. He would have wanted to show his dad that something was going right in his life. But no. Victor had only told him about the baby, not about the wedding.

They were coming to the steps of the métro, and Victor couldn't do it here. In fact, he should wait until the dinner was over. It was going to be too awkward if he broke up with her before dinner. Picking up the stroller, he carried it down the steps of the métro. At the bottom, Margaux went through the turnstile first and he followed, carrying the stroller over the bars. Paris métro stations were a nuisance for parents.

At their destination, they walked in silence, closing the distance to Guillaume's apartment with Victor still pushing the stroller. Margaux sighed. "Papa signed the papers for us so we could move into the apartment right after the wedding. Where did you book for our honeymoon?"

"*Euh.*" He cleared his throat. Margaux rang the intercom at Guillaume's place, and they were buzzed in immediately. As they waited for the elevator, Victor answered. "I haven't booked anything yet."

"Victor." Margaux's face pinched in a frown. "It's just like you to be so irresponsible. You know if we don't book soon there will be no honeymoon."

He couldn't resist retorting, "I'm not irresponsible. You're the only one who thinks I am. I run a company, and if I were irresponsible, the board at Brunex Consulting would never have urged me to run one of their branches."

The elevator arrived, and Margaux took the stroller from him, shoving it in with more force than necessary. "You're not going to start getting involved in middle management now? I thought we talked about this. How will you make any money?"

"No, *you* talked about it. I have plenty of money already, and I'm interested in building companies from the inside. Seeing what I can do to make them grow. Besides—" He turned to her, a muscle throbbing in his jaw, "it's not middle management. Running a branch is senior management. And I think I can do a good job of it."

"Well, you're wrong," she snapped. "You've had these sorts of ideas in the past, and they never worked out. It didn't matter when we were together before, but now I'm going to be home taking care of the baby, and you need to be the responsible one." The doors pinged open, and Margaux pushed the stroller out of the elevator and turned down the hall, with Victor trailing behind. She knocked on the door to Guillaume's apartment.

"I don't want to get married."

Margaux whirled to him, her face drained of color. For once she was not composed, and the look of shock eclipsed the outrage. The door opened.

"*Salut,*" Penelope said. She gave a slight tug on the stroller, so she could pull it in and peek at the baby. "You brought Matthias. That's just...*parfait.*" Victor looked up in surprise at Penelope's tone and thought her eyes held mischief. Or maybe it was just her usual sense of fun. Penelope kissed Victor and Margaux on the cheeks. "*Entre.* Everyone's here. Or—almost everyone. We've got an old friend coming to dine with us tonight."

There came voices of protest from the living room. "Sorry guys," Penelope said. "No one knows about it. You're all in the dark, except Guillaume."

"It's always Guillaume who's in the know," Aimée taunted, breaking her usual silence. Everyone turned to stare at her in surprise. "Well, it's true. Guillaume, when are you going to kiss her, anyway?"

"Come on, guys. Don't be ridiculous." Penelope moved into the room with a wave of her hand.

The bowl Guillaume was washing clattered in the sink, and Penelope stopped dead in her tracks. His face was bright red.

Penelope's jaw dropped. "What...what?" Everyone was grinning at her, as she tried to articulate her protest. Finally, she marched toward the kitchen. "Prosciutto and melon, anyone?"

April was already there, and she met Victor's glance. She was grinning as well, but her gaze dropped when she met his, and her smile fell. Victor wanted to rush over and tell her that he'd decided not to marry Margaux.

Aie! *Margaux*! he thought. *What does she think about what just happened?*

Victor risked a look. Though Margaux's eyes glittered, she had plastered a smile on her face. No surprise there. She wasn't going to let anyone know there was anything wrong. In fact, she was likely going to try to talk him into changing his mind. Well, he would stand firm. He had been blind to it before, but Margaux had always called the shots in their relationship. Victor had been too concerned with fitting into her family to notice. In fact, it had always felt like the most amazing stroke of luck that she liked him at all. Now that he thought of it, he was well out of this relationship.

Margaux's voice broke through the hum of conversation. "It looks like Matthias is waking up. Victor, could you give me a hand with him, please? Guillaume, do you mind if we use your bedroom?" Guillaume nodded, and Victor felt a jolt of nerves. He'd already decided he would stand firm. It was just not going to be easy.

Victor got up and followed her down the corridor toward the bedroom, feeling April's stare on his back. It looked like Matthias was still sound asleep, so this really was an excuse. As soon as they went into the room, Margaux flicked on the light and turned to him.

"Perfect timing." Her voice was icy. "You are joking, of course."

"I'm sorry about the timing," he said. "I didn't intend to tell you until we were on our way home."

Margaux gripped the stroller handle until her knuckles turned white. "What do you expect me to do now? We've sent out all the invitations. I will be completely humiliated. And what about Matthias? What about all these promises of being in his life? *The perfect father.*" Her sarcasm needled him, as he suspected she'd meant for it to do.

"Don't worry about Matthias," he said, ignoring the first part about the wedding invitations, which he couldn't do anything about. "I plan to be in his life. I *will* be a good father to him."

"So you're really serious about not getting married?" Margaux shoved her hand on her hip, frowning, and he lifted his palms in a gesture of helplessness. What could he say, really?

"Well, you can forget about being in Matthias's life. If you're not going to marry me, you will never see him again." Margaux yanked the door open and Matthias's wail came from the stroller. Marching down the hallway, she entered the living room with Victor trailing behind, still in shock. *I will lose the relationship with my son?* He had no doubts about her carrying that threat out.

"It seems I can't calm Matthias down," Margaux announced in a tight voice, her eyes darting around the crowd. "I'd better take him home." April sought out Victor's gaze again, her face inscrutable.

Penelope rushed forward and reached for Matthias. "No, you must stay. Here, let me take Matthias. You can relax and have a drink. You haven't even eaten yet."

Victor thought she seemed more determined than usual, and he wondered what that was about. He should just let Margaux go. It was one way to avoid listening to her diatribe the entire way home. Maybe he could walk April home instead.

Margaux shook her head. "I really must be going."

"But you see, he's already calmed down. Look—he's smiling at me." Penelope cooed into Matthias's face, and Guillaume came and stood by her side, looking down at the baby. As if to confirm, Matthias gurgled.

"He's really cute. Here. Have a glass of Schweppes." Guillaume slipped the one he'd been holding into her fingers before she could protest.

"Besides," Penelope said, "the surprise involves you."

Margaux raised an eyebrow and glanced coolly at Victor, but she took a sip of her drink and didn't seem ready to rush off anymore. *Shoot.*

Penelope had seated Margaux by Guillaume on the opposite end of the table from Victor, and there was an empty chair on the other side of Margaux. She'd put April next to Victor, and he tried to catch her eye to smile at her, but April returned a tight-lipped smile and looked away.

Guillaume brought out the roast beef and potatoes, and they passed the dishes around until everyone had been served. Before they picked up their forks, Penelope stood. "I'd like to make a toast. Théo, can you fill Morgane's glass?"

When Théo had poured the red wine, Penelope nodded at Arthur. "Actually, why don't you share the news first, then I'll make a toast."

April looked at Arthur with dull eyes, and Victor wished she would look at him instead. He wished he could talk to her.

Leaning back in his chair, Arthur said, "I had a meeting with Mr. Chambourd today." At that, April shot her head up. "He has decided to replace one of his paintings in the gallery and include a new canvas, titled, *April à Paris.*"

April gasped, and Victor was relieved to see a genuine smile on her face at last. "I can't believe it," she said.

Penelope lifted her glass in a toast, Matthias in her other arm. She seemed to be a natural with children. "And so this is my toast. To April, her talent, and her painting in the gallery. May *April* take *Paris* by storm." She grinned at her own pun, then said, "*Tchin tchin.*"

Everyone raised their glass and drank to April. Margaux raised her glass too—she would never be so rude as not to participate—but her face was stormy. Victor knew only good manners were keeping her there. Guillaume gestured for everyone to sit, and the dinner began.

The doorbell rang. "*Enfin*," Penelope exclaimed and shot out of her seat, rushing for the door. "You made it," she said, when she opened the door, and Victor heard an answering masculine voice. So the surprise was a person. Probably someone they all knew from high school. He glanced at Margaux, and for the second time in one day, she'd lost her composure. Her face was white, and her jaw had dropped open. Suddenly, the visitor was even more interesting.

"I didn't know you had a baby," the man said from the hallway. It sounded like he was flirting.

"I don't," Penelope replied, a note of glee in her voice, as she led the way to the dining room. "*Alors*, some of you will recognize our guest, but everyone else, I'd like you to meet Franck Duboise. Franck, you know Théo, Martin, Auriane, Guillaume and Morgane, I think. Aimée is Guillaume's little sister, and Victor and April are friends. I believe you also know Margaux?"

Franck startled when he turned to his right and saw Margaux. "I...I think I know about everyone here. Victor, is it? And April? April's not French, is it?" His laughter rang out false. He turned to Penelope. "You didn't tell me there would be a crowd."

"What are you doing back?" Margaux spoke up, her color heightened. "You said you weren't returning to Paris."

Franck tried to avoid her gaze, and gave a hasty reply. "I didn't say I wouldn't visit. I just said I didn't want to move back. Where should I sit?" he asked brightly, then glanced down and saw the only empty seat next to Margaux. A look of annoyance flashed over his features. "I guess here."

"Franck and I ran into each other near his apartment building. I didn't know he lived there, and I happened to be in the neighborhood buying a book. We caught up on old times, and I couldn't resist inviting him over to surprise the whole crew." Penelope sat with a flourish and took a sip of her wine, looking for all the world like she was queen of it.

"Oh." Penelope popped up again, and reached across Franck to hand Matthias over. "Here, Margaux, I think you'll want to hold your baby again." Margaux took Matthias mechanically. She was still looking at Franck, and Victor couldn't decipher the expression on her face, but he knew there was something afoot.

"Looks like I'm late," Franck's voice boomed out. "Everyone is already eating. *Ah, merci,*" he added when Guillaume leaned across the table to serve him some wine.

Matthias jumped at the loud voice and began a thin wail, and Franck flashed the baby a look of annoyance. "Don't you want to put it somewhere else?" he asked with a sidelong glance, then turned back to the other guests. "We're trying to eat here, right?"

"I don't mind babies, do you, Guillaume?" Penelope's smile had disappeared but her look of mischief was still present.

"Not at all," Guillaume answered, and cut a large forkful of lamb.

Victor remained silent. It felt like watching a slow-moving train that he was certain was going to wreck. He didn't think he could say anything, even if he tried. April was looking at her plate, so no hope for any silent communication there. For the umpteenth time, he wished they could talk.

The table was more quiet than usual, as if everyone were waiting for something to happen. Penelope chewed thoughtfully, then said, "So, Victor, is everything all set for the wedding? You and Margaux? Who's going to watch your baby when you go on the honeymoon?"

Franck gave him a sharp look, and Victor shrugged, not appreciating Penelope's maneuver. "We haven't sorted out all the details yet." He certainly couldn't announce here that he was no longer planning to marry Margaux. And he still needed to think things through, because if he was going to lose his relationship with his son, this was not a decision he could take lightly.

"Getting married?" Franck asked Margaux, with a lift of his brows. "Good for you."

"Yes, it *is* good, isn't it?" Margaux replied in an icy voice. "*Some* people know how to do the honorable thing."

Victor saw several people pause to look at Margaux, then the truth washed over him with perfect clarity.

"It's funny how little the baby resembles his father," Penelope said. "Margaux has dark brown hair, and Victor has an olive complexion, and little Matthias is pink all around. And look at his hair. There are red highlights." She laughed, and Guillaume smiled fondly at her, clearly appreciating some inside joke.

"I mean, you're a redhead, Franck. How does that come about? Do you need to have a redhaired parent to have red hair, or can it come from recessive genes?"

"Recessive genes," he snapped, gripping his wineglass. He swallowed the wine in one gulp and stood. "You know what? I see what this is." He whirled on Margaux. "It's probably all your idea. Another attempt to trap me, but it's not going to work."

Margaux stood as well, Matthias gripped tightly in her hands so that he started to cry again. "Isn't it just like you to walk out again? Why don't you be a man and face up to your responsibilities for once?" She marched over to the stroller and set Matthias in it, her gestures surprisingly gentle despite her anger. There were too many emotions swirling around, and Victor was frozen in place. He couldn't have spoken or moved if he'd tried.

Franck, seeing Margaux strap the baby in and appearing as if she were going to follow, began to look trapped. "I'm leaving," he announced, heading for the front door. Margaux was not long behind. "No you're not. You're going to hear me out this time." She pushed the stroller in his wake and caught the door before it closed behind him. Victor heard her voice as it floated down the hallway. "You may want nothing to do with your baby, but you are going to listen to what I have to say for once."

The door clicked shut, and there was silence at the table. Penelope was biting her lips, trying not to smile. "More broccoli?" Guillaume asked, and lifted the bowl.

Slowly, the conversation at the table resumed, and Victor dared to look at April. She was trembling, her hands on her lap. He wasn't sure exactly what he was feeling, but neither of them seemed to be able to finish the meal. He leaned over to whisper, "Can I take you home?"

April nodded, and he stood. "*Euh*...Penelope, Guillaume...I'm sorry to leave your dinner early, but I thought I would see April safely back to my grandmother's apartment."

"Of course," Penelope said, and it was almost comical how everyone began talking at once, assuring them it was a great idea. The very thing to do. Victor was sure they all wanted him to leave so they could discuss what had just happened, and he was in just the humor to let them. He pulled April's chair back so she could stand, and they went to get their things. As soon as the apartment door closed behind them, a muffled conversation erupted in full force.

Chapter Twenty-Five

❧❧❧

N either said anything until they were on the street. "So the baby's not yours then, is it?"

Victor shook his head and made no reply. When they'd gone a little further, April asked, "How are you doing? How do you feel about that?" When he didn't answer right away, she ventured, "Disappointed?"

"Yes, actually." He walked in silence, and April felt her heart sink. This must be a huge blow to him. He'd really loved the idea of being a father. She wondered if he would still marry Margaux just so he could stay in the baby's life, though it wasn't his. She didn't think so. He'd practically said the only thing keeping him with Margaux was the baby. *Oh dear. I hope I didn't misread him. Perhaps it was just an excuse because he has no feelings for me.*

As if he had read her mind, Victor said, "Well, yes and no." He took a deep breath. "Yes, because I'd started to get used to the idea of having a baby, and I was excited to be a dad. I always wanted to be a father, but I didn't think I would be a very good one. Matthias showed me that I could be."

April gave him a sidelong glance. "Of course you will be a good father," she said softly.

"I will miss Matthias. But—" Victor caught her gaze and held it before turning forward again to allow a couple to cross their path on the sidewalk. When they were alone again, he stopped and faced her. "I have to say. Right before we arrived tonight, I told Margaux I wouldn't be able to marry her."

April looked up in surprise. "You did? But...that's not what you said before. Your biggest priority was creating a family for Matthias."

"I know. But I realized I didn't love her, and I probably wouldn't grow to love her over time. It's one thing if you can see the potential in a relationship. But I saw *no* potential. I saw that it would be wrong to bring my son—I mean, a baby—up in a love-less relationship."

April felt a wild joy coursing through her, but she kept her expression neutral. Until he made a move, she would make none. "How did Margaux take the news?"

"She said she would not let me have a relationship with Matthias if I didn't marry her."

"That's horrible," April exclaimed. Then, after a pause, "What would you have done?"

"I hadn't decided yet," he replied. "Now, I guess I won't have to."

Victor began walking again, and April didn't want to press the issue any further. "So. Exciting news about my painting getting accepted, right? If I can earn anything off it, it will help me with my finances. I think China is probably out of the question right away, at least not until I'm able to go back and earn some money at home first. I hate that my dream has to wait. I feel like I'm letting my dad down by not going right away."

"You'll go, though. I know you will," Victor said.

"Yeah." April fell silent. She was glad Victor believed in her, but it felt empty in a way. Nothing had changed. She wouldn't give up her plan of studying art around the world, but...she wished it weren't so easy for him to let her go. She gave herself a mental shake. This line of thinking would get her nowhere. Even if he liked her well enough to ask her to stay, she couldn't. She wouldn't abandon her life's plan for a guy. Even one as great as him.

Victor interrupted her musings. "So when and where is the gallery opening anyway?"

April took a deep breath and forced some cheer into her response. "It's next Saturday night. It's in a small gallery near the Panthéon. I'll text you the address. Are you going to come then?"

He looked at her in surprise. "How can you ask? I wouldn't miss it for anything." They'd approached the street that led to his grandmother's apartment, and Victor stopped again, as if he were reluctant for their walk to end. Turning to her, he said, "April, I need to figure some things out. I need a few days to get things sorted in my head."

She was aware of his nearness, his masculine cologne, and she felt how easy it would be to reach her hands out and lay them on his chest. His presence was reassuring, a solid wall of strength that had saved her twice from brutality, and had been a buffer against the loneliness of being in Paris. When she was with him, she felt she wasn't alone, and she couldn't remember the last time she'd felt that way.

Victor's gaze skipped down to her mouth, then back up to her eyes. She stayed still, and did not reach her hands out like she wanted to. He'd said he needed time and that was what she'd give him.

Finally, he stepped back. "We're almost at Mishou's." His voice was husky. "Let me get you home."

WHEN VICTOR SAID goodbye to April, he walked past the métro station, continuing onward. The streets were lively, with people spilling out of pubs, along with the music, into the night. One group of Dutch tourists, dressed in bold colors, greeted one another with laughter and a foreign tongue. He crossed onto a smaller side street and continued toward his house, instinctively knowing the direction, though he didn't know the street. He'd been close to kissing April tonight, now that he was free, but that would've been like his old self. Just doing what felt good in the moment. This time, he needed to do it right, and the right thing would be to give himself time to get used to the idea of not being a father. Matthias was not his.

Lost in thought, Victor hardly realized how far he'd walked until he looked ahead to see the Louvre looming in front of him, its cornices and ornamental chimneys lit by spotlights. The museum made him think of April's art. Of course her painting would be chosen, now that they'd found it. It was amazing. *She* was amazing. He wanted to promise her that she would have the means to travel to all these countries if he had any say in the matter, but he suspected she wouldn't want anything she hadn't earned herself. That was tricky.

Winding around the Concorde, he saw a billboard for China Air. *Where April wants to go*, he mused. He knew deep down that not only would nothing stop her from going after her dream, but nothing should. It would mean saying goodbye. He passed the darkened storefronts, his reflections somber.

What if I went with her?

The thought whispered to him at first, until it grew, took hold, and began to form itself into a plan. Brunex Consulting had its eye on a boutique located in Shanghai. *What if I went there?* he thought. *What if I went to Shanghai instead of taking the branch in Paris?* He could put himself in place as director and see how well he did growing a foreign company from within.

What would that life look like? he wondered. He'd already done research on becoming a silent partner in his own company so he could take over the Paris boutique. This would just be a little further away, but he could still keep an eye on his company from there. And sure, the financial risks might be a little greater since he'd have to start over in a different city, but he had so much saved up. And what a sad life it would be if all he cared about was making more. Didn't April say that when they first met? There had to be something else motivating him besides money. Now was the time to prove there was.

Victor began the walk up the Champs-Élysées. That was what he would do. He'd go where April wanted to go and find work wherever it was, and he would live the adventure Mishou always encouraged him to live. And he'd live it with the woman who was meant for him.

April. He filled his lungs with air.

She would never agree to this unless they got married. She'd made it clear that she wouldn't live with anyone before marriage, and that was something he could respect. But would she say yes? And so soon? Victor didn't even need to ask himself if it was too soon. He was certain April was the right one.

The people walking on the Champs-Élysées at that hour were dressed to go out. Two women crossed his path, and the brunette eyed him provocatively, which might've tempted him at one time. Now it just felt empty. He cut across the broad avenue to reach the side street. There was only one way to know how April felt. He would have to ask. And Mishou had promised him he could have her ring when he was ready...

Victor faltered. How could he think about leaving Paris when his grandmother needed him? She was getting older, and she had no one else. She had the right to have her family nearby in her later years. He picked up his pace, turning right on his street. He had walked the whole way.

What was he going to do about this? There was only one thing to do. He needed to ask Mishou for advice.

❧

Wooden steps led to the gallery, and April went up, early as requested. Mr. Chambourd wanted to speak with her and the other artists who were exhibiting. Her heart thumped with excitement and nerves. She looked around and saw that the room was empty, save the small group congregated at the end of the gallery in front of her painting. She couldn't keep a grin from her face as she walked toward them. Françoise came across the room to meet her.

"You're the only non-French person showing."

"So...not Ben?" April rubbed her arms.

Françoise put her arm around April's shoulders. "He's just lucky you said you wouldn't press charges. Come. Mr. Chambourd started to explain informally how this is going to work. The sales will be done in an auction. Today the interested buyers will come and look, and the auction will be on Monday."

"Why separate the two?" she asked. "Why not have the auction the same evening?"

"I think it's to create a desire for the paintings. Let people decide which ones are the most important to them and make them impatient to have them. But...why don't we go hear for ourselves."

Two more students walked in, and Arthur came with Penelope and Guillaume. "My friends, *Maître*," Arthur called out to his mentor, who gave a brief nod. April smiled at Penelope.

Mr. Chambourd gave a final glance around and welcomed everyone to the showing. He introduced the artists to each other, pointing out each painting, then reiterating what Françoise had already told her, though he went into more detail. "The reason we're doing this in auction format is because none of you have a quote on the market to earn a decent price for your painting. The buyers we have coming in are art connoisseurs, and they love to find new artists early on. They're always looking for the next big talent to develop, no matter what nationality you are. The sales prices are often higher than an ordinary gallery showing would get you, and some of you are going to go far with what you earn. Of course, there are always a few cases where I've misjudged the art, and after the auctioneer opens the bid...there are no bids."

April sought Penelope's eye. *My worst nightmare*, she thought.

"My colleagues and I generally tend to have good eyes, however. We're reasonably certain your canvases will sell well." Mr. Chambourd clapped his hands. "The gallery opens in five minutes. Go have a drink and try not to look too stressed. You'll want to fit in with the buyers as much as possible, but if someone wants to meet the artist, we'll bring them to you."

Penelope came over while April was accepting a glass of champagne. "Where's Victor?"

"He wanted to bring me over, but he didn't realize I would have to be here early. He had some things to tie up at work, then he plans to visit Mishou before coming over. He wanted to talk to her about something."

Penelope nodded. "So..." The one word was pregnant with meaning, and when April didn't try to enlighten her, she was forced to ask. "Victor has no baby."

"No baby," confirmed April.

"And?" Penelope waved her head back and forth, eyebrows lifted.

"And what?"

"Anything happen? *Un petit bisou, peut-être?*"

"Well." April blushed, but smiled. "I will tell you about my kisses when you tell me about yours."

"What do you mean?" Penelope suddenly grew wary.

"Guillaume is one hundred percent smitten with you."

"I have no idea what smitten is, but whatever it is I'm sure he is not." Penelope folded her arms.

April shrugged, her grin in place. She wouldn't tease her friend if she weren't fairly certain Penelope felt the same way about

Guillaume but just had trouble accepting it. "No one believes that except you."

Penelope pursed her lips and blew out. "*Phbbt.*"

The crowds began piling in at that moment, and April had no more time to talk to Penelope or do more than raise a glass at Guillaume and Arthur. Mr. Chambourd called her over twice to speak to potential buyers, and the other artists who had learned about her father came to ask her about his painting and what he had taught her growing up. Everyone knew who he was.

She began to feel a growing sense of unease around nine o'clock when Victor still hadn't showed. He had promised he would come. Maybe he got held up, or Mishou needed him for something. She managed to keep a smile plastered on her face when Mr. Chambourd called her over to meet a third person, a Colombian buyer who wondered if she also did portraits since hers was the only painting that had a prominent figure in the scene. Answering in the affirmative, she gave him her card.

At ten o'clock, April pulled away from a student who had kept her talking for nearly a half hour, mostly about his own training and how good his painting was, and she cornered Penelope and Guillaume, who were standing close, deep in conversation. "I don't know why Victor isn't here. Has he said anything to you?"

Both shook their heads. "Have you tried calling him?" Penelope asked.

"I've been afraid to leave my place here in case I'm needed, but perhaps I can run to the bathroom and try to call him from there."

"Do that. I'll tell Arthur you've stepped away for a moment in case anyone asks."

April hurried to the corridor that led to the bathroom and pulled out her phone. There were no messages. She dialed Victor's number and let it ring. It went to voice mail. She tried a second time and let it ring. When it went to voice mail, she hesitated, then left a brief message. "Victor...I'm not sure where you are. I thought you'd be here. Hope everything is okay." She hesitated again, then hung up.

Walking slowly back to Penelope, she shook her head, mouthing the words "no answer" before another student came to ask about her father. Suddenly, everything felt futile. The reminder of her father every two minutes, plus the fact that Victor hadn't come. It was only then she realized how much she'd counted on sharing this evening with him. How much she'd counted on sharing her life with him.

The night dragged on and more buyers appeared. She supposed that was a good thing. She had no idea whatever happened to Victor, but he never bothered to show up. Perhaps he'd changed his mind about how much of a friend he wanted her to be, now that there was no barrier in place. Perhaps he thought she would get the wrong idea about him now that he had no fiancée. Well, fine. She would be *just fine* on her own.

Finally, the last of the crowds left. Penelope and Guillaume had departed a while ago, Penelope giving April a compassionate squeeze on the arm. It was going on midnight, and Arthur was still in conference with the gallery owner who had partnered with Mr. Chambourd. By now, he had a bony woman with a blonde ponytail draped over his arm, who must have been the famous girlfriend. Some of the other students had already taken off, but April stayed. She guessed it was in the mistaken belief that Victor would eventually show. How pathetic was she?

At last, April went to shake Mr. Chambourd's hand and kiss Françoise on the cheeks. Pulling her wrap around her, she went toward the exit, her footsteps echoing on the empty stairs. At the bottom of the steps, her phone rang, and she scrambled to open her bag and pull it out. She almost dropped it. *Victor.*

"April," he said, when she answered. His voice was hoarse and almost unrecognizable.

"What is it?" She was breathless, waiting, but he didn't speak. "What is it, Victor?"

"It's Mishou."

April waited, but he didn't seem capable of speaking further, and she could hear his quiet sobs. Finally, she prodded, "Where are you? I'll be right there."

"*Hôpital Cochin.*"

Chapter Twenty-Six

❧✿❧

April rushed into the hospital lobby and came up to the reception desk. "I'm here to see..." Suddenly she realized she had no idea what Mishou's real name was—first or last, which was crazy since she had been staying at her house. "I actually don't know what her name is. An older woman was brought in. I don't know what she had but it was an emergency."

The woman at the desk looked at her like she was slow. "I can't really help you without more information."

April felt a flash of annoyance. The woman could be more sympathetic. She pulled out her phone and sent a text to Victor.

I'm here. I don't know Mishou's name or where to go.

A second later she got a reply: *Wait right there.*

April moved away from the front desk and looked around. People were milling about; some crept along in hospital gowns, while others rushed in for a visit looking the picture of health. She looked toward the corridor that led to the patients' wards, and the somber lights hit her, along with the faint smell of antiseptic. She had a visceral reaction, remembering her own father's slow progression of illness. April looked at her feet. She would rather be anywhere but here, but there was no way she was going to let Victor go through this alone.

In another minute, the elevator doors opened in the middle of the corridor, and Victor walked out, his face drawn. He gave a half wave, and she walked toward him, resisting the strong urge to pull him into a hug. Honestly, she wasn't sure what he needed the most.

"What happened?"

"Thank you for coming." Victor put his hand on her back to guide her into the elevator. His touch was reassuring. He had not withdrawn completely then.

They rode the elevator in silence, and she respected his need to speak when he was ready. When they exited on the third floor and turned left, he led her past hospital rooms into a small lobby attached to the ward. They sat, and she was relieved to see they were the only ones in the room. He would be able to talk.

"She had an AVC. A small one," he said, at last.

"I don't know what that is," she replied.

"It must be a French term. It's when the blood flow to the brain has been cut off. It happened to her, and she lost consciousness. I came to the apartment to talk to her before coming to meet you, and it's a good thing I did, because no one would have been there to help her if I hadn't." Victor pinched the bridge of his nose, and April risked putting her arm around his shoulders. She held it there before pulling it back.

"A stroke then," April mused. "A small one. How do you know it's a small one if she lost consciousness?"

"Because she woke up before the firemen arrived—" He saw her look of confusion and explained, "In France we call the firemen for medical emergencies because they're better trained than the ambulances, which are privately owned. So she woke up before they got there and was already starting to talk, but she wasn't making any sense. She kept asking if the market was still open because she needed to go and buy more fresh fruit."

"So you accompanied her to the hospital. What did the doctors say?"

"They did an IRM." Again, he saw the confusion and said, "Like a radio but it shows the tissues instead of the bones."

"Oh. An MRI, then, instead of an X-ray. That's how you say *radio*." Her medical vocabulary was rapidly increasing, but she would rather not be in the circumstances that brought it about. "What did the MRI show?"

"That there were some burst blood vessels, and the firemen had already given her blood thinning medicine. They would clear on their own."

April thought for a minute before venturing cautiously, "It seems like she's going to be okay, right? Did she start making sense before...well, I assume she's asleep, and that's why we're in here."

"She did start to make more sense, and even told the nurse that he looked tired and not to worry about lifting her because she could climb on the table on her own. It was just like her. And yes, she's sleeping now."

"But you're still worried," April said.

"Yes," he said, and rubbed his face. "She's so fragile, and I realized I need to be more present in her life. I need to move her in with me, or into an assisted living if she permits it. She can't stay in the apartment on her own." He leaned back on the chair and April followed, her eyes scanning his face.

So Victor didn't expect her to stay in the apartment with Mishou forever. It only made sense that it was temporary, but it felt sad all the same that she was no longer going to be part of their lives. Not in an integral, daily way like she'd been. It was time to think about moving home, no matter what happened with the art show, no matter if her painting sold. From there she could figure out her plans for China and all the rest. It was too bad she could no longer ask for any help from Ben. But that bridge had been burned.

She was so lost in thought, Victor's hug came as a shock. Without a word, he slid his hand behind her and reached around to pull her into a hug, his head cradled in her neck. All her senses screamed. She'd been holding back her feelings with an iron grip, unsure if he felt the same way, and even now she didn't know if this was a hug of friendship or something more.

Victor lifted his head off her neck and kissed it softly. Then he sought her gaze and leaned forward to kiss her. As April responded to it, sparks went off behind her eyelids. She began trembling.

After a too-short kiss, he pulled away, his glance darting to hers. "I shouldn't do that. Not here. But I just want you to know I'm not rebounding or anything. I'm a little in shock from Mishou, and even a little from Matthias, but I'm not confused about how I feel about you. I..." He pulled away some, but kept his arm around her back. "I was hoping you weren't confused about how you felt about me."

A smile trembled at her mouth, and she shook her head. "I'm not."

His face brightened. "Well then." He gave her another kiss, but this one firm and short. "But that's enough of that."

April felt that, perhaps, a little more might not be a bad thing, but she didn't argue. Mishou was sleeping and recovering in the room two doors down, and there was enough to think about.

"Do you mind if I sleep a little right here next to you?" Victor asked.

April shook her head and he settled down, his arm still around her, though in a half hour he was not likely to have any more feeling in it. She gave a smile as she felt him relax into her. *So he has feelings for me.* She sighed quietly, fighting to calm nerves that were too jumpy. What did this mean? Did he actually love her and want her to stay?

Victor jerked upright. "I forgot to ask about the gallery show-ing. Did you sell your painting?"

"No, it will be sold by auction on Monday morning. So I'll see then."

"Where? And when?" he asked, but he had such a calculating look in his eyes, she had to say something.

"Victor, I forbid you to buy my painting."

"*Mais, pourquoi?*" He snuck another small kiss.

"Because I need to see that my painting will sell even with strangers. That it's good enough for people who have no vested interest. And this is the only way to know."

"All right, I'll respect that," he said, a cross between a grumble and a murmur. "*Je t'aime.*" That was definitely mumbled, so she wasn't even sure she heard him correctly.

She felt him relax into her again. Would she stay? *No, I don't think I can. I mean, maybe six months or so while I save up and plan, but I can't give up my father's wish for me. It's become my own desire as well. I wonder if Victor would wait for me.* She sighed again. *Probably not.* But she felt herself relaxing, too, and decided that now was not the time to worry about it.

Victor awoke a couple hours later and woke her up, too, as he pulled his arm from behind her back and shook it. He went to check on Mishou, then came back and sat next to her, leaning his head against hers, but keeping his arms on his lap. She did the same, and found it wasn't awfully uncomfortable, dozing upright in metal hospital chairs. Not when she was sitting next to him.

"Mishou's sleeping," he murmured. Then they both fell asleep too.

AT SIX IN THE MORNING, Victor breathed in and stretched his arms, and April shifted and started rubbing her neck. "Victor, I need to get home. Can you let me know how Mishou is doing and whether I can come back to visit this afternoon?"

His heart lifted at the sight of her at his side with her

disheveled hair, pink cheeks and luminous eyes. Victor nodded and caressed her cheek before leaning over to give her a quick peck on the lips. He really needed to get a hold of some coffee. And maybe a toothbrush.

"Thank you for coming and for staying here with me all night."

"Of course." April turned to meet his gaze. "What else would I do?" Picking up her beaded purse and silk wrap, she said, "Give Mishou a kiss for me when she wakes up."

After April left, Victor looked in his grandmother's room. She was still sleeping, and he went in search of some breakfast. By the time he'd eaten and come back upstairs, he found his grandmother awake and beaming at him from the hospital bed. "I guess I'm getting old."

"*Non*, Mishou. Not yet." *And please, God, may we have many more years together.* "But you know, I do think it's a good idea that you move into my apartment."

He expected a little bit of resistance, but he didn't expect his grandmother to lay her hand on his, with more strength than he could imagine her having, and give an emphatic no. "It will not be good for you to have me in your home while you're there with your young wife. It's not healthy for the marriage."

"Mishou, I was on my way to tell you...many things, but one of them was the fact that I wasn't getting married, and the baby is not mine."

"Of course you're not getting married to that girl. I was talking about April." Mishou patted his hand kindly. "You're a sweet boy, and I'm glad you've found someone who is perfect for you."

Victor's jaw dropped. "How did you know?"

His grandmother didn't deign to answer that but just said, "The ring I promised you is at the jewelers being cleaned, and you can pick it up tomorrow."

"Mishou, I hadn't even had a chance to ask you for it." And

then disbelief, surprise, admiration...all held his tongue in check for a moment before he added, "We can't really get engaged this soon. I mean, I only told her how I felt last night."

"Foolish young man," Mishou said fondly. Then she raised an eyebrow. "Foolish in love, I mean. You can't see it as clearly as I can with a lifetime of love and a few missed opportunities behind me. The two of you were adrift until you found each other, and you both fully come into your own when you're together. Go and get that ring. The receipt is in my wallet." She patted the side of her bed, searching for her purse, then pointed to it on the window ledge.

"And put me in the assisted living on Avenue Foch where Antoinette Vaudrat lives. I know I can't stay on my own anymore. It's not practical, and I'll be as happy at Foch as I will anywhere. Go with April to China for six months. She needs this. April needs to fulfill her dreams before she can settle down happily. I promise to stay alive until you get back. The doctors will tell you that I still have plenty of *force*."

"How do you know about China?" Victor felt like a puppet in the strings of a master. His whole world was being planned before his eyes, and normally the feeling would make him want to run. For once in his life, however, he just wanted direction. He wanted this to work out and to be with April, wherever she was.

"Two women can't live in the same apartment for several weeks without learning a few things about each other." Mishou chuckled. "Even if her French is almost impossible to understand."

"I can't leave you for six months," Victor said, but he was torn.

"Nonsense, *mon fiston*." Mishou reached up and laid her hand on his cheek in a gesture that was filled with the tenderness of a lifetime of love. "I'll be disappointed if, for once in your life, you don't do the thing your heart is telling you to do—to take a risk."

"*Alors, Madame Brigot*. How are we feeling today?" The doctor entered with two interns in his wake, and Victor and his grandmother weren't able to speak anymore. They would need to discuss all this in more detail, but Victor was pretty sure that, once again, his estimable grandmother was right.

§&

APRIL TOOK a seat at the auction in the back of the room where she saw the other students congregating. She hadn't seen Victor since she left him yesterday morning because the doctors had ordered tests for his grandmother and thought it would be wise to have no visitors for the rest of the day, apart from family. So he stayed with his grandmother, and she stayed away.

April hoped he would respect her wishes and not come and try to buy her painting this morning. She'd been unable to touch breakfast, she was so nervous to know whether her artwork would sell, whether it was worth something, and whether she would have enough money for the next phase in her life.

The *Commissaire Priseur* opened by bringing out the first painting—her own.

What? she thought. *That's not supposed to happen. This is too fast.* Her scattered thoughts took her in every direction, and she slumped in her seat. *Maybe it's because he thinks it's the worst painting, and it's not likely to sell.* Her heart was beating in her throat. *Well, here it goes, anyway.*

"Ladies and gentlemen, I present *April à Paris*, painted by April Caleigh, *une fille d'artiste*. She's the daughter of Henry Caleigh, the postmodern painter. *April à Paris* is done in a contemporary realism style, and the setting is on a residential street in Paris, the courtyard of a Haussmannien building in the eighth arrondissement. As you can see, if you've gotten a glimpse at the artist back there, this is a self-portrait that includes all the whimsy of a first-time visitor to the City of Light, set in a more traditional Parisian environment. I'll start the bidding at five hundred euros. Five hundred euros, ladies and gentlemen."

"A thousand." A man in the seat directly in front of her raised his white board.

"Three thousand." This came from a woman on her left, a telephone plastered to her ear.

"Three thousand, five hundred euros." A third bidder was standing on the side of the room.

April held her breath as the silence stretched. Then, from the woman on the phone, "Seven thousand euros."

There was a collective gasp, and even the auctioneer looked surprised. It did seem to April to be an unreasonable jump. Why not bid four thousand? Would it end there?

But no. The man in front of her bid "Eight thousand, five hundred." April looked more closely at the back of his head. He looked like the Colombian man who'd asked her about doing portraits.

"Nine thousand." Again from the woman on the phone.

"Nine thousand, five hundred." From the man on the sidelines.

"Ten thousand." April's gaze shot over to the woman on the phone, and then to Mr. Chambourd, whose profile was visible toward the front. He had an arrested look on his face, then one eyebrow lifted.

"Fifteen thousand." The Colombian man spoke up in a loud voice. April glanced at the woman, who was speaking into her phone, but she finally shook her head. The man on the side remained silent.

"Going once. Going twice. SOLD to bidder number twenty-three." There was polite clapping as April felt a few eyes on her. The only thing she could think of was how fast she could get out of there. She needed to leave as soon as possible, but that would probably be rude.

Fifteen thousand? It seemed like a great price, but April could hardly revel in it. The art school in Shanghai was ten thousand for six months. It was well-known and did not come cheap. And then there was the flight. She might get one for one thousand, but

JENNIE GOUTET

what about food and lodging and just general living expenses? Four thousand for six months. Impossible to live on. And—she had forgotten to ask what percentage the auction house kept.

"SOLD!"

April snapped to attention at the hit of the gavel. The next painting had sold for four thousand, so hers had been a good price, after all. But it was not going to be enough. Her thoughts flew from one consideration to the next, one worry to the next.

She flexed her fingers, reflectively. *Stop*, she thought, at once. A sense of peace came over her. *I earned money from my art. That is incredible. And the rest will somehow work itself out.*

The applause for the last sale ended, and April felt she had been there long enough not to attract attention. While the auctioneer brought out the next painting, she slipped out. She'd expected to see Penelope, but she was not there. Instead, April exited onto the street and began to walk toward the métro. Victor had sent her a text before the auction to wish her luck and to ask her to come to his apartment afterwards. Mishou was well enough that he could come home, and he wanted to see her. It was an effort not to break into a jog.

"April." She whirled around at the sound of her name.

She stilled when she saw who had called her, her heart in her throat. "Ben. What are you doing here?"

He came forward, his usual cockiness replaced by a look of embarrassment. "It was me in there. Well, not in there, but I was one of the ones bidding on your painting."

She couldn't help the displeasure that she knew covered her features. "Why, though? Did you win?"

He shook his head. "I tried. I had a certain amount of money, but the bidding went beyond that. I'm sorry."

"Don't be. I wouldn't have wanted you to buy it. I wanted a stranger to buy it. I need for my painting to be bought on merit, not on pity." April thought back. "So you were on the phone with that woman?"

Ben tried to catch her eye, his gaze pleading. "Yes. I wanted to make amends and make sure you had enough money to carry out your dream of traveling. As for myself, I'll be heading home. My parents weren't too happy when they found out that my painting was pulled. I had to explain why."

"Mmm." April was not going to be overly sympathetic.

"Anyway, I just wanted to say goodbye." Ben leaned forward in the usual way to kiss her cheek, but she shook her head.

"Why don't we just shake hands." April saw his misery and softened. "Listen. I forgive you, and it all worked out well for me. Don't let this one thing ruin your life."

Ben turned to go, lifting his hand halfway in farewell, and April headed to the métro.

Chapter Twenty-Seven

T he old apartment building was the same as it had always been. No lingering nightmares of Lucas or getting attacked. She'd not even suffered feelings of oppression in returning to the place where she'd lost her father's paintings—the greatest loss she'd experienced after the loss of her father himself. At least the pain was not too fresh. April closed the distance to the entrance and pulled herself up, her stride lengthening. *My father lives on no matter what happened to his paintings.* Her eyes filled with tears of awareness and gratitude. *His mark is everywhere throughout my own work.*

She opened the wooden door and entered the courtyard. There was the spot she had painted—the painting she'd sold! She still needed to process that bit of good news, along with the surprising emptiness of no longer having it in her possession. How did artists bear to part from their work? Her dad had always told her to disassociate her feelings from her work, but evidently this was a learned process.

Victor buzzed her in as soon as she hit the intercom, and as she climbed the stairs, her thoughts took a different turn that had nothing to do with art or emptiness. Her breath quickened in anticipation. The last time she'd seen him, they had fallen asleep side by side in the hospital lobby, and her feelings had run the gamut from wild butterflies to a cocoon of serenity.

Victor opened the door and wasted no time in pulling April into a hug, lifting her up off the ground. It would've felt like a brotherly bear hug if he hadn't shoved the door shut with his foot, set her down, and kissed her until she was breathless. *Whoa!* Her pulse raced as he held her, and her knees turned to jelly.

"Come." Victor pulled away, and she stumbled forward, stunned by the sudden change and the space that was now between them. He grabbed her hand, leading her into the living room. "Let me tell you about Mishou. Then I have something to show you. Well, two things to show you." He grinned.

"Mishou must be doing better or you wouldn't be looking like that," April announced, feeling as giddy as he looked.

"Mishou is fine. She'll be discharged in another week, and she said to give you a kiss, which I obeyed as soon as you walked through the door."

"Although I don't think she meant *that* sort of kiss," April said.

"Oh no, I think that's exactly the sort of kiss she meant." Victor laughed. "Okay, sit. No. Stand here. I have too much energy to sit." He grabbed both her hands. "I'm sorry I'm nervous. What I wanted to tell you is that Mishou is completely herself and that she had some advice to give me, which I've taken to heart. I plan to do exactly what she suggested, except that it involves you, and you get to decide too."

April was breathless. "It involves me?"

Victor stared at her for a long moment without answering. Then he took her hand and led her to his office, where he opened the door and walked through.

"What—" April gasped in shock as soon as she got a full view of the spacious room. Victor's modern paintings had been removed, and in their place were all six of her father's paintings, repaired so meticulously, you could only see the damage when you walked up close. She wasted no time in doing that.

There was the Chilean fishing boat with the dock covered in beige chipped paint, the toddler running through the bluebells and purple wildflowers, the cocker spaniel looking up at the small boy, and the scenes of their garden painted in summer, fall and winter. Each one had been set in a frame to match.

"How did you...?" April started crying, and that was Victor's cue to pull her into another embrace. They stood like that, the months of friendship bringing them to this moment, where it teetered on something deeper. She drew a long, slow breath and basked in the feeling of being cherished.

"My painting sold, you know," she said, her voice muffled in his sweater.

She felt him nod. "Fifteen thousand." And before she could ask how he knew, he added, "Penelope gave me Arthur's number so I could follow up."

"And you didn't bid. You left it alone." She felt him nod again. "And instead of trying to save me from financial ruin, you just gave me the most important thing I could possibly have on this earth."

He squeezed her tighter, and she could hear the grin in his voice. "When you put it like that, I sound like a regular hero."

"Nothing regular about you, Victor. But yes, you're a hero."

Out of the blue, she felt his heart speed up—felt it pounding through his shirt. He gripped her harder but didn't say anything, and she began to feel a little alarmed. "Um...is everything—"

"And you'd marry a hero, right? Someone you considered a hero?" Victor sounded as though he had something stuck in his throat.

At this, April pulled back, slipping easily out of his embrace as his hands fell to his side. She looked at him closely. "I don't understand."

With shaking fingers, Victor reached into his jeans pocket and pulled out a ring, which she didn't dare look at. Instead she kept her eyes trained on his.

"It's Mishou's ring." Victor swallowed. "She always promised it to me when I found the right girl, and she had it cleaned before she got sick—"

"For Margaux."

"No." Victor gave a shaky laugh. "Not for Margaux. For *you*. She just knew. I mean, I don't want to pressure you, April. It's sudden, I know. Who gets married after only a couple months of knowing each other? But then sometimes you just know. Please say something."

"Victor, I—"

"I'll come with you to China." It all came out in a rushed breath, and Victor put his hands on her arms, his gaze meeting hers. "I haven't had time to put everything in place, but I'm planning on taking a position in Shanghai with one of the subsidiaries, so I can be with you when you go."

April's mouth dropped. "*You* will come with *me*?"

"I want to. If you'll have me. It's just...I know you're the right one for me. Your dream is the one that can't wait very long. You need to do it when you're this free and this determined. I just know this relationship won't work if it means sacrificing your dream."

Victor looked down, suddenly unsure. "Maybe one day I'll need you to follow me somewhere, and I hope you'll be willing to do that. But we can start with following you, and that's fine."

April realized her mouth was still open and she shut it, but her eyes were fixed on the stubble on his chin. *Victor wants to marry me. I would get to be with him forever. He would be my home.* The words kept looping through her brain, but it was too overwhelming to give an answer.

At her silence, Victor took her by the waist and pulled her close. "You once said you'd never live together without getting married, and I can't really come to China with you and not live with you. Plus it would..." He cleared his throat. "It would be hard to wait."

The spell that had kept April speechless broke. "Yes!" she squealed, jumping up and throwing her arms around his neck. "I will marry you, and we'll go to China, and then...and then we'll see from there. I mean, yeah, I want to see other places, but we can figure out the timing on all that. I just need to at least *begin* the adventure. And never in my wildest dreams did I imagine I'd get to begin it with you."

Victor smiled broadly and kissed her again before pulling away, his brows furrowed. "And, regarding family? I mean, just to put everything on the table. You want to be a mom one day, right? We could..."

"Definitely." April grinned up at him. "Matthias wasn't yours, but there will be a sweet little boy or girl who will be one day. Perhaps not right away. Maybe we could go to Colombia after China, since the guy who bought my painting—"

"—for fifteen thousand euros."

Her eyes twinkled. "For fifteen thousand euros, which, by the way, is enough to pay for art school and airfare to Shanghai, but not enough to pay for cost of living."

Victor shrugged and lifted his eyesbrows. "Well, I suppose I could take care of that."

"I didn't know I would come to Paris and end up with a sugar daddy." April laughed and Victor joined her.

"I can only guess what that means." He put his hands on the sides of her face and whispered, "I love you."

Their eyes held, and she covered his hands with her own. "You feel just like home to me."

The door buzzed, shrieking through the stillness of the apartment, and April jumped. "Who is that?"

Victor pulled away from her, a smile hovering on his lips. He walked toward the intercom and announced, "*Entre*" before buzzing the entrance open. When he turned back to her, his eyes glimmered with mischief. "Who else? Penelope and her band. I just felt we couldn't celebrate our engagement without our new friends."

Once again, April's mouth was agape. This was becoming a regular thing. "Well, it's lucky I didn't arrive any later, or you wouldn't have had time to propose!"

"I *was* getting nervous," he confessed.

Slipping her fingers into his, April said, "I'm so glad you invited them though. It will make it seem real if we can share it with them. They've been good friends to us, haven't they?"

The door buzzed, and Victor went to open it. "Come on in," he said, as Penelope and Guillaume entered with Aimée, Morgane, Théo, Martin, and Auriane piling in behind them.

"I've brought champagne," Penelope said gaily, lifting the bottle high.

"And I've brought more," Théo said. "Because one is never enough."

"How did you know I'd say yes?" April asked, hands on hips.

"Oh." Penelope shrugged. "With the two of you, it's been plain right from the start. There was no way the answer would be anything but yes."

Victor went to pull the long-stemmed champagne flutes from the counter in the kitchen where they'd been hidden and handed one to each person as Penelope wiggled the cork out of the champagne bottle. When it popped, Guillaume tilted his glass to catch the bubbly liquid running over. She quickly filled the rest of the glasses.

"I think we need a toast," Guillaume said, taking the lead, and Penelope looked at him in surprise. Aimée smiled and lifted her glass in expectation, and everyone else followed suit. April and Victor raised their glasses last.

"To young love," Guillaume said, to a chorus of cheers. "To a made-for-each-other, unmistakable, unbreakable, irresistible love," he said. More cheers.

"To first kisses," he said, to even louder cheers.

Penelope protested. "I don't think that was their first kiss."

"I wasn't talking about them." And before Penelope could react, Guillaume scooped one hand around her waist and pulled her flush against him. He leaned down to kiss her until her hands dropped to her sides and she kissed him back. There was another chorus of cheers, and April couldn't help but laugh out of sheer delight. Guillaume finally pulled away, looking pleased and proud, and Penelope stared at him in astonishment.

Guillaume exhaled. "Sorry about that, Victor. I didn't mean to steal your thunder, but this was something that had to be done."

Victor shook his head, laughing. "Be my guest. I already got my girl."

"And now, if I may give a proper toast," Guillaume said, lifting his glass. "To friendship, and to a love that will last. Victor and April, may you have every happiness in the world. I have no doubt that you will."

Everyone raised their glass to toast and took a sip. April wrinkled her nose from the bubbles.

There was a short silence, and Penelope broke it first. "Well, you could have given me some notice," she said, her voice severe but with a smile hovering on her lips.

"I've given you all kinds of notice for the past eight years. I figured it was time to act," Guillaume replied. "We can talk about everything later, *mon amour*."

"Oh, so it's *mon amour* now," Penelope said. April looked around the room at her friends laughing at Penelope's inevitable capitulation, as they engaged in friendly arguments, punctuated by animated gestures, and raised their glasses to April's happiness. Her joy overflowed.

"*Shh*," Guillaume whispered to Penelope. "This is about April and Victor."

"Yes, it is," Victor said. He put his arm around April's waist, and they basked in the glow of unmistakable, unbreakable, irresistible love—and friendship.

LETTER TO READERS & ACKNOWLEDGMENTS

Thank you for reading *A Sweetheart in Paris*. I'm glad it found its way into your hands, and I hope you enjoyed it. Leaving reviews on Amazon is a huge help to us authors, as is sharing about the book on Goodreads and Facebook, if you're so inclined. I appreciate your support, which allows me to keep writing more books.

As a side note, I thought you'd be interested to know that the story about the art students pulling a prank (their version of subtle rebellion) on the Nazi visitors is a true story. My husband has three relatives who studied at the *École des Beaux-Arts*, so we have it first-hand.

I'm lucky to have had help from Angie Brooksby on all aspects of the art world, from creation to sale, particularly as it relates to France. If you'd like to see her paintings—and I'm sure you would because they're stunning, and many of them are of Paris—you can find them at angiebrooksbyarcangioli.com.

I also want to give a shout out to a few other friends and colleagues who kindly read and critiqued the rough draft of this book. Thank you so much, Emma, Jaima, Julie, and Paco for your time, insight, and sage advice. You all made my book so much better, and I'm grateful. I would be remiss if I did not mention Stephanie Parent, the editor and Su from Plumstone, who designed the cover. You guys did excellent work.

If you'd like to keep up to date on my author news, you can access the newsletter signup on the sidebar of my website, jenniegoutet.com. My books to date are *A Sweetheart in Paris*, *A Noble Affair* (contemporary), *A Regrettable Proposal*, *The Christmas Ruse - a novella* (Regency), *Stars Upside Down* (memoir).

On the next page you'll find the recipe for the *tarte à la mourtarde* (also called *tarte à la tomate*, or simply, Dijon mustard tart). It's good, and you'll get the benefit of Mishou's instructions right in your own kitchen.

Tarte à la Moutarde

Crust :

125 grams cold butter (about 1/2 cup)
    2 cups flour – I use a gluten-free mix
    1 teaspoon large grain sea salt – if you don't have large grain, use ½ teaspoon
    1 egg – this is important with gluten-free flour, but can be left out for regular flour
    1-3 tablespoons cold water, as needed

Filling :

2-3 cups grated Swiss or Emmental cheese (enough to fill the quiche crust about half-way).
    2 heaping tablespoons Dijon mustard
    2-4 ripe tomatoes, depending on the size
    1 teaspoon dried basil, or 1 tablespoon fresh
    salt and pepper to taste
    olive oil to drizzle (optional)

Pre-heat the oven to 350°F / 180°C. For the crust, put the ingredients in the Cuisinart and mix, adding one tablespoon of water at a time until it forms a ball. Place a sheet of parchment paper underneath the dough, and put another sheet above, and roll the dough into a circle until it's about 1/8" thick. Slide the crust on to the quiche pan, using the parchment paper, and trim the excess (both crust and paper).

Slather Dijon mustard over the bottom of the quiche, paying attention not to put too much on the sides. (*Maille* is my favorite brand). Cover the mustard with the grated cheese until it fills the crust half way. Slice the tomatoes and scallop those on top of the cheese so they overlap. Sprinkle the basil, salt and pepper and bake the *tarte* for 30 minutes.

Drizzle olive oil on top, if you wish, and eat the *tarte* warm with a side salad.

Made in the USA
Monee, IL
03 March 2021